Thigh High

Thigh High

Bonnie
Edwards

APHRODISIA
KENSINGTON BOOKS
http://www.kensingtonbooks.com

APHRODISIA BOOKS are published by

Kensington Publishing Corp.
850 Third Avenue
New York, NY 10022

ISBN-13: 978-0-7582-1774-5
ISBN-10: 0-7582-1774-9

First Kensington Trade Paperback Printing: February 2008

10 9 8 7 6 5 4 3 2 1

Printed in the United States of America

CONTENTS

TWINKLE TWINKLE
LITTLE THONG

To Laura Langston and Vanessa Grant.
May the Muse remind us we write, therefore, we rock!

1

DM's voice rolled over her, whiskey smooth, pebble rough. With the deft hand of a master, he took her into the realm of the sensual. Throaty and hot, the distinctive sound rolled like rumbling skies around the master cabin. The poetry he read of love, loss and betrayal followed paths he created along her searing need, until she found her most needful flesh and, with a lover's touch, tipped herself over the edge toward release.

Fingers slid through slick, tender flesh, moist and plump. Around. Around. Trickles of need whispered to her womb deep and empty.

Her whole life was empty these days. But she couldn't think of that, not when release beckoned. Her breath slowed, deepened as her lungs reached for air. Her heart thumped, pulse beats rose as sensation took over again, thought drowned.

His voice came back seductive and deep and pulled her again into the quiet of rising expectation. She closed her eyes as his voice entered her, hot against her heart. The remembered weight of a chest pressed to hers, of thighs pushing with power between her own, flesh sliding into flesh, pulling along nerve endings so taut they screamed. His voice in her ear, strong, sexy and low, carrying her along. Taking, stroking her neck, her chest, nipples and down with slow strokes of his tongue.

With two fingers inside, she rolled her precious pearl of nerves with her other hand until she crested, weak and small.

Music rose all around, sweeping through her as the last pulses ebbed. It was enough. It had to be.

She wasn't about bar prowls for sex, and she couldn't have a relationship. Not now, maybe not ever again.

Rolling to her side, she listened to the song he played for her, just for her, full of pain and loss. When it was over, she threw back the covers and went to wash her hands.

DM's voice came back on, quieter, more seductive than before. The man was good. The man was cool. The poetry was gone now, replaced by his rolling commentary on the blues songstress highlighted tonight.

Victoria's CHOK blues-in-the-night radio disk jockey was the hottest thing this place had going for it. Well, him and the guy over on the houseboat side of the marina who stared at her all the time.

Francesca Volpe couldn't remember squat about numbers. Never could. So she wrote important ones down until they stuck in her memory. Sooner or later, she'd remember the combination of this safe. But sooner wasn't now, so she yanked at the piece of paper in her shorts pocket and flattened it out on the wall in front of her while she dialed the combination.

Finally, the safe door clicked open.

Blown away by the fact that she even had to use a safe, she dug way into the back. Fiona's thong was in here somewhere.

Cold, hard diamonds against warm, soft velvet filled her hand, and she lifted the scrap of material gently. Fiona should have kept the thong in the designer's box, but no; her sister had decided the rich didn't give a rat's ass about their possessions so she didn't have to either.

The thong caught on a corner of a thick manila file. Anxious not to tear the velvet, she set it down, then pulled out of the safe everything that could possibly be in the way.

She took out a fireproof box that contained so many important papers her head swam. It held her sister's will, her sister's house deed, her sister's insurance policy. Next came file folders, then a copy of her parents' will. Everything came out, even the ownership papers for the yacht.

A yacht, for cripes sake.

Frankie Volpe was standing in the saloon of a yacht with four staterooms. Up to her armpit in a wall safe and she still couldn't believe it. Go figure!

And since when was a living room called a saloon? They belonged in old westerns, not on million dollar floating palaces.

She leaned in tight to the wall and winked at the scruffy brown dog that had all but adopted her. "Hey boy, how you doin'?"

He cocked his head and wagged his stubby tail. She'd decided he must've had it caught in a door when he was a puppy. It wasn't cropped exactly, more like he just lost the tip. He was her kind of dog, lost, lonely, a little rough around the edges, but lovable.

"Ah! Got it. Finally." She pulled out the thong and set it carefully on the coffee table in front of the leather settee. Looked more like a built-in sofa to her, but she still had a lot of boating terms to learn.

She considered the thong. Diamonds, glittering and cold, littered the front vee of black velvet. She shivered to think of all those sharp edges so close to the joy button. *Oh, ugh.*

The deep safe had been stuffed full. She took care to set all the papers and files back into the safe in reverse order, to be sure it fit.

When she turned back to talk to Scruffy, all she saw was his stubby tail and wet feet heading topside. He'd snatched the thong off the table and taken off with it!

"Hey! You little pervert! Give me back that thong!"

But he was gone when she got to the deck. His bouncing short tail was just visible as he raced along the floating dock toward the houseboats tied up a couple of docks over. A small community of houseboaters called the marina home.

Her former doggy pal must live over there in one of the houseboats.

She took off at a dead run after him, not caring that she was barefoot; night was falling and the floating dock was strewn with heavy gauge rope and chains. She picked her way as quickly as she could through the obstacles, keeping one eye on the scruffster as she went.

She wasn't quick enough. He disappeared for a full minute, but she'd bet anything he'd taken off for the waterfront park on Dallas Road. Oh shit, if he got to the off-leash part of the park, he'd drop the thong for sure.

She ran faster, no longer needing to watch him except in her mind's eye. He was a playful mutt, sure to have doggy pals. She imagined a tug of war, the velvet tearing into several pieces, the diamonds flying in every direction. "Shit! Shitshitshit!"

Her thighs burned with her run, her lungs strained, but her heart knew she'd lost him. She bit back a sob, gathered strength and picked up her pace again.

She reached the bottom of the ramp, steep now because it was low tide. Grabbing onto the rail for support, she dashed up the incline. She dragged in a heaving breath. Her chest blazed hot, and she could swear she felt the beginnings of a heart attack.

Oh man, how did she ever get this out of shape?

She wheezed once more and launched her aching self up the ramp, metal surface rough against her bare feet. The hard metal honeycomb was there to prevent slipping in heavy weather, but for bare feet, it was a killer.

She reached the halfway point when the dog reappeared at the top of the ramp and headed straight down toward her, tongue lolling out of his mouth.

Lolling out of his empty mouth.

She stopped, put her hands on her knees and dragged in a deep, burning breath. Her grateful lungs expanded.

"You . . . you . . . lost it . . . I'll . . . I'll . . . kill . . . kill . . ."

He licked her hand as he trotted past her down the ramp. At the bottom he turned right toward the houseboats.

Frankie dragged her body the remaining few feet to the top of the ramp, then searched the immediate area, but there was no thong in sight. He'd disappeared for long enough to bury it, or tear it up or, worse, hand it off to another dog whose owner would recognize the diamonds for what they were. A bonanza.

Lightheaded, she sank to her butt and laid her head to rest on the rail support. That thong was worth fifty thousand dollars!

She had to get it back.

If she was lucky, they'd find it when they did the dog's autopsy. She scanned the marina laid out below her.

The floating dock was cement and ran from right to left with several docks running perpendicular, like straight fingers out into the harbor. Each finger contained several slips. To the left was the marina side or the visitor's pier with visiting boats of varying sizes. Farther down were the fishing boats. To the right of the ramp were three fingers for houseboats. A subdivision of them, in fact.

She'd liked them, and the idea, at first sight.

But the sight she wanted now was of the dog, heading to the one he called home.

His bouncy rear end showed up as he reached the third finger.

A man, correction, *the* man who'd been watching her every time she was within view, whistled to Scruffy. The dog bounded faster.

She couldn't lose sight of the dog again, so she dashed down the ramp as fast as her bare feet on the rough steel would allow.

Whistling for the scruffy little dog might not mean a thing. Maybe the hunk was just another soft touch who fed the beast, the way she did. Either way, he hadn't seen her mad dash because he turned away and sat on one of the lawn chairs on his deck. He faced away from her toward the inner harbor and put his feet up on the deck rail. Settling in for the night, she assumed. Great. He could help her search for the thong.

Daniel Martin cracked open a beer and settled in to watch the ferry to Seattle churn out of the harbor. One beer before work took the edge off, warmed his throat, soothed his nerves and put him into a blues frame of mind. He'd gone from domestic brands to beer from all over the globe to test the effects of each one. Tonight's was Dutch. He tilted the bottle away, glanced at the label out of habit, ran his tongue around his teeth to gather the flavor then took another sip. Not bad.

He put his feet up on the rail of his float home and nearly dropped his brew when Barkley jumped into his lap. "Easy there, boy, you'd think you'd know better than to squish the package. Oof! Get off." He picked Barkley's back paw out of his crotch with a grunt. Instant relief.

The dog licked his chin.

"Is that . . . is that . . . your dog?" asked a husky, heavy-breathing female voice from behind him. He craned his neck around and dropped his feet to the deck at the same time.

It was the hottie he'd noticed from the yacht on the marina side. "You could say that. He's been mooching off me so long, I guess he does live here."

Good thing his paw hadn't damaged the goods. The goods

in question sprang to life, as usual, at the sight of the compact, dark-haired dynamo.

The woman was built just for him, he was sure of it. And it was about time she showed up. They'd been glancing each other's way ever since she'd washed ashore.

He grinned, thinking the dog was good for at least three doggie snacks for delivering her. "Has Barkley caused trouble?"

Her chest heaved in and out a couple times, breasts rising and falling with each heave. He did his best not to look, but she was in a bikini top that left little to the imagination. And Daniel had a great imagination. "Down, boy," he said, not sure if he was talking to Barkley or his libido.

"He took a thong. And I didn't see where. It's not anywhere near the top of the ramp, because I followed him."

"I see. Was it leather? He's got a thing for leather." So did Daniel, but it wasn't the time to mention it. "Shoes, that is." Maybe after he got her shoe back for her, she'd be grateful.

"Not a shoe. A thong." She looked exasperated. "You know." Deep heave. "Underwear." Her breath was still labored, still entertaining him with soft jiggles of flesh and cleavage.

The image of her fine behind parted by a thin strip of leather made him sit up fast and straight. He put his hands up in surrender. "Oh, I see. As much as he loves leather, he loves women's underwear even more." The count was now officially up to four dog biscuits. "His favorite day of the week is when Bitsy Mayer, two slips over, does her laundry. He takes her panties all the time."

"I don't give a rat's ass about Bitsy somebody's underwear."

He played at being offended. "Bitsy does. She's on a fixed income and the underwear she favors is expensive," he quipped.

His reward? A reluctant lopsided grin that winded him with its hesitant charm. He went on, digging for more. "They come with that heavy-duty flat panel in the front to firm the belly and some kind of stitching up the back to make the most of her butt."

Damn things cost him a fortune every month. "I'm beginning to suspect Bitsy enjoys the idea of me shopping for her undies." He gave an exaggerated shiver. "Bitsy's sixty-eight."

Her raised eyebrows put an end to the fun. Her smile disappeared. So, okay, she wasn't impressed with his comedy. He'd always been better with the blues.

But still, a lady shouldn't have to fight with Barkley over her underwear.

"Are you sure you want your thong back after he's dragged it all over the pier? He chows down on them sometimes. Tears the crotches right out."

"Yes, I want it back! Regardless of the condition. He ran up the ramp with it, and I've got to get it back. Do you know if he has a hidey hole anywhere? Does he bury stuff?"

She looked about to cry.

"Hey, it's a thong. I'll buy you a new one." He liked that idea. Much more fun than buying for Bitsy.

"It's a special thong. My sister needs it. She's on her honeymoon and she called to have me send it to her." Her voice got higher and more agitated with every syllable. She sounded desperate now.

"It's not yours?" That was too bad; he liked the idea of fantasizing about her in a thong. He'd never seen the sister.

"You can buy your sister another. I'll take you to a nice lingerie store I know." That could be fun.

She looked about to spit nails. "I've got to find that one. It's special."

"How special?"

"Very. Look, it's got sentimental value. She bought it to celebrate her engagement and planned to take it on her honeymoon. Now she's *on* her honeymoon and she wants it."

"I see." He pretended to think hard when all he could really think about was the spectacular rise and fall of her breasts. He didn't want to be a pig, but he was a red-blooded male and there they were: round and pert with the nipples that pointed upward like two perfect pearls. "You could still buy her a replacement," he suggested.

She took another deep breath, but this time he figured it was one of those looking-for-patience deep breaths that women did so well, not an out-of-breath-from-running kind of heave.

And a woman looking for patience was not likely to agree to a date. "I'm sorry, but I don't have a clue where he'd bury it. But I can help you look for it first thing in the morning. I get home from the station around five A.M."

It wouldn't kill him to stay up a few extra hours after his shift to wait for her.

"You're leaving?" She looked at the beer bottle rising from his lap, condensation slipping and sliding down onto his hands. Kinda looked like his . . .

"Yep. I'm on the air at midnight. It takes fifteen minutes to get to the station." He stood. "I take an hour to prep, so I'd better get moving. I can wait for you to wake up before I hit the sack for the day. But if you wait until much after seven I'll be pretty useless. So, I'll see you bright and early?" The question was all about her name, not about when he'd see her.

"Frankie. I'm Frankie Volpe. And I hate early mornings. So, if I don't find it, I'll still be searching the park when you get home. Look for me there."

"You sure that's a good idea? That park's not the healthiest place to be after eleven or so. It's used by all the normals until then. A lot of people take their dogs for the last walk of the night along the path."

"I'll be fine. I've been in tougher neighborhoods and survived." Her eyes glittered and her chin came up, stubborn and cute as hell.

"What's this thing look like anyway?"

"It's sparkly. Very sparkly. Black velvet. With rhinestones all over it."

"Sounds like it would hurt."

She rolled her eyes. "Looks even worse," she said, and gave Barkley a scowl before she turned and headed back down the float.

"You must love this sister a lot if you're willing to search all night," he called after her.

She waved a hand without turning back.

"Barkley, man, I owe you big time. Frankie Volpe is definitely the catch of the day." Then he remembered she hadn't cared to ask his name.

"Hey!" he called again, aware that everyone on this side of the marina could hear him. "I'm Daniel and I'm on CHOK radio, the blues show from midnight to four. Give me a listen tonight. Maybe I can figure out where Barkley hid it."

She gave him a salute and took her fine ass up the ramp.

2

CHOK radio. The blues show. When Frankie got to the top of the ramp, it hit her. His voice was different off the air, but still sexy and deep. His on-air voice was intimate and coaxing.

Daniel Martin. DM, the blues DJ. The man whose voice filled her master cabin with earthy sexuality.

She heated from her chest to the roots of her hair. It was one thing to let the man into her head, to use his sexy drawling voice to lead her into release. It was quite another to meet him under such mundane circumstances.

Kind of took the pop out of her whole fantasy life.

Jeeze.

An hour and a half later, Frankie pawed the ground around the roots of yet another tree and came up empty. The pine needle scent had long since lost its freshness. She'd been under these damn trees so long she felt like a mushroom. Sticky pine pitch clung to her palm, filled with needles that stung like thorns. Her knees were a mess.

Hard as she tried and feeling more miserable than a dog

pound executioner, she couldn't figure out a way to broach the subject of cutting Daniel's doggy pal open. It wouldn't have to be a big cut, she reasoned, just from the bottom of his ribs to his little useless peter. The thong had to be wedged in there somewhere, just waiting to pass on through.

A creature with more legs than she cared to think about crawled through her hair, but she didn't even flinch this time.

She'd never felt so dirty. But she refused to let some dirt get between her and finding the treasure. Besides, real dirt in the great outdoors was healthier than digging through, say, a dumpster in an alley.

Admitting that, yes, she'd even dumpster dive to get the thong back, she returned to her search. She felt around for some freshly dug earth, but everywhere she put her hand felt compacted under the spiky, dry pine needles.

She could go back to the yacht to get a flashlight, but she didn't feel like explaining her midnight treasure hunt to the weirdos hanging around. The types of people who inhabited the park at this time of night weren't to be trusted with a dollar, never mind a thong studded with diamonds.

Which brought her back to the DJ and his dog. A dog's belly was no place for diamonds that could cut. It would be a kindness to operate. Surely Daniel would see that and agree. He struck her as a reasonable man. She'd pay for the whole thing, of course.

Maybe if she grabbed the dog off the deck of the houseboat she could dognap him and take him to an emergency vet clinic. At least for an X-ray. She felt better immediately. Yes, an X-ray would be the best option.

Her panic had discombobulated her to the point of forgetting that X-rays existed.

She could trust a vet with diamonds. They probably swore some kind of oath or something. Like doctors. If they did have to operate, maybe she could be in the room to get the thong when they retrieved it.

Her hands were scraped, and one finger still bled from a sharp piece of glass she'd tossed to the side. Her numb, dirt-encrusted knees protested as she patted the ground around her. She'd had it up to here with kneeling and crawling through and around trees.

Nerves skittered along her spine. The park was much quieter now than when she'd begun her search. When she'd first arrived the place had been full of normal folk out with their dogs, or biking and inline skating along the waterfront path, but now it was a different story. Daniel had been right. The oceanfront pathway was a haven for walkers and joggers who made the most of the evening.

But after eleven, even the stalwarts had disappeared into the trendy James Bay neighborhood and expensive condo buildings that lined the inner harbor.

Ten minutes ago a young couple disappeared under the tree next to her. The moaning and rustling had begun almost immediately. She was tired of waiting for them to finish. Polite was polite, but she was antsy to get back to the marina to get the dog.

She listened hard and heard some definite panting coming from under the huge tree. The idea of digging around under there when they were finished grossed her out. What if she squished a condom in the dark?

The sex-generated moans were kind of a turn-on, though, so she settled in with her back to the tree trunk and waited. The sounds of lovemaking arrowed to her pussy and made her wet as the couple got further into each other, letting the real world fall away.

She'd had that kind of heat once. Hot loving that filled her world. As Blaine had filled her body, he'd taken her heart, her soul. She blew out a frustrated breath and set thoughts of Blaine aside. He was gone and good riddance.

But man, could he turn her on.

Of course he could, she reasoned. With his smouldering good looks he'd been able to practice with every other woman he could find. His bad-boy attitude meant he found plenty.

"Oh baby, yeah, do that. Suck it, suck it good."

Since it was the man's voice, Frankie was able to visualize what the woman was sucking. She sighed.

She missed sex. She liked sex. She wanted sex.

She'd left home suddenly and hadn't packed her vibrator. It was still in her nightstand in her abandoned apartment.

Which was probably rented out months ago. Her furniture would've been sold. She hadn't thought of clearing out the place, just got her ass out of there. She'd grabbed Fiona and run, scattering her family like petals on a breeze.

She'd gather them again someday. For now, she snorted, thinking of someone getting a deal on her old bedroom furniture and finding her underused battery-powered joy machine.

Ah, yes, the weight of a lover on her chest, the push–pull of a hard pair of hips fused to hers. She wanted it again.

She wanted it now. The rustling under the next tree continued, the voices low and crooning.

Sweat trickled down her neck into her bikini top. She swiped at the moisture, sure she left a dark smudge across her chest.

"Oh yes!" the young woman squealed. "This feels so good . . . and you're sooooo bad. . . ." Her voice heaved with each breath, giving it that breathy quality that said she was ready. Frankie remembered saying much the same thing in much the same way.

From the sudden silence, she guessed the bad boy had found his mark and slid home. Was that the delicious sound of skin slapping skin?

Enough! She couldn't bear to hear any more, especially when her hands were too filthy to use on herself and her vibrator was long gone. Frankie rolled to her knees and crept as quickly and as silently as she could around the far side of her tree. The other couple, wrapped up in each other, would never hear her.

Pathetic, that's what she was, listening to other people making love. She wasn't sure when she'd become too uptight to look for some action, but she had. Her pitiful vigil under the tree proved it.

That damn Barkley had a lot to answer for.

Scraped knees, a cut finger and a throbbing need all lay at the feet of that perverted little beast.

She could make the dog's owner take care of some of these problems. The very scrumptious Daniel the DJ. The way his on-air voice wove through her into her deepest fantasies proved he knew his way around a woman's body. She could ask him to kiss her scraped knees, bandage her finger and take care of her deep-down throb as soon as he got home.

After all, she'd gotten off on just his voice a time or two.

A night with the appealing DJ might be just what she needed to calm her jitters after six months of crazy. His voice alone took her deeper into her sexual fantasies than her vibrator ever had. If his voice was that good, imagine how good his hands and mouth would be.

"OH! BABY!!!" One last squeal of rapacious delight caught her ears as she hurried down the path toward the lights of the marina.

Daniel put on Etta James's newest and got back to his daydream about Frankie Volpe. She was hotter up close than he'd thought. He'd watched her for the last two weeks and wondered why she was alone on such a big yacht. Boats that size tended to require crew, but he hadn't seen anyone else onboard.

No one else in the marina had seen anyone else either. The *Boondoggle* had been a matter of a lot of discussion on the houseboat side of the marina. All anyone knew was that the boat had docked in the middle of the night amid a shroud of secrecy and a fog of misinformation.

If the harbor master knew anything about the owners of the yacht, he wasn't saying.

All Daniel had been able to do was stare hard at the redheaded powerhouse from afar. Up close, Frankie was enough to make a man weep.

Her eyes raked a man bare. Her tongue, sharp edged and quick, could flay a man wide open. But all that served to do was make him want more of her. All of her.

He liked spitfires. And he'd bet Frankie Volpe could spit more fire than any other woman he'd ever met.

She'd been pretty upset about that thong Barkley had taken. When he got home, he would take a run through the park to see if she was still there. Not likely though. No sane woman would wander a dark park at this time of night no matter what neighborhoods she'd survived.

He doubted she would ever find the thong. Barkley must have the instincts of a politician for burying dirty laundry, because Daniel had never found anything he'd taken. The mutt had to have found the perfect hiding place for his secret stash of underwear. Like a pervert who collected panties off clotheslines, he was determined to get away with it for as long as possible.

If Barkley had actually eaten the thing he'd have to get him X-rayed. Rhinestones were sharp.

But the mutt hadn't eaten Bitsy's underwear, only stolen them, so it wasn't likely he'd eat Frankie's.

Etta's song ended on a mournful wail, and he went back to his microphone.

"Twinkle twinkle little thong, how I wonder where you belong," he said, "wish I may, wish I might, see you twinkle in the moonlight," he added as an afterthought. He chuckled low and intimately with the hope Frankie was tuned in.

Fire crackled under his skin at the idea of seeing her in a sparkly velvet thong, her ass cheeks high and round, divided by a silky black line that traced her from back to front.

At least now he could strike up a conversation whenever she was on the float. His schedule was so different from most people's that he hadn't found a convenient time to talk to her before. Either he was on the way to work while she was returning home or she was long gone when he woke up. His morning was afternoon for most people.

But timing wasn't an issue with Frankie. She knew his crazy shifts and would expect him to be on an odd schedule. He couldn't wait for his shift to end. If he could get her past the thong mishap, he might have a chance with her.

"Twinkle twinkle little thong, how I wonder where you belong," Daniel said in a croony bluesy voice that tracked heat from her heart to her deepest belly. The man had a voice that stroked through to her vitals. The in-joke about her missing thong made her smile.

"Wish I may, wish I might, see you twinkle in the moonlight." She laughed out loud at that one. The man was funny and hot—a potent combination. She hoped he was visualizing her in a sexy scrap of black velvet, because she'd love to show him the real thing.

She opened her laptop and searched for the radio station's phone number. Eventually she found her way through the automated answering system to the booth and talked to a person who identified himself as Daniel's producer. He told her to turn her radio volume down, then put her on hold while she waited until the next song ended.

Thirty seconds later Daniel answered.

"Hi! It's Frankie." The shower she'd taken had cooled her, but now she was hot all over again.

"Any luck with your thong?" His voice warmed to molten lava. And she heard "I want you" under the words. She shivered with anticipation.

"No. And I'm afraid I have to ask you to help me round up your doggy pal so we can get him X-rayed."

"I thought of that myself, although he usually doesn't eat the underwear he steals. If he does, I've never seen it come out again." He chuckled. "I'm wincing because that didn't sound right. Not the kind of conversation I usually have with a woman I want to impress."

"You want to impress me?" She grinned and let the smile show in her voice. Flirting was such fun. The spice of middle-of-the-night phone flirting added to the days of eye contact.

"Hell, yes, I want to impress you. As long as you're free to be impressed."

"I'm free. You?"

"As a bird."

With those important preliminaries out of the way, she tucked the phone close to her chin. "I like your voice. That impresses me. I love the music you play. That impresses me." As did his shoulders, his caramel-colored eyes and the shock of sun-tipped hair that fell over his forehead. His pecs, his arms, the lazy but focused way he watched her whenever she walked up the ramp.

He must think she didn't see the way he tipped the brim of his ball cap up to watch her. It was subtle, that tip, but since she'd become aware of him, she'd caught it every time.

"I'll be off soon; do you think you could round up Barkley and bring him to the station? I can call a vet clinic from here."

"Will he be inside or on the deck?"

"He's got a dog house on deck. Should be there."

He hung up suddenly, but no sooner had he disconnected

than she heard his voice, sultry and warm, on the radio again. She turned the volume back up and smiled as he joked about the thong one more time.

This time he made it sound like a shoe rather than a panty.

She put a call in to Fiona and left a message for her not to expect the thong for a while. Her sister had protested long and hard about going to a remote wilderness camp for a honeymoon. But Bernie, her longtime fiancé, had perked right up at Frankie's suggestion. Raised in the city, Bernie had wilderness fascination big time.

Next up on the honeymoon whirlwind was a safari in Kenya. Anything to keep her sister out of the limelight. With Bernie on her side for a change, Frankie felt confident they could keep their whereabouts a secret for at least another month. She hoped so. Being on the run sucked the big one.

Having connected with Daniel, she looked forward to spending more time here. Victoria had a lot going for it. The city was small, clean, beautiful and out of the way for her. No one would think to look for her here.

Daniel's voice seduced her as she dressed quickly. It was clear the man loved what he was doing. The blues called to him, in spite of his sense of humor. He loved the music, loved the intimate format of his show. Yes, he seduced and cajoled and turned her mind to the wild thing. But while she dithered in front of her closet, dreaming about the man behind the voice, his dog may be suffering.

What did a woman who wanted to impress a man wear to a middle-of-the-night run to an emergency vet clinic?

The man in question had definitely noticed her chest earlier, so she pulled on a fresh pair of shorts. Keep it simple, girl.

3

Daniel sat beside her in the waiting room with Barkley on his lap. They were surrounded by dismal-faced, tired people whose pets were suffering real emergencies. But if Barkley was trying to pass diamonds through his system, it could soon be a matter of life and death.

"He seems fine, don't you think?" she said for what must have been the hundredth time. But they'd both been saying the same thing since she'd arrived at the station with the dog.

Daniel nodded. "Perky as usual. I think we're on a wild good chase here. If he had a gutload of rhinestones, I think he'd be miserable by now."

She petted the dog's head and gave him a good scratch behind the ears, torn up by the prospect of Fiona's thong causing Barkley distress.

The doctor arrived and they stood. She clasped Daniel's forearm and gave it a squeeze in support. The doctor smiled. "No foreign objects show up. Whatever he did with your thong, miss, he didn't eat it."

Relief washed over Daniel's face, and he gave the dog an affectionate buss on the head. "Thanks, Doctor. That's a relief."

A couple of people in the waiting room brightened at the good news and gave their congratulations. Frankie's worry meter rose a notch.

She looked at Daniel, busy petting Barkley's head. "Where could he have put it then? I searched under every big tree I could fit under." Except for the love nest. Her cheeks warmed.

The memory of the amorous couple heated her through.

The doctor moved on to his next patient.

"You need to think back about how long he was out of your sight," Daniel said. "How far into the park could he have run and still buried it so completely that you couldn't find it?"

"Good point. It was only a minute or so, maybe two. There's no way he could have run as far as I went. It must be closer to the top of the ramp." She hadn't thought to check the water. He might have dropped it into the harbor. "I didn't see him drop it into the water, but he might have."

Daniel walked to the desk with his wallet open, but she insisted on paying the bill for the X-ray.

"No, Frankie, I should have had Barkley under better control. It's just that everyone knows him. He was left behind last year, and we all fed him until he settled in with me."

"I shouldn't have allowed him on the yacht in the first place. He thought he was welcome to make himself at home." And she was the one who'd got bent out of shape about getting the thong back. "So, we'll split the bill," she said, handing off the cash.

She regretted that she couldn't tell Daniel the truth. But, really, a diamond-studded thong? She still rolled her eyes at Fiona's indulgence. Her sister was the one who needed to be leashed.

Maybe Frankie could find one of those electric collars and put it on her sister's neck. It could give her a jolt anytime she got within fifty feet of a jewelry store.

"Let's go home, buddy," Daniel said, setting Barkley down.

He reached for Frankie's hand and she slid her palm into his larger one. Slow heat and heavy desire sparked awareness between them. His eyes warmed with promise when she caught his eye.

Barkley danced at Daniel's knee until they exited the clinic. He watered three bushes on the way to the car. Daniel chuckled. "Yes, he's definitely behaving normally."

His hand felt large compared to hers. Strong and surprisingly calloused. "Callouses?" She tugged on his hand and inspected his palm in a pool of light from the clinic's window.

"Yes, I do a few repairs on the boats and float homes. Not everyone's still capable."

She'd noticed some older retirees on the houseboat side. "That's sweet." Sexy, funny and generous with his time. Oh boy, she could be in trouble here. "You call them float homes not houseboats?" Another term she'd need to learn.

"That's right, they float on tons of hollow concrete. That's why they're as stable as they are."

She nodded. "So folks don't get motion sickness on them?"

"Depends on how sensitive the person is. But with a two-story home the second floor moves a little more. You're not afflicted, are you?" Warm concern drenched her, and she felt absurdly pleased and excited to be able to tell him no.

"I've got a rock-solid stomach onboard. I've never felt anything but happy to feel the roll under my feet. Considering I didn't grow up around boats, that's pretty cool, huh?"

"Pretty cool." His grin was warm and promised warmer. Her body responded with slick heat, and moisture pooled in her panties.

"It's late," she said, checking the color of the lightening sky. "Or maybe I should say, it's early. I'm bushed." She yawned, unable to hide it.

Since she hadn't had a job in six months, she'd finally come around to her natural sleep rhythm and had begun to sleep in later and later. But still, she'd been up for hours now and dawn was fast approaching.

He opened his car door and nuzzled her hair as she slid into the seat. "We'll look for the thong together after we get some sleep," he said, his voice throaty with steam.

A thrill of anticipation chased down from her head to her pussy. "Are we doing that together too? Sleeping, I mean."

He cocked an eyebrow. "If you'll have me."

"I'll consider it," she said with enough spark to keep him guessing.

Barkley jumped into the backseat and curled up to sleep immediately. "Funny," Daniel said, "he usually demands the front passenger side to himself."

She clipped her seat belt into place while Daniel crossed the front of the car to climb in behind the wheel.

No sooner had he buckled in than he grabbed her hand again to set it to rest on his thigh. Under her palm, the rough denim heated while his muscle felt firm and hard. She squeezed lightly.

"I'd like to see the inside of your float home, Daniel. I've never been in one before." Better his place than hers. Company on the yacht would be a huge mistake.

He slanted her a glance that melted her. "If I show you around in there, it could take all night."

"Good, I like all-nighters." Once she got started taking care of this itch, it could take awhile. Six months was a lot of time to make up for.

After that, she couldn't think of a thing more to say. The atmosphere in the car turned quiet and soft and felt like expectation.

Warm, gentle anticipation. The best kind.

Her stomach sent thrills of desire up to her chest, and she decided Daniel was a slow, careful lover. She sometimes liked rockets like any other woman, but tonight wouldn't be about rockets. Tonight with Daniel felt slow. Quiet.

Promising.

She settled into her seat with a sigh, her nipples hard and scratchy under her newest lace bra. Barkley snuffled in his sleep in the backseat. "Think he has any idea of the trouble he's caused?"

"Since his brain's the size of a walnut, or smaller, I doubt it." He twined his fingers with hers and moved their hands to her lap. The pad of his thumb found her pulse and circled there. Her heart rate jumped, but his hand was warm and gentle. Soothing her with easy promise.

Oh yes, tonight would be all about slow.

To help speed things up she thought of pulling his roving thumb to her crotch. Her pussy creamed and pulsed with need, her clit plumping as he teased the delicate flesh at her wrist. She shifted to widened the space at the top of her thighs.

Daniel, damn the man, didn't take the hint.

The dashboard lights glowed red, giving the object of her lust a devilish glow. His eyes gathered the red, and she imagined sparks of fiery need deep in their depths. If he didn't touch more than her wrist and hand soon, she swore she'd unzip her shorts. Maybe then he'd get the hint.

He turned into the short drive that led to the parking area for the marina. As they traveled the length of a playing field that ran alongside, she pulled her thoughts to more mundane things. There wasn't much she could share about herself, but she remembered something.

"I wanted to buy one of these cars a few months ago." Before her life had exploded. "But I was turned down for a loan."

"You're living in a yacht the size of Texas and you couldn't swing a car loan?"

"I'm, ah, yacht-sitting." The lie everyone had agreed on

only felt a little wrong. "It's just as well about the car because I found myself unemployed shortly after being turned down."

He grinned and winked. "Then I guess you'll be around for a while. Things do have a way of working out for the best."

She chuckled and turned her face to her window so he wouldn't see the glow he'd put in her cheeks, or the guilt in her eyes from the lies she'd already told. There would be more, too, she was sure of it.

Her belly jumped with worry. She'd never been a stone-cold liar, and she didn't expect to be able to keep it up for long. The best she could hope for was that they'd tire of each other before the truth became awkward.

"Think we'll be able to find the thong tomorrow? I need to get it back." If it was anywhere the sun could catch at the diamonds it would be picked up, if not as a curiosity by a child, then as a fabulous find by a discerning adult. The diamonds were of such quality any woman who'd ever gazed in a jewelry store window would see the truth.

Her belly sank.

If word got out that an honest-to-goodness diamond-studded thong had been found at the Dallas Road oceanfront, she'd have to get gone. For good.

She glanced at Daniel, and her desire ticked up a notch.

So what if the truth came out first thing in the morning, she'd have this time with him now.

He pulled the car into his parking spot at the top of the docks. Barkley jumped into her lap from the backseat and put his front paws on the armrest to look out the window. His back paws dug into her naked thigh.

Daniel trotted to the passenger door and opened it. Barkley, true to his name, set off down the ramp at a dead run, voicing his joy at heading to his own bed.

"I used to yell at him to shut up, then I realized I was making as much noise as he was. Most of the time, my neighbors tune him out."

A chorus of other barks responded to Barkley's, and she chuckled. "I wondered why there was such a racket every morning at this time." Now she knew all the dogs on the docks welcomed him home.

He closed the car door and slipped his hands to her shoulders. "If I don't do this soon, I'll lose what little mind I have left."

"You've lost some of your mind?"

"Shut up and let me kiss you."

She looped her arms around his neck, cupped the back of his head and pulled him to her. "About time, Mr. DJ."

His lips were hot, hard and demanding. More demanding than she'd given him credit for. Daniel may be a gentle name, with no hard sounds or harsh syllables, but it said nothing about the man's potency. Nor did his soft eyes and his I'm-so-fuckable voice.

No, no. Daniel was a great kisser, full of gusto and hot demand that fired each of her cylinders into rocket launch mode. Rocket sex? Oh yeah, he knew rocket sex.

And she felt liftoff.

She had no idea where she'd come up with the slow sex scenario, but she was dead wrong.

Someone groaned, whether it was her or him, it was loud enough that they pulled apart, locked gazes and went back for more, this time with Daniel lifting her against the car so he could press his hardness against her softness.

And soft she was. And wet, and open.

And needy.

Six months' worth of needy.

"Get me to a bed, Daniel. Now."

He swooped her into his arms, and she heard another groan. "Am I too heavy?" But she didn't want to get down, didn't want to have to walk down the ramp.

And especially didn't want to get to the bottom of it where she'd have to decide between right and left. And right and wrong.

Turning right would mean going to his place and his bed.

Turning left would mean another lonely night in the *Boondoggle*'s master cabin, thoughts whirling as fear built.

As for right and wrong: She knew it was wrong to sleep with a man she'd just met. But with Daniel it felt right in places she hadn't explored in too long.

In the end, she didn't have to walk the ramp because he said, "That wasn't my groan, it was Barkley growling."

Sure enough, there he was, sitting patiently at the top of the ramp. His stubby tail swept the dirt, eyes bright, head cocked to one side. Tonight was unusual and he seemed to know it.

"He wants his routine back. Going out to the vet in the middle of his night has confused him. He's waiting for me to hit the sack, the way I usually do."

"Usually? This is usual?"

"Not at all, Frankie, not at all. But I hope it continues long enough for all of us to get used to it."

She nuzzled the spot between his earlobe and his shoulder. He smelled of warm flesh and good man, and she couldn't resist a lick.

"Keep that up and I'll stumble." At the bottom of the ramp, he turned right toward his float home. So much for her right or left, right or wrong quandary.

Her heart hammered, and she licked him again to see if she really did have the power to make him stumble.

Barkley scampered ahead of them, hopped onto the deck and disappeared into his doghouse.

Next time she tasted Daniel's neck, she gave his earlobe an experimental suck. This time, it wasn't a groan she heard, but a growl. And Barkley was nowhere to be seen.

4

Daniel set Frankie down on deck, next to the barbecue. The sky was rife with stars failing against a dawn-pink sky, the air spiced with the sea and soft quiet.

She kept her arms looped around his neck. He slid his palms down each side of her rib cage to hold her hips. He squeezed, happy to find she was womanly where he wanted. Too many bone racks had wandered through his bed, and he liked a woman with flesh. Frankie was perfect. A package of taut womanly curves that fit into his hands as if she were made for him.

Her face tilted up to his, eyes gleaming in the pearly dawn light, full of mystery and come-get-me.

"I don't know anything about you. Where you came from, where you're going, or why you're here with me," he said, avoiding the trap of falling into her eyes. Patting himself on the back for his quick thinking, he left the leading statement where it lay between them.

"I'm here for the same reason you are." She stretched up and kissed him, her lips soft, yearning and ripe. She tasted of coffee and need, and he lost all the questions he thought to ask.

"Just so we're clear, it's been a long time for me. Life's been hectic and I'm a touch . . . raw. Best bet here is to let tonight be about tonight," Frankie said, "with no promises for tomorrow."

"Works for me." He hadn't missed the neat sidestep she took around his curiosity, but he was so hard and she was so pliant, he let his body, and hers, be in charge.

Besides, Frankie was doing something with her tongue under his ear that had him lifting her to waist high.

Need swamped her as Daniel hauled her up to his waist. She wrapped her legs around him and let him carry her through the door and into the living area of his home. An impression of masculine efficiency flashed by, but checking out the decor would have to wait. He took her straight through the kitchen to his bedroom at the front. The drapes were already drawn, the bed turned down.

She worked on his buttons while he walked her, straddling him, to the bed. Her fingers worked fast, because even as shaky as they were, it had been far too long, and all she wanted was the feel of his hot flesh under her palms.

In ten seconds she got it. "Oh, you feel good," she murmured as she slid her hands under his shirt. She cupped his pecs and sighed with the rightness of his smooth skin. A sprinkling of hair between his pecs narrowed to his waistband. Silky, springy hair. She shuddered as she ran her fingers through the heated silk. She grinned in the dark. "I love chest hair."

"Good." He released her and she plopped onto the bed. He followed her down, but before she could settle he straddled her hips, pinning her into the soft mattress.

Vulnerable, she caught her breath, aware of her mistake. She was here with a stranger and no one in her life knew it. Big-city smarts had faded to horny stupidity in the face of six months of abstinence.

But Daniel wasn't into hurting her, she realized in a blink.

He wanted her naked. He copied her rapid work at buttons and whipped her shirt as wide open as his. "Front?" he asked.

"Yes."

He found the catch to her bra and clicked it, then swept the cups off her. "Dark, like I thought," he said as he palmed her. "Big, full nipples."

She moistened at the admiration in his gaze, the slide thick and wet between her legs.

He positioned her nipples in the apex of two fingers. With quick squeeze-and-release manipulations, he brought each nipple to hard in record time.

Oh yeah, this man knew his way around a breast. To show him how much she liked what he was doing she flung her hands up toward the headboard and arched up into his palms.

Encouraged, he squeezed and plucked, sending arrows of heat to her dripping pussy. "Oh, that's good," she said on a tightened huff of breath. She squeezed her thighs together for the little comfort she could find from the aching need.

He balanced on his heels and undid his belt buckle. She held her breath while she watched the smooth play of his hands and fingers. No turning back now.

Thank God.

She sat up and palmed his ribs while she found and sucked one of his nipples, then the other. He caught his breath and stilled. She nipped the flesh lightly. "Yes, do that."

She delighted in his responses to every lick, every suck of her lips and tongue. Her belly tightened with anticipation.

He slid off the bed, yanked down his jeans then kicked off his sneakers. Then he stood and let her look her fill. And her fill was what she'd get. The man was spectacular. Fully erect and thick, his penis would fill her and then some. She felt her inner muscles quake as the message zipped from her eyes to her brain and down to her weepy pussy.

"I'm going to have to be very ready."

He chuckled. "I'll make sure of it."

She just bet he would.

"Now I want to see you. Strip out of those shorts, Frankie, and show me your wet, tight, lickable pussy."

Her hands stalled on her zipper. She swallowed. "Oh."

"Never been kissed?" His eyes lit up like a kid in a candy store. She wanted to be everything he hoped for.

"Not very well." Fact was, she'd been shy and awkward and the whole thing had seemed forced anyway. As if Blaine was doing what he thought he should instead of what he wanted. Which had been to shove himself inside, root around for a moment then pull out to shoot all over her belly. He liked to see the mess. That is, if he got the condom off in time.

She always thought he'd seen too much porn and got off more on the cum shots than the act itself. She was already more turned on with just a few touches and kisses from Daniel than she'd ever been with Blaine.

Daniel's warm palms on each knee brought her back to bed, to the here and now and what they were doing.

"We'll see if I can do better." His voice stroked like rough suede down her spine. She melted under the intensity in his gaze.

"Do you like . . . doing *that*?"

"Say it." Desire filled his voice, his eyes, warmed through his palms and burned the flesh of her knees. "Say what it is that you think I like doing. Say it."

She thrilled at the soft command. "Do you like licking pussy?"

"Strange question, but yes, I like it. Love it. You'll come, I promise. If I'm really good, you'll come more than once and then I'll get to slide all the way home and we'll both go off like rockets again."

She couldn't form thoughts let alone words, so she unzipped as quickly as she could and let him help her out of her shorts and panties.

Then he spread her legs to indecent and settled at the foot of the bed.

From this angle all she could see was his incredible focus. She wanted to watch his face as he studied her, but shyness washed through her so she stared at the ceiling instead.

Stars twinkled where there shouldn't be any, and then she realized he'd stuck the Big Dipper over the bed. Glow in the dark stars reflected their stored light. She smiled at the whimsy and liked Daniel even more. "You're making me see stars," she said.

"Jeeze, and I haven't started yet." His humor eased its way through her shyness, and she felt her body bloom open.

"I like you, Daniel."

"I like you, Frankie."

The bedside clock ticked into the silence. "Are you going to start now?" she whispered.

"I'm trying to catch my breath. You're so beautiful, Frankie, I'm not sure I can do you justice."

"Now you're teasing me." She raised up to her elbows and looked between the vee of her knees. Daniel grinned back at her.

"No, this is teasing," he said. He dropped his face to where she waited.

Daniel felt pretty good about how he'd kept the awe out of his voice. He often depended on humor to hide his real feelings. Fear of the microphone, fear of losing his train of thought and fear of losing his audience were all kept at bay with jokes and light talk.

But this woman scared the hell out of him, and there weren't enough jokes or humor in the world to help him fake it.

He could see she was nervous, maybe shy. But she'd made it clear what she wanted, and she wanted a night of good sex. He already wanted more, but for now it was enough to give the lady what she wanted. Tomorrow could take care of itself.

She lay spread before him like a banquet, all pink rosiness, plump and oh-so-juicy. He lifted each of her legs and draped them over his shoulders. No need for finesse; he didn't want to give her time to backtrack or shy away.

He pressed the flat of his hand on her low belly, then tracked the landing strip of dark curls to just over her clit. Her belly quivered so he pressed deep to let her know there would be no squirming away from him. He rubbed at the apex of her mons to encourage her bud to peep out from its protective hood. A little more encouragement and out it popped like a plump pearl.

He blew across it, feeling her belly react and flutter under his palm. She stayed quiet, waiting.

But he could see moisture gathering, creamy and scented in a way that made his blood boil. "I like your scent, Frankie. Like hot need and warm woman."

He nuzzled the side of her inner thigh, where some of her juice had smeared. The hollow between her outer lips and her inner leg was as good a place as any to start tasting her. She jerked at the first lick, but he pressed his palm into her again until she calmed and relaxed.

His cock pounded, his blood rushed in his ears as he set the tip of his tongue to her outer lip. She flinched at the touch but soon eased her muscles again. "You'll come soon. And then you'll want my mouth all over you."

She rolled her head from side to side. He imagined her biting her lip to keep from crying out. But she couldn't hold back a moan as he worked her into a frenzy. She gushed into his mouth while his tongue delved deep into her. She tasted of ambrosia and the earthy taste of horny woman.

His thumb stretched to cover her clit and he rocked her into a soul-searing come that exploded on his tongue and lips. She grunted and pressed toward him while he lapped and held her at the peak.

She rolled her hips and cried out. One arm slammed across her mouth to cover her screams, while she used her other hand to hold his head in place. Her fingers bit into his scalp while she bucked and lunged and came and came.

Before the inner muscles stopped clenching, he rose to the bed and crawled up her trembling, shattered body, grabbed her hips and widened her cradle. While she quieted he slid on protection and positioned himself at her entrance.

"Slide home, Daniel. I want you in."

The invitation sounded like the opening of heaven's gate and he took his place inside.

5

Frankie woke to the sound of a phone ringing and then the sound of a groggy male voice answering. Daniel.

She snuggled into the heat of his side and tried to drown out his whispered conversation, but his voice began to clear, get sharper, louder.

She peeped open an eye as he pulled himself to a sitting position. This put her face interestingly close to his cock.

His morning erection filled her vision. She grinned and tipped out her tongue. Musk and salt burst on her taste buds.

The man was as hot and delicious and good for her as an old-fashioned bowl of oatmeal on a cold morning. The taste of him warmed her belly and woke her completely.

His voice changed as she slid her mouth over the top of his cock and down as far as she could go. He shifted his legs to give her room to seek out his sac. And a full sac it was, too.

Full and hard and yummy.

She rolled to lie between his open legs so she could lick his balls and tease at the hair there. Whatever he was talking about was already done. She heard the phone click off.

"Good morning," he said. His palms cupped the back of her head, fingering through her hair. "This is good, Frankie." He moaned. "I'll come if you don't stop."

She considered it, but the musky flavor had woken her own need and she took one last swirl around the head of his lovely penis, dipped her tongue into the slit to taste the dew of pre-cum he offered then rolled to her back.

"Climb on, big man, and ride me," she crooned, pressing her breasts together for her own morning offering.

He reached for a condom and stretched it over his burgeoning flesh. Sitting on his haunches, he pulled her to his lap and let her slide slowly onto his spearing cock. Playfulness in full force, he bounced her up and down. "Giddyup."

She laughed and took over, bouncing and bucking, letting him in deeper and harder, closer to her heart than she'd ever intended. A one-night stand was looking to be far more, and she let herself enjoy the idea of a full day in bed with him.

Daniel had no idea who she was, where she was from or how she'd ended up here, and that's the way it had to stay. With some luck, though, she could have this time with him.

If he never learned the truth, she'd never have to doubt him. Doubting Daniel was not something she ever wanted to happen.

Because this was all she could give him.

But give it to him she would. The way he was giving it to her. Hard, fast, deep and strong. Bouncing gave way to rocking, and rocking gave way to holding her pubis to his while he moved slickly in and out of her. His thumb rubbed her clit and took her into a crashing orgasm.

He crowed with a come that bounced off her inner walls and tipped her into her favorite kind of deep, inner clenching. Powerful shudders racked her as he pressed up and into her, as he sought to keep her on the edge for as long as possible.

The man was a master.

* * *

Two mugs of coffee later, she waited on deck while Daniel finished dressing. He had an idea where to look for the thong, and she was antsy to get going. The afternoon stretched on either side of them. The first half had been about outdoing each other in the orgasm department. A contest she'd won handily. She had at least four to his two and had the sore pussy to prove it.

From this side of the marina the sounds of people living their lives on live-aboard boats and float homes took on more of a familiar neighborly sound. She could hear television shows in the distance. Two slips away, she saw a woman hanging her wash on a line that bisected the deck of her converted boat. It had the look of a Chinese junk about it. As she'd noted more details about the surrounding homes, she noticed more of the quirkiness of the people who chose to live aboard. Every conceivable type of vessel that could be converted to a home, had been.

Some were obviously built for life on the water, others had once been working vessels with haphazard additions and renovations to turn them into live aboards.

Daniel's was fairly new and had been built as a float home. He had everything here that a regular house would have, including laundry facilities. He was hooked up to city water and sewage, just like a regular house.

Fascinated by the lifestyle, she scanned for similar homes to his and found several, all painted in muted tones. The more quirky places, the homemade ones, seemed the most likely to be painted in brilliant yellows, red, purples and some combinations that would make an interior designer's stomach turn.

No one would ever look for her here. She blew out a breath and enjoyed her first truly peaceful afternoon in six months.

Great sex, good coffee, and a humorous man with a magic tongue, lips and cock; what more could a woman ask for?

She decided to enjoy the respite while she had it.

Strong arms slid around her waist and she sank back into Daniel's embrace. He took her coffee mug with one hand while his other copped a feel. He tweaked her nipple, sending sparklers deep and hot to her center. She heard him sip the last of her coffee next to her ear and smiled.

"Ready to go, you coffee thief?"

He turned and called the dog out of his doghouse. "Barkley, you're the real thief, now cough up that thong."

"I thought we established the fact that he couldn't cough it up when we got that X-ray."

"Good point." He stepped onto the dock, then held out his hand. She liked that he wanted to touch her in such a simple way. One of the joys of a relationship was having a strong hand to hold. "There's a trash can just at the entrance to the park. I've seen Barkley drop stuff there. Next time I look, whatever he's dropped has disappeared. I think there's another animal that drags it away."

"You mean he's supplying some wild creature with women's panties?"

"Not panties so much as sparkly things. Barkley will take girly shiny hair bands, or glittery stuff or pieces of shiny plastic. He's a pain in the ass." He slanted the scruffy canine an exasperated look.

"But he's *your* pain in the ass."

He snorted in good humor. "Yeah, he's mine. Aren't you, you little thug?" Barkley danced in a circle, then peed on a pylon.

"I've passed this trash can a hundred times and I've never seen anything but a dog near it."

"Lead the way," she said. He took her hand as they walked along the cement dock to the ramp. Everyone who was outside waved to Daniel. A couple of people commented on the sunny day. All of them appraised her with interest.

"They're staring at me."

"Because you're from the *Boondoggle* and it's making them nuts that they don't know anything about you and you've been here two weeks."

"Oh." She sighed and swung his hand between them. "That's not going to change any time soon. I don't shout my business to anyone."

"They're also curious because I don't often have women sleep over."

She heated and squeezed his hand. He pulled her to a stop at the bottom of the ramp, set his hands on her shoulders to make her face him. "Yes?" she asked.

He kissed her. Not in an Oh! baby, we had a great time together kind of way. Oh no! Not Daniel. He had a hidden theatrical flair. He kissed her, then dropped her into a dip that made her belly drop to her toes and brought out a chorus of cheers and whistles from his neighbors.

When he set her back on her feet, she slapped his shoulder in a show of affection. "You're a wild man." His sense of fun brought out her inner clown, and she turned to the onlookers and gave them a deep curtsy.

To another set of catcalls and whistles, they turned and headed up the ramp, Daniel's hand on her butt, just in case anyone doubted she was his.

She laughed. "How long have you lived in the marina? And what made you decide to live in one?"

"I like the people. Some of them are a little on the odd side."

"Eccentric, you mean."

"No, they just like to live their way. It's a frame of mind, mostly."

"It's like living in an RV park on water."

"Sort of." He swung her hand as they turned and headed up the ramp. "I'll be sorry to leave."

"You're going somewhere?"

"Not yet, but I'm always putting out feelers."

"You want to move from here?" The city's downtown core was compact, easily accessible and fun. The harbor was one of the most beautiful she'd seen. The architecture alone was worth a visit. Stone government buildings, a glorious Victorian-era hotel and a causeway for strolling around a U-shaped inner harbor made the city unique.

"I hate to, but if I want more money I need a wider audience."

"And you want more money." Dread weighed like an anchor in her belly.

"Doesn't everyone?" He grinned and looked back the way they'd come, then out across the harbor. "I want a real home, with a wife and kids. Late night pays the bills, but not enough for the life I want. Not to mention the shift's a killer for relationships."

It was midafternoon and they were out for the first time today. "I can see how that could be a problem. If I had a regular day job, I wouldn't be here with you now. Guess we're just lucky."

"Very lucky." He snugged her close to his chest and kissed the tip of her nose. "I'm very lucky."

She smiled up at him. "Me too."

"The trash can's over here." The chain holding it to a concrete slab was rusted from dogs leaving their mark.

"You've never actually seen another animal drag things away?"

"Some animals are shy. With good reason. I think this one's a rat."

While she shuddered at the idea of Fiona's thong being fondled by an honest-to-God wharf rat, Daniel grasped opposite sides of the can and slid it a few inches. "There's a hole."

Right under the trash can. She jumped back, convinced the

rat waited, beady eyes glaring, sharp rat teeth ready to tear into her exposed ankles. "Oh, ugh! Daniel, be careful."

"He's more afraid of us than—"

"Yeah, yeah, you sound like my father explaining spiders to me when I was five."

He stopped shoving and stared at her. "You had a father?"

"Of course I have a father. Had a father," she corrected for caution's sake. "I was named after him." The family had splintered six months ago, and her heart still ached from the pain. She and Fiona were the only ones to keep in direct contact. For now, at least.

Daniel chuffed and pushed until the entire hole was exposed. He knelt beside the can.

"You're not putting your hand down that hole, are you?"

"I don't have a shovel. Not much use for one when you live in a marina."

"I'll run to the beach and see if I can borrow a sand shovel from someone."

But her suggestion fell on deaf ears, and Daniel shoved his hand into the rat's den up to his elbow. She couldn't help but think of herself in the saloon with her arm inside the safe.

"That would be fine, but it's not a sand beach. It's full of boulders and rocks."

She'd forgotten.

"It would be a stupid rat to have only one escape route," Daniel explained. "I'm betting he took off the minute I shoved the can." The sun caught the movement of muscle in his back and shoulders as he stretched into the hole and felt around.

Great shoulders, and a fabulous butt. And a heart as kind as all get-out. She didn't know another man who'd stick his hand where the sun never shone just to help her out.

Her heart warmed and cracked open at Daniel's kindness.

Barkley, fascinated by the idea of his human pal stretching

out on the ground under a smelly trash can, danced around like a crazed whirligig, yipping and growling near Daniel's head.

She scooped the dog into her arms.

"I've got something." Daniel pulled, then sat back on his haunches. In his hand, smudged with dirt and covered with leaves and other bits of debris, was Fiona's thong.

Barkley jumped out of her arms the minute she started to sag to her knees beside Daniel. She kissed his cheek, his ear, then planted a powerful one on his lips in thanks. She slipped the thong from his hand into hers and balled it up so no passerby would see it.

"You're the sweetest, kindest man I've ever met, Daniel Martin. Don't ever forget that."

"Don't you ever forget it, Frankie." He stood. "I need a shower, right away."

"I'll go call my sister and let her know."

"Want to toss that in the wash?"

"Thanks, no. I'll do it by hand." Then she'd put it back in the safe where it belonged. She only hoped she could convince Fiona to return it. She loved her sister, she did, but there were times she could smack her upside the head. With a two-by-four.

Barkley continued to dig at the hole and began unearthing a treasure trove of junk. "Get away from there, Barkley." Daniel slid the trash can back into place. "Don't want anyone to step in this hole and break an ankle."

"You're a thoughtful man too."

He flushed at the newest compliment. "That phone call earlier?"

"I didn't hear much. I was focused elsewhere."

"Thanks for that, by the way." His grin was lascivious. "I've been called to a meeting in an hour. The program director wants me to come in."

"Sounds important."

He frowned. "Could be."

"If they gave you a raise, would you be happy to stay doing late night? You sound so happy on your show. As if you can't think of anything you'd rather be doing."

"As far as job satisfaction, I have that in spades. But satisfaction doesn't pay bills. And it isn't just the money, it's the odd hours too. I can't see a relationship working with radically different shifts."

"A relationship is that important to you?" she asked, not certain which answer, yes or no, she'd rather hear.

On his way to his meeting, Daniel considered Frankie. She had an odd way of showing relaxed interest in him while keeping her history and personal information to herself. She was pretty good at keeping secrets. All he knew about her was that she loved coffee, liked his dog in spite of Barkley being a pain in the ass and knew how to make the most of her erogenous zones.

She'd been named after her father, but he'd noticed a slip of the tongue when she couldn't decide if he was alive or dead. She also had a honeymooning sister who was as yet unnamed.

He'd asked her to stay a few more days, because he wanted full and immediate access to her. She'd hesitated long enough to make him think she'd refuse, but in the end she'd agreed. She was yacht-sitting only a few docks away, but he still wanted her at his place.

She seemed content to stay once she'd considered it. But those moments when she'd made him wait for her answer had been hard for him. Surprisingly hard.

Lucky for him he'd remembered that trash can. If he hadn't thought of it, she might have gone back to her place right away.

Frankie was fun and got his stupid humor, and he loved

making her laugh. In bed and out of it. When Frankie laughed, the room lit up, her smile went wide and her throaty chuckle grabbed him by the heartstrings.

Funny thing was, that fact didn't scare him. Loving Frankie was not scary at all.

He'd never been in a relationship with a woman who was free to accommodate his schedule. Normally, he was a hit-and-run kind of guy, mostly because the women he met were caught up in their own lives and careers. Taking time to see him for a couple hours here and there turned into booty-call sex, and eventually those things fizzled out for lack of anything else substantial going on.

He was great with being a booty call, but with Frankie he wanted more.

He pulled into the parking lot and turned his mind to the upcoming meeting. His numbers were good, his audience growing, and he hadn't pissed anyone off lately, so he had no idea what the meeting was about. Butch, the program director, had been unusually reticent about sharing information when he'd called, and with Frankie doing the wild thing at the time, Daniel hadn't asked for specifics.

Maybe he should have.

He hoped to hell this was about a raise. He wanted a home. A raise would give him the chance to go for it. With Frankie squarely in his sights he felt more than ready to settle onto terra firma.

Reaching for the door, his hand caught the light from overhead. His naked hand. No rings. He had a visual of a gold band there. *Must be my feminine side*, he thought. People talked about men having them. He snorted. Stupid.

He walked through the foyer and headed for Butch's office door, trying like hell to get his mind back on the meeting. The station was a different place in the afternoon. Light and noisy with people running to and fro, gathering and laughing to-gether at the front counter and near the staff room door, coffee mugs in hand.

A few of them waved at him. One, the morning man's pro-ducer, gave him a broad smile as he walked by.

That was odd. He was normally persona non grata to that guy.

When he got to Butch's office door, he leaned inside the door frame. "You're way too ugly at this time of day. Tone it down, would'ja?"

"Fuck you." Butch looked up and grinned. A grin that said they'd spent a lot of years together in a crazy-making business and survived. Together.

"Why the rush to see me? Good news I hope."

"Sometimes good news is bad news."

Daniel took a seat in front of the desk. "So, this isn't about a raise, I take it?"

"Not exactly. It's about a move. Good news for you, bad news for me." He frowned. "And maybe even bad news for you."

Daniel leaned in. "Now you're dicking me around."

Butch shook his head. "No. Chicago. A transfer."

"No way."

"Way."

"Shit!" Chicago, the market every bluesman not based in the south wanted. Wait'll he told Frankie. All he could think of was sharing his news with her. He flashed on an image of her face, lighting up as he told her. "Wait a minute, what's the bad news?"

"It's the morning shift."

Which meant a lot more money. But he'd have to give up the quiet of the night, his solitude in the booth. Butch's face hadn't shifted away from the frown. "What else?"

"They want to team you up."

"Shit," he said. Morning chatter shows aimed at morons and tweens. And banter.

He hated banter.

"I don't play well with others." Not on the air anyway. "Especially not in the morning."

"I remember. But this is an opportunity you shouldn't pass up. The money's good, Danny."

He swallowed when he heard how much. "How soon do they need to know?"

"They'll be surprised if you hesitate. Let me know tomorrow." Butch paused. Looked him in the eye. "I'll repeat that you shouldn't pass this up, but I know you'll hate it."

"Every minute, but I'll get used to it." He closed his eyes, while his gut did a roll of disgust. "Any idea who I'd be paired with?"

Butch's gaze shifted left.

That did not look good.

"Shit. I'll let you know in a couple of days." Tomorrow was too soon.

Butch said, "If I could give you more money here, I would."

"I know." He didn't press for more information on the partner. He didn't need any more bad news to color his decision. Either he wanted a morning slot and the livable wage or he didn't. The partner wouldn't matter. "Whatever you could give me wouldn't be enough for what I want anyway."

Butch leaned back far enough on his chair to lift the front legs off the floor. "Do tell. What is it you're after?"

Daniel stood.

"A woman?" Butch demanded, curiosity lighting his ugly face.

"Maybe."

"Women aren't maybe's, they either are or are not the right one. Which is she?"

"Put that way, I'd have to say . . . fuck you. Fuck you very much." He stepped out of the room and laughed as Butch hollered out his office door.

"I hope to hell she makes you squirm, Danny! Squirm!" But the words were said around a chuckle.

Daniel was already looking forward to dinner with Frankie before he had to come back for his shift. He had a lot of thinking to do.

Daniel sipped a beer while Frankie flipped burgers on the grill. It had been ages since she'd cooked for a man. She'd made the patties bigger than she would have made for herself. Without warning, his arms came around her and she felt his warm hug and hard body behind her. "I wanted to take you out for dinner to show you my generous nature."

She grinned and leaned back into him. "You already have." A generous man in bed was a lot better than one who tossed gifts a girl's way. "And I wanted to impress you with my burgers."

"So far, I'm impressed with everything about you," he said. The affection in his voice was clear and warmed her. She felt the same way.

"I like this routine," she said. "Sleeping late suits me. I'm not an early bird. When I was working I was always running late. I hated getting up early."

The burgers were ready. "Pass me your plate," she said.

He held out both plates to her and she slid the meat onto the buns.

After several compliments on her cooking, which made her glow with feminine pride, he polished off his burger and a huge helping of salad. "So, you haven't asked how my meeting went." He swiped a napkin across his lips and chin.

"I'm dying to hear but I didn't think it was any of my business." She wanted what he wanted. Whatever made him happy would make her happy.

He slid his hand across the glass-topped patio table and stroked her knuckles with his fingertip. "I'm glad you want to know. And it's crazy, but already it feels like your business."

"Oh, Daniel." Her heart wanted to burst with joy. But hard on that feeling came a nugget of fear. It was too soon. Crazy. Impossible, given the circumstances. "I care for you too—"

He interrupted her, taking her words and running with them. "I've been offered a transfer to Chicago."

"Chicago?" Frankie tried to put a smile on her face, and her lips cooperated just fine. It was her eyes that must have given her away. Her eyes and the hollowed-out, disappointed tone in her voice. Anything that would make him happy would make her happy.

Anyplace but Chicago.

"It's everything I want. Have always wanted." He held her with nothing more than the tip of his sexy finger, wreaking havoc on her knuckles. Then he saw beyond her lips. "What's wrong? You look strange."

"I'm just surprised," she blustered. "I've never thought of anyone being thrilled at the idea of moving to Chicago." She had to remember that the familiar and boring to one person was new and exciting to another. Like Bernie and his wilderness fascination. A native Alaskan wouldn't find trees and mountain streams nearly as big a thrill as Bernie.

"You've been there?"

"You could say that." She had to give him a smidgen of information now that she'd been so transparent. "You'll love the blues clubs. There's a place on North Michigan that's fantastic." His other hand reached out and he took both hands in his. She stood and picked up the empty plates. "I'll tell you about it sometime."

He followed her into the kitchen, carrying the rest of the

dishes. "So, you'll tell me about blues clubs and where to go in Chicago, but you won't tell me anything about you."

She put the plates on the kitchen counter. "I can't. Not now."

"But you will? Sometime?" There was nothing but gentle persuasion in his voice. No demand, no pressure, no avid curiosity.

"Thanks for giving me space, Daniel. I . . . appreciate it."

"You've got me wondering if you're in the witness protection program or something equally sexy."

"Sexy?" She laughed. But it was forced. There was nothing sexy about being on the run. No matter who you were running from, or why. "So, you're taking your show to Chicago. You'll be a smash. The blues fans are in for a treat."

"This is a morning show. It's more money and a wider audience."

"No blues in the night?"

He shook his head, and something that passed for happy but wasn't flashed in his gaze. She recognized the look because she'd been wearing it for some time. Even good things could have sharp edges that cut.

"It'll be traffic reports, contests, wake-up music and banter." The edgy expression disappeared, replaced by a now-familiar and welcome desire. He took her in his arms, slid his hands to either side of her neck. The kiss he gave was light, coaxing, and sent her thoughts spinning. His thumbs rotated on either side of her throat, caressing and smoothing her skin, creating sparks of desire low in her belly.

"You can fill me in on the blues culture in Chicago later. But right now what will you tell me?" His voice was hypnotic, charged with need.

She leaned into him and accepted his kiss. Deep, hungry, delicious. "I'll tell you what I want you to do."

"That is?"

"Love me, Daniel. You're so good at it." She cupped him through his slacks, slid her palm up the rigid steel she found there. Her mouth watered, her pussy wept.

She offered her neck; he took it.

She offered her breasts; he suckled them.

She offered her slickest, neediest parts. He dropped to his knees and took her where she needed to go.

6

Without a morning phone call, they were able to sleep in as long as they needed, but Daniel woke first. He slipped out of bed without disturbing Frankie. She'd listened to his entire show and waited up for him. That was a first with a woman. But then, he was having a lot of firsts with Frankie.

When he'd tiptoed into the kitchen, he'd seen the glow of candles from the bedroom. Frankie had been shopping. Dressed in a soft creamy-colored merry widow complete with garters and stockings, she'd taken his breath away.

He finished in the bathroom and checked on her. Still asleep. The floor of the bedroom was strewn with various bits of satiny lingerie that made his cock rise again.

He could wake her with a quick slide inside, but she needed to sleep. He'd kept her up for hours, and she must be tender from all the attention. He put the coffee on, then peeked in at her once more. Frankie was still asleep, breathing heavily with the sheet in a two-fisted clutch under her chin.

When the coffee was ready, he filled his mug, stepped out on deck and stretched. He rubbed his naked belly and gave Barkley a whistle.

He considered the offer of the Chicago gig. More money versus giving up the best job he'd ever had. The late-night time slot suited him. He'd been cheered by Frankie's comment about how the hours suited her too.

More and more about Frankie engaged him. Without knowing anything about her, he was drawn into her, wanting her time, loving her smile. Needing her laughter to round out his day.

She fascinated him. Mystery swirled around her. She looked close to speaking sometimes, but when he waited expectantly, she'd get a worried look in her eyes and change the subject.

Whatever was wrong, she needed time to come to terms with telling him. Pressing her for information was a bad idea. He'd often gone with his gut on these things, and his gut had never failed him.

All he could do was follow his own heart in this.

Which brought him back to what he really wanted. He wanted to stay in the late-night spot. Wanted to have full control over his show. Wanted to sit back in the dark of the night and do his thing.

But more than that, he wanted Frankie.

She was unemployed, and if not for the kindness of a friend, she'd be without a home. Which took care of conflicting schedules but increased the need for a better-paying time slot.

Daniel's time in late night needed to come to an end. His gut twisted at the thought, but he sucked it up. His father's voice rang through his head, reminding him that most people worked at jobs they hated. Life today demanded sacrifice if a person wanted a family.

Daniel had the sense that if he didn't soon do something toward getting the family he wanted, he'd miss out. Maybe he was coming at the family thing late, but that didn't mean he wanted it less than other men. Maybe because he'd been so slow, he wanted it more. And faster.

He thought of Frankie, asleep in his bed. His heart warmed.

He whistled for Barkley again, then peered into his doghouse. Empty.

And Barkley was nowhere else onboard.

The dog usually stuck close to his food bowl until breakfast had been served. Then he pretty much filled his day scrounging more meals from all the neighbors. That, and stealing underwear. Daniel whistled again. Listened for the bounce of his paws on the dock.

Nothing.

But in the distance he heard a bark, seriously pissed. Barkley. The sound came from the marina side.

He stepped onto the dock and walked along until he could see Barkley's scruffy cropped tail, standing straight up. His back end hopped up and down as if it were on strings. He was farther away than he sounded. He whistled again, but the dog ignored him as his barks got ferocious.

The closer he got the more he heard. Between barks the little guy was growling and snapping. Something was seriously wrong. Daniel set his coffee mug on a pylon and took off at a dead run.

Barkley went into an insane racket, snapping, snarling, and then, Daniel heard a yelp and cry that spurred him to run faster, harder. Now he was the one pissed.

Someone had hurt his dog.

Daniel rounded the dock where he'd last seen Barkley and slid to a stop. The stranger Barkley was harassing was on Frankie's yacht. Slouched cap, black jeans, bland windbreaker. The guy looked like background. Nothing about him would stand out.

Except for the camera dangling around his neck.

"Hey!" Daniel yelled. "Who the hell are you? And what'd you do to my dog?"

Barkley had wisely climbed onto the boat on the far side of the dock and stood barking on the cabin roof, well out of range of this guy's sneakers.

"I didn't do anything to your dog. Tell him to shut up, he's disturbing the neighbors." The guy put up his hands and gave him a *who me?* smile. Friendly and easygoing-like, and Daniel hated the slimy guy on sight.

"Get off that boat. The owner's not here."

"Yeah, uh, where is she? We're supposed to meet here today. You seen her?" The guy climbed down to face Daniel on the dock. His eyes scanned the marina, sharp and suspicious.

Barkley finally stopped barking but stayed where he was, growling in as menacingly a way as a fifteen-pound mutt could.

"There's no her," Daniel said reflexively. "Who are you looking for?"

"Hey, if she's not here, she's not here." He put his hands up in surrender and sidled around Daniel. "I'll catch her later." He headed off while Daniel coaxed Barkley off the cabin roof and into his arms.

"You okay, boy?" The dog licked his cheek and ear. If Daniel didn't know better, he'd think his little buddy was actually relieved to see him. Then he wriggled, wanting to jump down. Daniel let him go with a good scratch behind the ears. "You're getting an extra cookie for that, Barkley." At the word *cookie* the dog danced in a circle. "Whoever that guy was, he wasn't up to anything good."

They strolled back toward the float home together. Daniel picked up his cold coffee on the way past the pylon and kept a sharp eye out for the intruder, but he was long gone.

Frankie peeped one eye open, so sated she could barely roll over. She checked the time on the bedside clock. Daniel had let her sleep. She stretched and took measure of how she felt. Her legs were like overcooked noodles, her spine like butter, and the area between her legs felt slick as olive oil.

A gentle swell rolled under the house. Must be the wake from the *Victoria Clipper,* a catamaran ferry for foot passengers to downtown Seattle. Pleased that she already recognized the ebb, flow and pattern of harbor traffic, she sniffed the air. "Mmm, coffee."

Listening to the roar of a seaplane, she realized how familiar the sounds of life in the marina had become since arriving two weeks ago. People called out to each other, boat motors started, gulls screeched. The water rolled under her, rocking her gently in the bed.

She could get used to life on the water.

Back in Chicago, she rarely saw the lake. Never bothered to walk there. Daniel would like it, she was certain. Maybe he could take his float home and find a spot for it on the waterfront. She wasn't sure how that would work, but if she could help with the move, she would. Maybe they could put it on a barge or something and tow it.

A house on a barge would look weird going through the Panama Canal and up the eastern seaboard. Might be faster to ship it by train. Mind boggled by the turn of events, she stretched and yawned. Daniel, in Chicago, doing what he loved best. The thought pleased her in spite of the pang of regret she suffered.

Chicago. The bustle, the traffic, the . . . problems. So far away. But here, with the salt in the air and the quiet busyness of the afternoon, it was different. Slower, softer. So damn livable.

Then again, she was probably just feeling the afterglow of stupendous sex. She tightened her thighs in memory. Mmm.

Daniel.

Hot.

Mmm.

Suddenly realizing she hadn't heard a sound from within the house, she sat upright and peered out the bedroom door into the living area. No sign of him. He was probably already out on deck.

Her one-night stand had certainly changed. She hadn't wanted a relationship, but it seemed she had one anyway.

The idea brought a silly, girlish smile to her face, and she stifled an equally silly giggle with two fingers against her lips. People had no control over affairs of the heart. The best intentions could be waylaid by a smile, a lover's touch, a bit of shared laughter and a warm glance. Her heart thudded happily at the idea of another day with Daniel, and she let the giggle escape into the room.

Lighthearted, she slid out of bed. A denim shirt of Daniel's hung on a hook by the door. She pulled it on, sucked in the scent of him and gathered her lingerie off the floor. His face had been pure seduction when he'd seen her wearing it.

She rinsed her mouth, then used his toothpaste on the brush she'd brought from the yacht and did her best to freshen up as quickly as she could.

Daniel had a healthy appetite for sex, and she hoped the long night would turn into a long afternoon in bed with him.

With Fiona's thong safely washed and stored away, she didn't have anything to do, but Daniel. And doing Daniel was all she needed for now.

The transfer to Chicago had surprised her. He seemed taken with the idea, in spite of the obvious joy he took from working the late-night show. Ambition was a good trait to have. It was. It was just such a bitch that he had to show it now.

Damn.

She would have liked more time to explore all the traits Daniel possessed. As it was, she suspected he would like her to be pleased with the transfer news. She was, for him. But she'd miss him. How he'd gotten under her skin this quickly was a mystery, but there it was. She wanted him. Anywhere. Anytime.

Anyplace but Chicago.

Her belly bloomed heat and need as she listened for any sound onboard. Nothing.

Just as she finished washing up, a thud from the kitchen and Daniel talking to Barkley in a singsong voice made her grin. It was time to see what the day would bring.

She borrowed his comb and brought some order to her sex-mussed hair before heading into the kitchen.

As soon as he saw her, Daniel opened his arms in invitation. She moved into them and received one of the best hugs she'd ever had.

"You're good at this," she commented. "Just the right pressure and your arms enfold me completely." Such comfort, warm and inviting. She had to be careful not to want more. Not with Chicago on his mind.

He loved the way Frankie flowed into his arms, natural and easy as if she belonged with him. "Did you have an appointment today? On the yacht?"

She disappointed him by sliding away to help herself to a mug of coffee. "No, why?" Her voice was stilted. Odd.

"There was some guy looking for you." It still burned his ass that the guy probably kicked his dog. "I heard Barkley kicking up a real stink so I ran over. Halfway there, I think your visitor kicked Barkley to shut him up."

"Is the little guy okay?" She froze in the middle of sliding the coffee carafe back onto the warming plate, but she didn't turn around.

"He seems fine. Never heard him snarl and growl that way before, though. He took a real dislike to the guy. You're sure you weren't expecting someone?"

Her shoulders squared, and he wanted to turn her around to

face him, but he waited, sensing she needed time to process the news. She took a deep breath before sliding the carafe home. She turned back to him with a sunny smile and nervous eyes. "Who was he? Did he say?"

"Didn't say anything except he had an appointment with you."

She moved into his arms again, cradling her mug between his chest and hers. "You, ah, kind of caught me off guard last night with all that excitement about Chicago. If I had an appointment with someone, your exciting news made me forget about it." She sipped her coffee. "You make me forget a lot of things when you touch me."

His blood flowed south of his waist as she brushed her soft parts against his hard-on. Her eyes gave him an invitation he couldn't resist.

She set down her coffee and pressed her coffee-warmed hands to the flesh above his waistband. He sucked in his belly, then stole a kiss. He sucked her bottom lip, swept his tongue across her bottom front teeth, then slid inside her mouth. She tasted of coffee and excitement.

She moaned lightly and set him on fire with her response. "You have a way with kisses that makes my mind short-circuit," she murmured. She opened the shirt of his she wore and offered herself. Her breasts bobbed when he cupped them, full and already pebbled.

He swept in and took. Then he took some more.

Daniel's lips were magic. On her mouth, her breasts and *there*.

The *there* melted and opened. She shifted her feet apart to let him know where she needed his next touch. Fingers skimmed against her wet entrance, tantalizing her with brief swirls. Suddenly, he was there where she needed him, and he filled his hand with her freshly streaming pussy. A finger speared into her while she rolled her hips in a plea.

"Oh, you're good. Do that again."

A second finger slid home and she rocked against his palm, sucking sounds proving her arousal. She kissed him into silence when he looked ready to speak, then decided to take him way past the need to talk.

She dropped to her knees, regretting the loss of his fingers in her slit. But a girl had to do what a girl had to do. She worked his tented shorts open and freed his cock.

Jutting flesh greeted her, and she took him tip-deep into her mouth. She followed his lead and played lightly with the bulbous purple head, sliding and swirling her tongue. His shaft thickened with the attention, and she cupped his scrotum. His balls pulled up hard and she knew he was close. In spite of the orgasms through the night and early morning, Daniel was a wake-up sex kind of guy.

He groaned and held her head lightly while she played him.

"Bed," he groaned. "I need—"

But she knew what she needed and this was it. To know she could take him over the edge with nothing but her mouth gave her a power she loved. A power she craved. A power she had to use to keep his mind off the man he'd seen.

Because this had to be good-bye.

Something was off, Daniel decided, while his thoughts whirled and sensation threatened to take him over the edge into orgasm. She was anxious and hurried, whereas all the other times they'd made love, Frankie had been open and at ease. Once she got over her shyness and got rocking, that was.

She surged and sucked him, licked his balls and took them into her mouth. He nearly lost it then, but managed to hold on long enough to form a plan.

He burrowed his fingers into her hair and tugged lightly to pull her away. She moved, looked up at him with feverish need and tried to dive back into his crotch.

"No. Bed, now." He picked her up and she cuddled into his arms. He stepped out of the shorts around his ankles and carried her back to bed.

Following her down into the mattress he pressed his body the length of hers, twining their feet, his cock cushioned by the softness of her belly. He slid his hands into her hair again, holding her still. He stared into her eyes until she focused and quieted.

"What's going on, Frankie?"

"What do you mean?" She pumped her stomach muscles, sending fluttery sensations from his cock up his spine. Sweet heaven, the woman didn't stop.

"Don't play this game. As soon as I mentioned that guy on your yacht, you went from morning-after comfortable to let's get this over with."

Her eyes widened. "You're crazy." She moved her head from side to side to break his light grip.

He let her go and sat back on his haunches. "Maybe I am, and maybe some women can switch gears that fast, but I don't think you're one of them. We were about to settle in for a quiet day together. You know it and I know it."

"I know nothing of the kind." She stiffened, looking alarmed. He rolled away. She needed room. Whatever was wrong, it wasn't about him. It was about her visitor. Hell, even Barkley hadn't liked the guy.

"You put on my shirt," he explained. "If you weren't planning to spend the day with me, you'd have dressed in your own clothes. You'd have left for your place." He hated that he couldn't tell from one moment to the next whether she'd be here or not. It had been like that since she'd first come onboard.

She nibbled her bottom lip but kept silent.

"Who was the guy on the yacht? He had a camera, if that helps."

She groaned. "Telephoto lens, too, I bet."

"Yeah, come to think of it."

She bit her lip again. "I can't be seen, Daniel. If I am, all hell will break loose and I'll have to leave." Her hands fluttered over her chest in a gesture that screamed nervous fright. "I should go anyway."

"Go where? Whoever this guy is, he found you here. He'll find you again. What's going on?"

"What did you say to him?"

"He said he was looking for the owner of the boat. Asked if I knew where 'she' was. I said there was no 'her' and that the yacht owner was away. He seemed okay with that answer and moved off without giving me his name."

She nodded, and he could see her thoughts whirling. "I should still leave. He'll be back if he doesn't have anywhere else to look."

"Stay here. Keep out of sight for a few days. Wait it out in bed." He ran his palm down her chest, past her lusciously sexy belly and found her slickness.

She blinked and smiled. "For today," she said. "I'll stay for today. I have to consider my options."

"One of them being me." He slid two fingers into her, watched as she closed her eyes and raised her hips for more. Wet heat enveloped him as he moved his fingers in and out, taking her mind off the conversation. He pulled his fingers out and licked them.

She stroked his cock with languid care, making his belly tighten.

She sighed and opened her legs. The woman from last night, relaxed and free, came out from under her nerves, and Daniel settled in to enjoy every moment of her company for as long as he had it.

"Stay with me, Frankie; it's too soon to lose this."

"Yes, too soon."

He slid into her and rocked her into an orgasm that took him too.

Two hours later, she knew she should deal with the disturbing news of the man on the yacht, but she'd been *dealing* for six months and she was tired. Tired of running, of hiding, of trying to keep her sister out of harm's way.

Meetings out the wazoo. Being chased, harassed, photographed, her emotions left raw and bleeding. Her family had been blown to the far corners of the earth. It was all too much. She needed to crash.

What better place to land than here, with Daniel. The man with the golden touch and the softest, most versatile lips she'd ever come across. She giggled at the thought.

To come across his lips was something she planned on doing several times today. Beginning now . . .

He blew a raspberry on her belly!

Just when she was settling in for some serious lovin' he got silly. She squealed when he did it again.

"That's better," he murmured as he trailed his lips lower. Sensation speared her as he nuzzled at her curls. Buried deep in her folds her clit plumped and filled. Remembered response. Her body already anticipated the slow build of tension Daniel was so good at.

She shuddered. "That's so good," she praised, smiling inside at the raspberry. The man knew exactly what to do to make her forget her troubles.

No one knew she was here with Daniel. She was safe for as long as she stayed out of sight.

She closed her eyes and let Daniel's easy strokes carry her along to glory. He slid his palms beneath her hips and raised her to his face.

"Open for me, Frankie, I love to look at you."

She slid two fingers to her pussy and widened her lips for him. The tip of his tongue found her clit and rocked her hard with a fluttering that carried her over the edge. Held up this way, she couldn't move her hips but had to leave it to Daniel to press and take her higher before she fell, fell, fell into the abyss of exquisite sensation only Daniel could create.

Before the inner pulses died away, he shattered her again with an invasion of cock that stole what breath she had left. She took him in to the hilt and rocked him past all thought and deep into the world of sensation he'd created.

7

"I'm leaving him," Fiona said.

Frankie pressed the phone to her ear. "Oh, give me a break. Leave Bernie? Are you insane?" She was, Frankie realized. Fiona was nuts. "You've been engaged for three years and together since high school. You're *not* leaving Bernie." Besides, she'd been saying that same thing since they met. Frankie had hoped that having a longed-for wedding would stop the nonsense. But no, apparently her sister had tuned out the "til death do you part" section of the vows.

"We're stuck up here with nowhere to go but fishing. It's cold, it's wet and I want to go home." Home meaning more than the place they grew up. Frankie gripped the receiver tighter.

"I'd like our lives back to normal too. We have to hang tough a while longer."

Her sister sniffed into the phone. "You're right. It's just—it's been so long. And Bernie's having the time of his life. He's found a bunch of hunters and guys who fish to hang with. I'm lonely." A social butterfly, Fee wasn't used to being left to her own devices. Frankie took a deep breath and prayed for patience.

"You don't know how lucky you are to have Bernie." She surprised herself with the depth of her feelings. She was jealous! Not of Bernie, but of the trust her sister had in him. Dependable Bernie, always-there-for-Fiona Bernie. Frankie sighed and bit back hard on the jealous pang. "Bernie loves you, would die without you. Believe me, that counts for a lot."

"I know," her sister responded in a broken whisper. "Believe me, I know. I thought it would be different, that's all."

"Marriage you mean?" It was a supremely stupid question considering they'd been living together for years. Oh! The distress that had caused her traditionally minded parents.

"No, the other thing."

"All that is being sorted out. We have responsibilities and I'm seeing that we all live up to them. Well, as much as I can, anyway."

Fee chuckled. "You've always been good at being responsible. While I've been nothing but a screwup."

"Don't say that, Fee." Anyone would have gone crazy given their situation. "You took the news about the thong going back exceptionally well." That was a huge step for her shopaholic sister.

Fee's mood had changed from whiny to reasonable. Frankie made the best of it.

She leaned back against the shady wall of Daniel's boathouse. Wearing an old lady caftan topped with a wide-brimmed hat and sunglasses, she blended in with a lot of the population on the houseboats. From a distance, she hoped her getup would make her look thirty years older. She hoped it was enough.

"Poor Bernie," Fee chuckled. "He'll never see my pussy dripping in diamonds." An image Frankie could have done without.

"Yeah, thanks for that, Fee. Just what I want emblazoned on my brain."

Fiona giggled, her sunny nature restored. "So, how are things with you?"

She shouldn't think it, let alone say it out loud, but it felt so good she had to share. "I've met someone."

"No shit, who?"

"If you can believe it. A DJ."

"You mean you've been partying? Hooked up at a club? That doesn't sound like you." The sudden concern in her sister's voice warmed her. Maybe her family wasn't as splintered as she thought.

"No, not a club DJ. He's on the radio. He's good, Fee. I just love to listen to his voice. He does a late-night blues show."

"Does he know?"

"Of course not. I can't tell him." She wanted to. She was missing out on so much sharing. All the getting-to-know-you stuff that was vital in the early days of a—she broke off the thought.

"I guess you can't." There was a pause on the line, and Fiona moved away from some background television noise. "That's better. Listen, Frankie, I'm glad you've met him. You're way past due for some action, but you're right to keep it to yourself. You can't trust anybody." Her sister's firm, quiet voice surprised her.

Fiona was rarely the one who chastised.

Oh, but she wanted to trust Daniel. He inspired hope and confidence. If nothing else but these few days were in the cards for her and Daniel, she'd cherish them forever.

"Don't worry." She cupped her hand over her mouth for more privacy. "I may not be around for the next few days, Fee. A guy with a camera showed up on the yacht. For now I'm hiding out with Daniel, but if I'm discovered, I'll be moving fast." Leaving Daniel.

She patted Barkley's head. He'd taken to sitting beside her whenever she ventured out on deck alone. Her little guardian.

"Hiding out with him? He must be important if you're taking that kind of chance."

Again, she squeezed the phone tight. "He is, Fee. I have a lot of feelings for him already. He's kind and protective and hasn't asked me much, in spite of being curious. He's smart, too, and funny. He chased the guy off the yacht, told him I was gone away, even before he checked with me. Said Barkley didn't like the guy either."

"Barkley?"

"His dog. Scruffy terrier cross, cute and a real pain in the ass, but he barked at this guy and Daniel ran over to the yacht."

"Where were you?"

"Sleeping."

"In Daniel's bed?"

She let silence be her answer.

"So, the bed thing's good?"

"Fee!"

"You can tell me, I won't tell Ma and Dad."

She grinned and her pussy twitched in memory. "Rockets, Fee. Rockets like the Fourth of July."

Fiona laughed long and hard. "It's about time. If you could only find a way to trust him, he might be a keeper."

A keeper.

And this was the worst possible time to find one.

"He would be a keeper if he wasn't moving to Chicago." She told Fee about the transfer. "He wants the promotion to the morning slot. Although I suspect he'd prefer to stay on late night. It's weird."

"Is that what he said?"

"No, he said working the morning shift was everything he wanted, but he had a sad look in his eyes when he said it."

"When he told you about this promotion, did he ask you to join him? How serious is this?"

"When it looked as if he was going to ask me, I kind of changed the subject. Distracted him. If it was any other time, and especially any other place, I'd want to be with him."

"That's quick."

"Crazy, huh?"

There was a prickly silence. "Oh, Frankie." Fee's voice crackled with sympathy. "I hate fate. Sometimes it really fucks up."

"It sure seems to be giving me the gears." She cleared her throat and tried to put a smile in her voice. "Speaking of keepers, you have one in Bernie." She couldn't believe she was saying it, but boring old Bernie was dependable and honest and a far better man than Fiona would find now. Yes, thank God for Bernie. He kept Fiona grounded.

"I realize Bernie's a forever kind of guy." She sighed, long, hard and suffering. "About this safari in Africa. Do I really have to go?"

"You really have to go. Unless you can promise to keep a low profile when you get back from Alaska."

"But—"

"No buts. Bernie gets it, why don't you?"

On that note, Fiona growled her frustration and disconnected.

Frankie had been fighting an uphill battle with her sister for six months. With a touch of good luck, some of this traveling would open Fiona's eyes.

Frankie could only hope.

"Fiona is a sweet girl, Barkley," she said as she scratched the dog behind the ears, "but not particularly aware of the world at large. If conditions don't effect her, they don't exist." The dog looked up at her, brown eyes bright and curious. He tilted his head. "Don't get me wrong. She isn't cruel, or mean-spirited, she's just . . . small in her scope."

Barkly groaned and rolled to his back, presenting his belly for a rub. She obliged, happy to be outside, even if she was dressed in an ugly caftan that covered her from neck to ankles.

A seaplane roared out of the harbor, water dripping, sparkly and light, from its pontoons. Maybe she should be on the next one out of here.

But she didn't want to go. These nights with Daniel had twisted her up into knots of want. She wanted Daniel in bed, she wanted Daniel at the breakfast and dinner table, she wanted Daniel holding her hand, Daniel's arms, his trust, his . . . love. She wanted all of it.

But could *she* give *him* all those things? Without complication, without mistrust, without doubt. She definitely couldn't if he found out her secret. And the longer she stayed here the more likely it was that her secret would come out.

That would spell the end of this time with him. The end. No more Daniel. No more loving in the wee hours when the soft quiet of the waterfront seeped through her bones.

The pain of losing him seared her.

She tracked the seaplane, banking to the left, heading into the sun. Maybe tomorrow. Maybe she'd book a flight tomorrow. One more night with Daniel couldn't hurt.

She picked Barkley up and buried her face in his neck, fighting tears. He kissed the top of her head, then yipped and squirmed to get down. She let him go and swiped at the moisture gathered in her eyelashes.

"Your sister?" Daniel's voice startled her, while Barkley danced on deck.

"Yes, Fiona." She sniffed. "Thanks for the use of your phone." Her own might be traceable. She hadn't needed to explain, Daniel had simply passed her his cell phone.

"Ah." He nodded. "She has a name." He pulled a chair over to sit close. Leaned in. "Is there anything wrong?" His finger smeared across her cheek with a gentleness she loved.

"No, I just miss my family. We've grown apart."

"You can always mend fences."

She stayed cross-legged on the floor, back to the wall, hating that she'd made him believe there'd been a falling out. Every lie of omission, every half truth and misrepresentation ate at her. Daniel deserved better.

He grinned and made a show of raising his eyebrows. "Nice outfit. Sexy as hell."

"Oh baby," she quipped, then slid her hem to her knees in a peek-a-boo slide designed to make him laugh.

He did.

Humor. Comfort. Acceptance. All three flashed between them.

This was the way it was supposed to be between people who cared for each other. It pained her that she had to be dishonest.

"You're taking a chance being out here," he commented, with a quick glance around the harbor.

She cleared her throat. The man's intuition kept surprising her. He ran his fingers along the center part in her hair, then slid them through to the ends. "Tell me what's going on, Frankie. Whatever it is, I can help. I want to help."

She tilted into his hand seeking the comfort he offered, but taking none. The push–pull in her heart was making her crazy. Daniel pulled at her while her own problems yanked her away from trusting him.

"This is something I need to work out for myself. I'm the only one who can do it."

"Okay." His voice quieted. "If it's money you need, I've got some."

She warmed. "That's sweet. You have no idea what that offer means to me, but money from you won't help."

"Then what else can I do?"

"Take me to bed, Daniel. That's what I need." More of his Fourth of July rockets would set things right for the moment.

8

Daniel gathered her close and swept her up into his arms. It was clear she'd been to Chicago, knew the place intimately. She'd told Daniel about favorite places to eat, play and walk with an insider's knowledge. At one point or another she'd mentioned all four seasons, too, so the likelihood of her living there seemed a sure thing.

She got a nostalgic look in her eyes when he pressed her for details. She was in hiding, and all he could think was how lucky he was that she'd chosen him to hide with.

He'd pressed her about her fear of exposure, but given the *Boondoggle*'s silent, midnight appearance he figured he was lucky to have even this much time with her.

But he wanted more. He wanted her.

Here. Now.

For the rest of his life.

She must trust him to some extent to stay with him after the camera-toting man showed up on the yacht. But, still, he needed answers if this was going to continue. "The guy with the camera wasn't a cop, Frankie. You're not on the run from justice. You'd have been gone in thirty seconds after I told you about him."

He cupped the back of her head, dug his fingers into her hair and eased her head back to read her expressions. Her eyes widened with the action.

"No, he wasn't a cop," she vowed.

"Are you running from an ex-husband or boyfriend? A stalker?"

"I wish it were only one man." She eased her mouth to his and kissed him with delicious intent. She'd tried once before to distract him with sex and he was more than willing to allow it this time.

Because he planned a bigger distraction.

He swept Frankie, oversized caftan and all, into his arms. Barkley danced around his ankles but soon wandered off into his doghouse for a nap. "Apparently, the pooch has figured out we don't want his company."

She chuckled and nuzzled at his neck, nearly making him stumble.

He couldn't believe how much he wanted her. Now and always.

When she landed with a whump on the bed, he followed her down. "I want to help, Frankie. I want to be the one you turn to when you're scared. I want to keep you safe. I want to keep you, period. Marry me."

She blinked and the smile she'd worn since she'd seen him on deck slid off her face. "I don't know what to say." She frowned. "We hardly know each other." She made a show of counting off on one hand the number of days and nights they'd shared. She stopped at three.

"How long does it take to make a decision when your heart's in charge?"

She smiled, tentative and shy. "Are you sure it's your heart that's leading the way here? Or is it something else?" Her clever hands cupped him and gave him a light squeeze.

She could make him ache with no more than a touch.

"Okay, you want to keep things easy for now, fine. But it's making me nuts that some flake's making you nervous. Promise me one thing, Frankie." He slid between her thighs, cock nudging at her lips.

She closed her eyes and raised her cradle to envelop him. He pulled back.

"This isn't fair. You're using sex to extort promises." But she grinned and settled back into the soft pillows.

"And you use sex to distract me, so it's pretty much a given that we're both lowlifes and will use whatever means necessary to get what we want."

She laughed, but still didn't give him the "yes" he wanted. "So, will you promise?"

"What promise do you want?" Her palms bracketed his cheeks, and he knew she'd given him one more iota of herself.

"That you won't run without telling me. That if you have to leave, I'll know where you're going."

She blinked. "I'll tell you before I go, Daniel. I promise."

"But not where you're going?"

"I'll try if circumstances allow. It's the best I can do."

It was all he was going to get. It wasn't enough, not by a long shot, but with her determination to keep everything to herself he was smart enough to know this was the best he would get.

He slid into her welcoming warmth as he watched her eyes slide shut with the grasping entrance of his burgeoning cock. She loved this as much as he did. They were so good together.

He stilled to enjoy the softening acceptance of her tight channel. There was a moment of deep gentle clasps that he loved, and while he felt her walls expand and contract around him he accepted he didn't want to live without her.

It would kill him if she left without understanding how he felt.

"I love you, Frankie. God help me, I love you."

She took him inside her body while he gave her his heart.

He couldn't offer any more help than a place to hide if he didn't know what Frankie was running from. Trust wasn't an easy thing for a skittish woman to give, but the time they'd spent in bed had to count for something. She trusted him with her body, surely she could trust him with her troubles.

She still refused to accept money, even though he'd offered it again. The friend who owned the yacht must be taking care of her living expenses too.

He hated the idea that another man had taken responsibility for her, that another man was trusted when Daniel wasn't. That grated.

Hard.

He signed off for the night and ended his shift. Butch needed to know about the transfer. The morning drive. Shit.

Decision time. He vacated the seat in front of the microphone as the morning man arrived. Daniel put on the canned show they used for filler between four and six A.M. and nodded a greeting to Jace. The morning man was a good DJ, thorough and professional. A man obsessed about prepping two hours in advance, while his cohost usually sailed in just in time for the show.

"Jace, does it get to you that you and Jenna have such different styles?"

"You mean me coming in this early while she's barely in her seat on time?"

"Something like that."

Jenna was also like a runaway train. No telling where her mouth was going to take her. But from what Daniel had heard, her career was on the fast track.

"Yeah, it does. But what bites is the offer she's got from Chicago."

Belly rolling, Daniel pursed his lips. No wonder Butch wouldn't answer him. He knew Jenna was the kind of cohost Daniel would hate to work with. "Morning slot again?"

"Big raise, too." While Jace was being left behind. Disappointment radiated out of his slumped posture.

"I thought she had her sights on television."

Jace shrugged and went back to selecting his music. Without his planning, Jenna wouldn't have a clue, because music was not Jenna's thing. Banter was Jenna's thing. Daniel suppressed a shudder.

In the radio business weird shit happened every day. When stations changed formats, dedicated pros were overlooked or fired for new voices with sex appeal and a knack for hitting the right note for a new target market.

He couldn't figure out what the Chicago station saw in his style that appealed to them. Especially if they wanted to pair him with Jenna.

Daniel ambled outside to the darkness before dawn and headed to his car. No answers waited for him as he checked the sky. He loved this time. The streets were just beginning to flow with pre-dawn traffic. Early morning workers, the ones who avoided rush hour by rising earlier than everyone else, cruised the unclogged roadways.

There was a bakery he liked to stop at on his way home. Their croissants made his mouth water and the baker always put on the coffee for him.

"Where you been the last few days? I heard you sign off every morning, but you didn't come in like usual. You sick or something?" Lou was burly and hairy as a gorilla but had a touch like nobody else with the light, delicate pastry.

"Had to take my dog to the emergency clinic for an X-ray the other morning. Since then, I've been busy."

"Yeah?" Lou put his elbows up on the display case while Daniel helped himself to a coffee on the side counter. An early morning show from a competitor squawked in the background. Something about girls in bikinis on the expressway. And banter.

God save him from banter.

Lou chuckled. "I love these guys," he said with an amused shake of his grizzly gray head. He raised his hand. "I know it's the competition, but I hate that canned stuff you put on."

So did he. An old British rocker rambling about his glory days forty years ago wasn't his idea of good radio.

The morning drive team on the competing station consisted of a man and woman. She, in a rare twist, was the wild one, while he was the straight man. Usually, that would be seen as the stupid girl and the wise man, but these two made it work. The woman used acerbic wit and brilliant observation while the man was smoothly calm, if a little dense.

"They're babbling about girls in bikinis on the side of the expressway," Daniel said.

"Yeah, but they're funny."

Funny. He thought of trying to be funny for four straight hours when he was trying like hell to keep his eyes open and wake up.

He'd hate it, especially if he got stuck in a slot with a cohost like Jenna. He wasn't as obsessive about prepping as Jace was, but he sure as hell didn't sail into work at the last minute either. He liked to pick his music with a theme in mind. A night-inspired theme. A lonely theme. A quiet theme.

Morning drive time was never about quiet.

Lou gave him an appraising stare. "You look different." Rubbed his chin. "You gettin' some?"

"You talk to all your customers that way?" But he couldn't keep the happy out of his voice.

"Just you. Most of my customers are on the run, heading to work. You come in to sit and enjoy the quiet of the place before the rush. You like quiet, like me."

"Yes, I do." The quiet of the wee hours, the peace on the airwaves. The easy drive home against traffic.

He loved it.

"This woman, she good?"

"What do you mean?" His hackles rose.

"Oh, hell, not that way. That way's none of my business, but a good woman's hard to find. Especially these days. I had one once, but I screwed up bad and I lost out. Kick my ass every night when I crawl into those cold, empty sheets."

Daniel snorted. "You're always telling me about all the ladies you've got on a string." Most of the stories he dismissed as the ramblings of a too-hairy man's lonely mind.

Lou snorted. "There are times, my friend, when settling for second best is worse than having nothing at all." He checked that the coffee cream jug was full and headed back behind the counter. The baker in back hollered out that more muffins were ready, and Lou disappeared through the swinging door into the back.

Lou was talking about women when he'd said second best could ruin a life.

He had not been talking about career choices. Lou had once had dreams of being an artist, but he'd inherited the bakery. Now, his creative side came out in the pastry he loved to create.

Daniel loved what he was doing on air, but he loved Frankie more. Wanted her so bad he'd give up all the other, smaller things he loved just to have her.

He scraped the chair out from the table and headed out into the fresh morning. The city was more awake fifteen minutes later than when he'd gone into the bakery.

He thought of climbing between the sheets with Frankie

and grinned like a fool. He kept the vision of her front and center when he dragged out his cell phone and called Butch at home.

"I'll take the transfer," he said when Butch answered.

"What the fuck time is it?"

"Early." He heard rustling as if Butch was sitting up at the side of the bed. He wasn't sorry to wake him.

"No one but Daniel Martin, a tried and true blues fan, would have to think about it."

"I know." He refused to ask about Jenna. He'd deal with that when the time came.

"Why?"

"Sometimes life hands you beautiful things. Sometimes you have to give up stuff to keep those beautiful things. Choices are made."

9

_____

When he got home, she was there, warm and welcoming and still awake. "Didn't you sleep?" he asked as he lifted the covers and slid in, already hard.

"No, I always listen. I love your show. Even before I knew it was you, your voice seduced me."

He chuckled. "You're crazy." But he grinned at the compliment. He wanted to finesse her this morning, make her feel like a queen. The way she made him feel like he could take on the world and win. He grinned to himself, happy with his decision.

If he could have Frankie every day, he wouldn't mind that he'd given up the late-night shift he loved.

He could learn to love banter.

He _would_ learn to love banter.

"Maybe I am crazy, but I love your voice." She bit her lip. She rolled, and the warm scent of her from beneath the sheet rose to him. "What would you say if I told you I get turned on by listening to you?"

"I'd say tell me more." This was a new one on him. Most women wouldn't stay up late enough to listen.

"The way you talk makes me wet."

His interest spiked. He reached for her, then ran his palm along her flat belly and into her wet heat. She opened her legs so he could flutter his fingers against her lips.

"I hear that crooning quality you use when it's deeply dark outside. You're with me here"—she pumped her hips toward his questing fingers—"your voice strokes through me, deep into me. Yes! Like that. It rumbles around the room and I touch myself."

"Like this?" He rubbed at her clit with delicate swirls, the tips of two fingers barely inside. To tantalize her before a deep hard plunge, he wiggled them.

"Oh, Daniel! Yes! Just like that," she murmured, and widened her legs even more. He pushed the two fingers into her, feeling her inner channel grasp and hold and need. His thumb rolled over her plump clit again and again. "Ahh. I cream and come just on the sound of your voice. So hot, so cool. I love how you talk about the music and what it means to you."

He thought back over the show. Couldn't recall a damn thing in it that would cause this reaction. He'd talked about a thirties blues king that had died too young. The only recordings left were scratchy, almost too tinny for airing, but he figured if he let them go they'd be lost forever. He set his mouth to her neck and gently sucked some of the delicate flesh between his lips. Her blood rushed in a drumroll of heightened awareness.

"I think of your wicked tongue," she said, with an arch into his hand, "and your wild lips, and I can hardly wait for you to come home to me."

Heaven. This was heaven, and he'd found it with her. He shifted between her legs, then slid both palms under her ass and tilted her up to his mouth. Diving in, he stroked his tongue from her clit to her slit and deep inside. She crooned and thrashed around him, but he didn't stop. She swelled into his mouth as he felt her crest.

She jutted her pussy toward him, then rocked against his mouth in a raging orgasm. Clasping his head, she came in a wild gush that he lapped and held on his tongue. Exquisite juice burst on his taste buds.

He took the condom she had tucked under her ass and slid it on. With a roar of possession, he slid in to the hilt and held her as she rocked against him.

Quieting into a roll, he rode her to another come, then followed with a strong surge into her. He gasped her name just before he broke and shuddered against her.

"If this is crazy, then I want more." He pulled her close, deep into his chest. "You're the best thing that's happened to me. Crazy or not."

Her heart pounded against his as she kissed him hard. Her flavors blended in his mouth. Pussy and tongue swirled together as he tasted both.

Her color went high at the compliment. "Thank you, but you're only saying that because you've been too long without sex." She tried to make light of his declaration, and it piqued him.

She was more than an easy, available lay, and it was time she knew it.

"That may be part of it. But the reality is, you get me. You understand why I do what I do, why I want what I want, even why I play the music I play." He stilled, holding himself tight to her pussy, keeping their connection deep.

"Everyone loves the blues." She wriggled under him, but he held firm. "Everyone feels the blues. Everyone loses someone at some point." Her eyes went wide, the expression so soft he could lose himself in her gaze. Lose himself gladly.

"I guess they do." But losing Frankie wasn't on his agenda.

He slid out of her, then went to the bathroom. He stared at his reflection, gave himself a talking to. All he had to do was show her that being with him was better than running.

It meant a lot that she was still here. She'd had all night to run, but she hadn't. That meant he hadn't frightened her by saying he loved her.

All he had to do now was convince her that a move to Chicago was right for both of them.

When he climbed back into bed, she looked pensive.

She rested her head on his shoulder and sighed, her breath stirring the hair on his chest. "Have you ever been in a position where a wonderful thing happens, but there's a dark side you never considered?"

"Like a double-edged sword?"

"It's like a woman has a baby and it's 'Great, I'm a mom.' The other side of the coin is, 'Great, I'm a mom.' " She drawled out the words with sarcasm. "On one hand she's thrilled to be a mother and to start a wonderful adventure in parenting."

"On the other hand," he concluded, "she's not the young, carefree woman she was."

"Exactly!" She looked pleased with his observation. "Maybe deep down she's afraid, or feels unprepared for the responsibility. No matter what good fortune brings, life always smacks a person back down."

"You're right. There's rarely a time when there's no black cloud even if the silver lining's the fulfillment of all your dreams." To put the best spin on his promotion to the morning time slot, he hadn't shared with her his disappointment at walking away from the best job he'd ever had.

"Even the most stupendous good luck can turn your life upside down," she went on. "Not that you'd want to give up that stupendously good—luck, you'd just have to temper your reactions." She pursed her lips. "You'd have to be realistic."

She was dancing around something important, something big, but he'd have to be patient and let her come around to her own way of telling him everything. "All we can do is roll with the punches," he said in a bland tone designed to keep her talking. "If we fall down, we've got to get back up." She was going somewhere with this line of thought, he just couldn't see where yet. Bless her, though, she was at least trying to open up.

"Have you decided to accept the transfer?" she asked, which meant she'd moved on, away from talking about herself again.

"Yes. I called the program director on the way home." No point mentioning Jenna or how much he'd hate the work. With any luck at all, Jenna would move on soon, anyway.

Frankie rose onto her elbow and looked him in the face. "You'll like Chicago," was all she said. She blinked a couple of times, and her eyes glistened.

He pulled her to his mouth and kissed her, his thumbs on each cheek, ready to smear away whatever moisture might fall.

"I need to love you, Daniel. Right now." With that, she disappeared under the sheets to crawl to his jutting cock.

Wet heat enveloped him in one long, slow slide, and he drifted into sexual ecstasy. Payback. He'd arrange payback as soon as he could.

Five minutes later, he twisted so she was under him. A couple more moves and he was face deep in creamy pussy, while she pumped and licked at his cock and balls.

Her succulent, pink clitoris peeped out of its hood and he zeroed in, sucking and licking as she squirmed against him.

He spread her lips wide open to see her darkest pink. Spearing his tongue, he went in deep and felt her inner walls clutch and grind as he prodded. Fingers followed his tongue to keep her guessing, while he focused on her clit again.

Juice filled her as she came.

His orgasm screamed from his root to his skull and spewed

deep into her throat. Her hot mouth took all of him as he pulsed. She grabbed his ass, held him tight to her and careened off into another powerful release seconds behind him.

When he could breathe and speak again, he said, "I love you, Frankie; come with me." He flopped to the bed and tucked her head against his shoulder.

"I just did," she crooned as her eyes opened in silky satisfaction.

He snugged her hips close to his. "No, I mean, come with me to Chicago, Frankie. Marry me."

She patted his shoulder, eyes wide, satisfaction flaring into fear. "I—can't go to Chicago." She turned away, and he took the hint.

She wasn't ready to hear his plans. Not yet. But she would be soon. She was making progress in other areas, so he expected her to come around in her own time.

When he finished in the bathroom, he leaned on the door frame and considered her, covers up to her chin again, as she stared at the ceiling. "Frankie, this could work for us. I'm taking a day job for more money and normal hours so we can get married and build a life. I'm being practical as well as being head over heels in love with you."

"Yes, I see that."

"What *that* do you see?"

She peered at him across the miles of secrets that separated them and nodded. "I see that you're being practical by accepting the promotion. And I know you love me. In spite of my not being able to be completely open about what's happening with me."

"Then what's the problem? You're free, I'm free. We connect on so many different levels I can hardly believe my luck in finding you." He walked to the bed, trying hard to find a joke somewhere to ease his way into her mind, her heart. "I'm trying to find something funny to say, but I'm coming up empty. So, I'll do this instead." He slipped her hand out from under the sheet and placed her palm on his heart. "Feel it? It's pounding out of my chest. Fear. Frankie, I'm afraid you're going to disappear on me."

She looked at him then, eyes wide and filling. "Daniel, I can't go to Chicago with you."

"Are you running from an abusive husband? Are you in the witness protection program?"

"No, it's nothing like that. It's smaller in so many ways, but it's huge too. Life changing, and I don't want to involve you right now."

"But I am involved. Completely. Marry me."

Barkley's growling bark rose to a racket on deck; his nails scrambled for purchase as he sounded a familiar alarm.

"Who the hell would be here at this time of the morning?"

Frankie didn't respond, just grabbed his shirt she'd taken to wearing and dashed into the bathroom. She slammed the door while he slipped into his jeans and headed outside. The man with the camera Barkley had caught on the *Boondoggle* stood on the dock. His jaw was set in a stubborn, defiant cut. He squared his shoulders when Daniel stepped outside.

"What do you want?" Daniel demanded. He crossed his arms over his chest and bristled.

"I'm here to see if Francesca Volpe is a guest." The guy already had his camera up and ready. A steady clicking sound told Daniel he was already shooting.

"Never heard of her. Now get the hell out of here."

"Daniel," Frankie said from behind him. "It's all right. I planned to tell you anyway."

He turned, shielding her from the camera. She gave him a grateful smile, but her eyes were wide and sad. He wanted to throttle the guy for taking her from him. That's exactly what was happening.

Whatever the hell was going on, Frankie was already gone. He read the distance between them in her eyes.

The camera man moved lightning quick, trying to climb aboard. Barkley went for his ankle and grabbed his blue jeans, snarling and growling like a ten-ton beast.

"What are you doing here, Ms. Volpe? Slumming? What are you going to do now? Where's your sister, Ms. Volpe?" The questions came thick and fast. Obviously, this guy was no journalist. All he wanted was to badger her. "What have you done with all the money?"

She ignored the questions, stepped out around Daniel and bent to pick up Barkley. The dog quieted when she gathered him close. "I'm leaving. Now that you've found me, I'm gone."

10

"What's going on here? Who the hell are you?" Daniel demanded of the camera man. He got in the guy's face and slammed his palm over the camera lens. "And stay the fuck off my deck."

"I'm a photo journalist, Mr. Martin, and this is Francesca Volpe, winner of one of the largest lottery jackpots in American history. She won six months ago, made a ton of promises to charities and hard-luck cases then skipped out. She and her family disappeared."

Daniel couldn't take it all in. "She won what?"

"Sixty-five million, Mr. Carver, after taxes. More money than anyone has a right to."

Frankie scooted back inside.

"But what stinks up the place is the way she made promises then reneged on them!" The guy called loud enough so Frankie would hear his accusation. "What have you got to say about running out on burn victims and abused women, Ms. Volpe? Huh? What have you got to say? Why not tell me your side of it? Instead of hiding here?"

Daniel twisted the camera out of the man's grip, but not for long. He grabbed it back, and Daniel let go when he saw a strap around his neck. As much as he wanted to strangle the guy, he couldn't let the altercation get out of hand. "You're not welcome aboard. Get the hell off the dock and out of the marina. If I catch you bothering Frankie again, I'll punch your lights out."

The guy sneered. "Yeah, like I haven't heard that one a million times before."

He turned and headed back toward the ramp. But once there he stationed himself at the top, the telephoto lens aimed directly at the float home.

Daniel swore at the guy's smarmy arrogance and headed in to find Frankie. His mind whirled with everything he'd learned, unable to make sense of any of it. It was too unbelievable.

She was on the phone, trying to get dressed one handed with Barkley yipping and whining at her feet.

"Fee! They've found me again." She listened. "No, I don't think they know where you are." She hopped on one foot, only to land heavily on the side of the bed.

Daniel held the leg of her jeans up so she could slide it on. She tossed him a grateful smile.

"I'll call you in a few hours, Fee. When I decide where I'm going." She flipped the phone closed.

"And Chicago is not where you're going." She was leaving him high and dry. His gut clenched.

"No." She swiped a hand through her hair. "Daniel, I'm sorry. I can't go back to Chicago. Not now." She blinked, and he could swear she was trying not to cry.

"You came from there. You won your millions in Chicago." She nodded.

"You didn't tell me because you didn't trust me." She thought he'd want her for the money.

She reddened and avoided meeting his gaze.

"So, now what? You run again? Hide?"

"Yes."

"Why? Talk to me, Frankie, we've got time. The guy's retreated to the top of the ramp." His mind was working over what he'd learned.

Money, this was all about money.

He ran his hands through his hair. It would almost be easier if she was running from the law. He laughed at a sour thought. "You must have found it hysterically funny when I offered you cash."

She shook her head. "No, Daniel. I thought it was generous and thoughtful. And typical of you. You've been nothing but kind to me and I felt awful about lying. I took terrible advantage of you—"

"Like the burn victims? The abuse victims you promised to help?"

She looked as if he'd struck her. Her eyes went wide as she blinked several times, her chin trembled and her lips quivered. Then in an incredible display of bravado, she tilted her chin proudly. Rose to her full height. "I don't expect you to understand."

"Then explain." He yanked a kitchen chair away from the table and sat. Hard.

She wrung her hands. "Money changes everything. People go crazy. They expect money to fix whatever's wrong. It doesn't."

"It can fix a hell of a lot. Especially if you don't have any."

"People who've never had money have the most unrealistic expectations. They're the ones who get bitter."

"What about what that guy said?" He'd calmed down enough now to realize she was finally being open with him, and he didn't want to do anything to ruin this chance for them. This one last chance.

Pathetic, that's what he was. Blind to everything but the horrible notion that if she left, he'd never see her again.

Her eyes softened. "I'll make coffee."

"You'll stay long enough to drink it?"

"I can't leave here knowing you'll think the worst of me."

All he saw was Frankie, his Frankie, the woman he'd grown to love. The woman he thought needed him. For protection, support, love. She needed none of those things. She wanted for nothing.

More money than anyone has a right to. Camera man's condemnation rang through his mind as Frankie busied herself in his tiny kitchen. She looked like she belonged there, had since he'd carried her in his arms that first night.

"I've never been good with numbers," she said. "I even have a hard time remembering new phone numbers, so I hate having to change mine all the time." The water began to run through the coffeemaker, hissing and sprinkling. She turned and faced him, hands behind her back as if she needed the counter to hold on to.

"When I won I took three days to come forward. I spent the whole time writing my ticket numbers down and comparing them to the winning numbers, convinced I must have it wrong."

"What happened then?"

"I didn't plan anything until after the announcement was made. Then my life turned into a circus. My family, including long-lost second and third cousins, made demands of me and promises *for* me. They promised people things and expected me to go along, the way I always had. Before my life exploded, I was easygoing, not pushy or difficult. Mild-mannered, don't-rock-the-boat Frankie."

He listened as she explained how her life had crashed around her. "Charities came at me," she said, "begging for help. Most of them are legitimate, but a lot weren't. One I found out was set up the day after I came forward to claim my prize."

"They targeted you."

She nodded, wrapped her arms around her middle. "Because

I volunteered at a women's shelter. They thought I'd just sign checks without thinking."

"Once you found out they were a scam, you started looking twice at everything."

She nodded. "I had to get away. I set my folks up in a beautiful home in Florida with an income to live on. My sister Fiona and her fiancé Bernie got the wedding Fee wanted but could never afford before." Her lips twisted in a grimace. "But not until Fee went freaking *insane* buying everything and anything she could get her hands on."

"It was her thong." His palms broke out into a sweat. "They weren't rhinestones, were they?"

She shook her head so slightly he could barely see the movement.

"She got angry with me when I told her it had to go back. There's so much more that could be done with fifty grand."

He swallowed and nodded, light-headed at the idea of the rat's nest lined with diamonds.

The coffee was ready, and she poured them both mugs. Then into his she put one spoonful of sugar and a dash of cream. She already knew how he took it. She might be rotten with numbers, but she'd taken careful note of how he liked his coffee.

"It's been six months since the win. What now?" *What about us?* He wanted to ask, but couldn't. She'd had more demands made on her than he would ever know about. It was clear his marriage proposal was not one she wanted to deal with.

And he couldn't ask her again. She'd think he was like all the others who'd disappointed her with their reactions.

"I've got a law firm setting up a charity foundation. All requests will have to go through them."

"Good idea. And your sister?"

"She's coming around. Bernie's a good influence, rock steady and blind in love with her. Has been since he was fourteen."

"Did she really want the thong to wear on her honeymoon?"

"Yes. After she bought it, I realized how frenzied she was with the money. The shopping was manic, the splurging obscene. I sent them on Bernie's dream honeymoon. They're in Alaska at a remote hunting and fishing lodge. My sister's sweet, but she needs some time to think and calm down."

She nodded, as if trying to convince herself she'd done the right thing. "I'm sending them to Africa next. Bernie says she needs a reality check. That should do it for her. Fee will be fine once she realizes this kind of good fortune comes with social responsibility."

"That's something you've always known," he said, thinking of her volunteer stint at the women's shelter.

She nodded. "I want to share the wealth, do the right thing and help people, but I'll be damned if I'll allow unscrupulous people to take advantage of me."

"You've sacrificed a lot for this money." He took in her sadness, her slumped shoulders. "You even led me to believe your father was dead."

"I'm so sorry, Daniel."

"Has everything else between us been a—"

"A lie?" She interrupted him, then tilted her head to the side. Her voice dropped to a plea. "Never the loving. What we shared was real. I gave you everything."

She bowed her head, and the arms she'd crossed over her stomach trembled with her effort to hold herself together. She sniffed, and he saw her face crumple toward tears.

He was on her in a flash, wrapping her in his arms, holding her while she wept. "I've lost so much I loved, Daniel. Friends, family, my good name. People hate me for no reason."

"I don't, Frankie. It seems wrong to tell you I love you now. As if I'm taking advantage, but you have to know that while you've lost a lot, you've gained too. Here, with me."

It seemed even more trite that he'd been planning on giving up his job to take one he hated to have enough money to have her in his life. But he would have, in a heartbeat. He'd have made a morning slot work, even with a bimbo like Jenna in the booth with him.

He'd have done all of that if it meant having Frankie.

Now he'd lost her, and there was no sacrifice he could make that would keep her with him.

"I guess all we have to do is figure out how to get you out of here without that jackass following you."

She sniffed and smeared her nose on his shirt by his collar. "Okay, but what about your shift tonight? Do you have a replacement for emergencies?"

He set her away from him. "You inviting me along?"

She nodded. "Married people hang out together, Daniel. Don't know what you were thinking, but you asked me to marry you and I said yes."

"No, you didn't."

"Well, I would have if we hadn't been interrupted."

He kissed her, long and hard and deep. When he could think again, he came up for air. "I don't want to go with you."

Her eyes widened. "What do you mean?"

"I'd have given up my whole life for you, Frankie. I was willing to sacrifice a job I love to provide for us in a job I'd hate. Now I want you to think about sacrificing something."

"What's that?" She looked happily suspicious, if that were possible.

"Stop running. No more hiding. We're thousands of miles from Chicago. Since your windfall, other people have won big jackpots. They're in the spotlight now. Stay here with me. We'll build a life together."

She grinned. "Maybe I should track the new winners down, start a support group."

"Wouldn't hurt, might help." He pressed his hips against

hers, slid his palms to cup her ass. "Besides, if you didn't want to be found, you would have been gone the minute I told you about that guy on the *Boondoggle*, but you stayed anyway."

"I stayed because I was falling in love. With you. Your voice, your kindness, your sexy caramel eyes." She glanced around the kitchen. "I love it here, Daniel, and I love you." She kissed his nose, then his lips, quick and hard. "There's one other thing we can do."

"That is?" he asked.

"Call that journalist back down here. We'll give him the interview he wants, then he'll leave us alone. You're right. I need to stop running. I want to stop running."

"We'll weave your family back together, Frankie, you'll see."

"I knew the first time I heard your voice you were the best thing this city has going for it. I'd be happy if you stayed on the air, doing what you love to do. Every night, I'll be here waiting for my midnight blues man."

"Oh God, Frankie. I'm the one who won the real prize." He brushed the back of his knuckles across her delicate cheekbones.

"Daniel, you're the sweetest man on earth."

"No, just the luckiest." He hugged her close and swept his tongue into her mouth, then down her sweet neck and lower.

THIGH HIGH

To Nancy Warren, a dear and much-appreciated friend.
And to E.C. Sheedy, whose midnight adventures in
Emergency came in handy!
And for Ted, always.

1

"Oh man, he is so buff!" Kat Hardee commented, ogling her next-door neighbor. Her mail forgotten in her hand, she leaned on the mailbox at the entrance to the townhouse complex.

"I'll say," Celia agreed. "But such a nerd. It's a shame."

Celia lived on the other side of the man in question, Taye Connors, and Kat had forgotten she was standing there too.

"I didn't mean for you to hear that," Kat said with a burn on her cheeks. Knowing Celia she'd twist the comment into something it wasn't.

He climbed out of his SUV and headed to the door of his townhouse, briefcase in hand. He bent and picked up a package left on his front step. Wrapped in cozy brown cords, he had a great butt, even from this distance, and Kat found several ways a day to see it. From her back upstairs window she'd watch him put out bird seed. Through his tiny kitchen window she'd catch glimpses of him making dinner.

"He's not a nerd," Kat said in his defense. "I'm willing to bet under that tweed jacket is a lot of man."

"You think?" Celia assessed him with her man-hungry eyes.

Kat shifted. A second mistake. Taye's physique was not up for discussion, not with Celia. She was a shark when it came to getting what she wanted. Kat's comment had alerted her to something Kat wanted to keep to herself. For herself.

Not that she had the gumption to go after the man. Chasing a man had created havoc in her life once; she didn't need to do it again. Especially not now! She was finally in college and finally doing something for herself.

A man in her life would only mess up everything! She wrestled the image of Taye Connors's hot, sexy body back under her libido. Way under her libido. Locked in a vault under her libido. No way would the two meet again.

"How much would you bet?" Celia's curious, dangerously calm voice broke into Kat's wrestling match. The look Celia gave her was every bit as dangerously curious as her voice.

Dread leaked into her belly. "What do you mean?" Even she heard the fear in her voice. Celia had a way of making foolish behavior sound like fun. Lots of fun.

Celia clicked her tongue impatiently. She didn't suffer fools gladly. "What would you bet that he's a lot of man under his clothes?"

Everything inside her tightened: stomach, libido, vault, all waiting to see what Kat would say at the idea of getting Taye out of his tweed jacket, then his shirt, then his slacks. "You know I'm broke. I can't afford to bet."

"Hmm. Wouldn't have to be for money." Celia pulled mail out of her box and smiled in a way that made Kat nervous. "How's this? You get him naked and let me know how buff he is. I'll give you the weekend."

"Why?"

"I'm curious. The men I usually spend time with aren't like him. I go for bad boys. I've never done a man like Taye." She arched one perfectly waxed eyebrow and waited.

"Do you want him?" Celia and Taye: a good man with a bad, bad woman. He was nice, quiet. Kind. Gentle. A woman like Celia would eat him alive.

Celia shrugged one smooth shoulder. "Might be fun, if the bod's up to snuff. But I won't know that unless you tell me what he looks like under his clothes."

Kat secretly admitted to some curiosity and a dose of reluctant admiration for the woman's want-it, get-it attitude, but she did not want firsthand knowledge of Celia's lifestyle. She preferred a quieter life. She preferred to wait for a man to find her. She preferred not to think of Celia with Taye.

She wanted Taye.

If he took a walk on the wild side with Celia, Kat wouldn't stand a chance. He'd never look her way again.

Up to now, there had been some glances. Second and third glances. A couple of those glances had stretched into looks. Long steamy looks.

"I'd do it," Celia threatened in a sly tone, "but I'm going away for the weekend." The lascivious expression in her eyes meant she'd found a new man. But still, she looked at Taye as if she couldn't wait to get her mouth on him. "But there's always next weekend."

Celia's nipples rose under her low-cut sheer cotton blouse, then Kat saw her upper thighs squeeze and release. Damn it, Celia meant business.

She could let this go. It wasn't up to Kat to keep a nice guy out of Celia's clutches. Especially since Taye never did anything more than chat politely at the front door.

But she couldn't allow Celia to move in on a man Kat wanted. This was way past schoolgirl stuff. Taye's heart might be at stake. The round robin of why she should walk away and let it happen versus the disaster of Celia messing with him bounced around in her head.

She looked up the driveway one more time. He was dead-heading some petunias, bent over again, firm ass looking like a fine piece of fruit.

It wasn't her head that made her decision. It was her heart. Followed quickly by a libido that came to life with a roar.

"All right. I'll give it a try. But Taye going from small talk in the driveway to naked in my arms seems like a long shot."

Celia crossed her arms under her gigantic boobs and shook her head sadly. "Who said anything about naked in your arms? I didn't say you had to fuck him, I just said you had to see him naked. You can leave the fucking to me." She actually smacked her lips! "In fact, I'd prefer it if you did."

"No way. If I see him naked, you have to walk away. Completely." Temptation. The thrill felt good, gave her underused libido a jangle she enjoyed. A jangle of keys, one of which opened the vault under her libido. Once the vault opened, temptation gave way to lust. She was in now, no going back. "If I get him naked, there's no way we're not having sex. A naked Taye means he's mine. Got that?"

Celia rolled her eyes. "There's that puritanical side of yours again." She waggled her finger in a dismissive gesture. "Sleeping with the same man shouldn't interfere with a friendship, Kat. Men should never come between friends."

"No, they shouldn't." Because friends shouldn't sleep with the same man.

"Of course not." Celia firmed her lips into a moue. "Not unless there's more than sex going on."

Kat rolled her eyes. "That's not what I meant at all."

Celia continued as if Kat hadn't spoken. "If you were to get attached and start a thing with Taye, then of course I'd back off. But if it's just sex for convenience, then, honey, I'm up for a roll with our delicious neighbor too."

"So my choice is to seduce him into a relationship and keep

him to myself or play with him for a weekend and leave him wide open to you?"

The last time she'd insisted on a relationship with a man she was in lust with, her life had taken a rotten turn. She was just now repairing the damage.

But, and it was a huge but, she wanted Taye in a powerful way. If she never went for it, Celia would sleep with him. And if Celia slept with him, Kat wouldn't be able to. No matter what Celia said about convenient sex. Kat wasn't capable of sleeping with a friend's lover.

So, if she didn't get to Taye first, she would never have him.

Later she would swear she heard actual creaking as her long-closed vault door opened wide as lust rose in every muscle, ligament and artery in her body. Her heart picked up speed and her breath shallowed. She never could have imagined going head to head with Celia for a man's attention, but damn it, Taye was the one Kat wanted. Celia figured one cock was as good as another. It wouldn't matter a fig to Celia if she lost out on one cock, but it would matter a lot to Kat if she let Taye get away.

Celia watched as Kat fought her silent battle. Then she sighed, letting her breasts jiggle for emphasis. "For a woman as knowledgeable about sex as you are, you're a real prude sometimes."

"There are two sides to sex, the mechanics and the emotions surrounding those mechanics." Celia's comment rankled her into a sharp response. "I'm not a prude. I just like a connection with the men I sleep with. There's nothing wrong with that."

"Sex is a bodily function. A tool," Celia said. "Nothing more than comfort food. It doesn't mean anything." Celia frowned and pursed her lips.

"This is why I never go clubbing with you. I can't feel the way you do. It's not in me."

Heat glowed in Celia's gaze and her frown turned dark. "Be careful, Kat, you're getting awfully close to calling me—"

"I'm sorry, I didn't mean to sound judgmental," she interrupted, slinging her arm around Celia's shoulder. "Like religion and politics, there are some things friends shouldn't discuss."

"Just remember, it was your need for a connection that got you married and divorced by what? Twenty-two?"

Her spine stiffened. "Point taken."

"And you're twenty-five now. Three years divorced and you're still clinging to attitudes my grandmother would laugh at."

"I've met your grandmother, Celia." Kat crossed her arms. "And using a Las Vegas showgirl as a moral compass has left you jaded and cynical."

"I meant my other grandmother." Celia speared her with an intent stare. "Are you going to get Taye Connors naked or not? If you do, will you sleep with him?"

Ticked off by the mention of her disastrous marriage, something she'd only confided after two bottles of wine, Kat rose to the challenge. "Yes!"

Then to make matters worse, she let Celia's mocking stare goad her further. "If I don't sleep with Taye Connors, I swear I'll go out clubbing with you."

"And you'll find a man when you do?"

"You want me to sleep with a stranger just to prove I'm not a prude?"

Celia clicked her tongue. "Okay, you don't have to go that far. But you do have to come out and have some fun. You're working yourself too hard." She went back to assessing the man in question. "Must have had a delivery from his mother again," Celia said with a sniff. "The guy's a high school science teacher, neat as a pin, who gets care packages from his mom. That spells nerd to me."

To Kat it spelled sweet. She checked out his butt again with a deep lean around the light standard to get a better look. Sweet and hot, she thought, setting out for the short walk to her front door.

With a sultry chuckle that set Kat's teeth on edge, Celia sauntered into step beside her. As irritating as Celia could be, she had a good point. Since her divorce her education had come first. Add that to the fact she hadn't found a man worth more than a second glance and the itch Taye created inside her burned.

If Celia had an itch, she scratched it. She wasn't as picky about male company as Kat was. Being seriously attracted to Taye set up all kinds of conflicting emotions. She had more than enough reasons not to pursue a man right now, but if she didn't take a chance with Taye she'd lose out.

To Celia.

She wasn't prone to adventure and intrigue. She was no drama queen. Chasing Taye was a bad idea, but she couldn't leave him to Celia.

She would have to remember all the lessons she'd learned during the end of her marriage. All her realizations would serve her well now. She'd put too much into her marriage, had given, given, given. She wouldn't make the same mistake with Taye, she vowed.

Turning her back on the idealistic young woman who'd married her high school sweetheart should be easy. All she had to do was have sex without commitment. She could learn to do that. She would learn to do that.

She just had to figure out how to convince her heart to go along for the ride.

2

Taye elbowed open his front door and backed in. The package in one hand and his briefcase in the other made maneuvering awkward. Even more awkward was the blood that rushed to his cock when he caught sight of his neighbor, Kat Hardee. She could buckle a man's knees with a glance.

As usual she was at the mailbox when he got home from school. Today she'd chatted with Celia for much longer than she normally did. He'd fiddled around outside in the damn flower bed so long he'd started to feel stupid. And now here he was caught halfway in the door doing a juggling act with his cock going up in flames.

He stalled halfway inside his front hall, shoulder holding open his door as he watched her stroll across his half of the front lawn, mail dangling from one elegant hand. Her breasts were the kind that sloped down to a point, with all the weight on the underside. Natural and heavy, they swayed with each step. She never wore a bra when she was at home, probably thought they were uncomfortable. But the free and easy sway tortured him.

He froze, hoping she'd stop and talk for a minute or two.

His imagination could make a lot of use out of a five-minute chat. Embellish it for hours, take it places she never suspected he wanted it to go.

"Hi," she said, in the shy, hesitant way she had.

"Hi," he responded with a quick juggle of his briefcase to hide his rising hard-on.

"Tough day?" she asked. Her lips parted in a smile that raised his temperature. The woman had no idea what she did to him.

"Not bad. Yours?"

She made a face. "My sociology prof hates me, but other than that, it was okay." Her smile went tentative as she noticed his juggling act. "A gift?" She nodded in the direction of the package that threatened to topple out of his arms.

"I'm not sure. I don't know where it's from. But I order a lot of books and stuff off the net. Probably something like that." Oh Christ, he sounded like such a nerd. Wake up, asshole, you *are* a nerd.

"Oh." She hesitated, and the moment stretched as he lost his train of thought. Blood loss from the brain turned him speechless. Puzzling over the fact that she was the first woman to create the effect on sight, he waited and hoped the flow would reverse.

Nope. No reversal. Not yet.

If she looked closer she'd see his hard-on, thick as a tree trunk, trying like hell to spear out of his pants. He shifted his briefcase once more. The mystery package wobbled again.

"Well"—she hesitated and flushed her exclusive shade of pink—"I'll leave you to find out who sent it to you." She walked into her own place, leaving him hot, flustered and calling himself an idiot.

The box teetered out of his hand and bounced against the door frame. Thank God she hadn't seen that. Not only did he sound stupid when he spoke to her, he was clumsy to boot. He set his briefcase down and slid the box free of the door so it could close. He scrubbed at his scalp, wishing he had the smooth patter other men used.

He'd never been a hound dog with women, but he'd never been tongue-tied in the presence of one before either. Rock hard and speechless. He shook his head at the effect Kat had on him, but there was nothing he could do about it.

If he stayed late after school, it was worse. He missed seeing her at the mailbox, but as he unlocked his front door, he would see her through the sheer curtains in her kitchen window. She'd be hunched over her table, surrounded by books, working on a laptop. She'd have the harried, harassed look of a cramming student.

The hunch in her shoulders made him want to run his thumb down her spine in a straight rush. Loosen her up. The fantasy would move on to where he'd massage her stiff neck muscles until she sagged off the chair onto the floor, where he'd strip off her panties and eat her into a sated marshmallow, re-laxed and easy. He salivated at the thought of getting his mouth on her juicy, salty pussy. *Get a grip! The woman doesn't know you're alive.*

He should have asked her in for coffee the first day he'd moved in, but he'd been distracted and busy. By the time he'd taken a good look at her and noted the beauty she really was, the days had moved into an awkwardly long stretch.

She had retreated into polite nods and shy hellos, and he kicked himself for not moving faster right at the beginning. The more he saw of her, the more he wanted to find a way to break the ice and start over.

He'd compounded the error by allowing her to enter his dreams and get his libido cranked to the stratosphere. When-ever he saw her, his damn cock took charge, leaving him self-conscious and awkward. But every night, he wanted her more. Every day, he behaved less like himself around her.

With his juggling act going awry he could have asked her for a hand getting the package into the house. If his brain had operated properly, they could have been sharing coffee right now. He could have shown her the real Taye, not this gawky man he'd become.

Frustration ate him. Next time he wouldn't freeze up. He'd be his usual calm, cool, collected self and ask her out.

The box sat on the floor, mocking him. The label had a smudge that covered the shipper's name and he didn't recognize the return address. But like he'd said, the package could be from anywhere. He dug out his pocketknife and sliced the tape that held the box flaps closed.

Inside he found shipping foam peanuts, but no bill or receipt to give him a clue as to who sent the package. He dug deeper and came up with a . . . double-headed cock about fourteen inches long.

"Holy shit!" Erect, full-veined and flesh colored, it could rock a woman's world.

He dropped it back into the box to lie on the bed of pink and green foam bits. He picked up the plastic package again and let it dangle at eye height. "Who the hell would send this?"

Double your pleasure, he read, *with this lifelike aid to sexual fulfillment.*

Lifelike. He snorted. If fourteen inches was what it took to get this woman off, whoever she was, a real cock wouldn't begin to do it.

He dug deeper, pulled out a tidy package of thigh-high stockings. *Stay ups,* he read.

He held the package up to the light from the front door window.

Black.

Fishnet.

Hot.

He dumped the rest of the peanuts out onto the floor. He had to find out where this stuff came from or at least where it was supposed to go. No matter how tired he was when he ordered off the Internet, he would not make a mistake like this!

A paper fluttered onto the floor. He'd opened the box wrong side up. The receipt was at the bottom. If he'd opened it right side up, the paper would have been on top and he might never have seen the contents.

Kat Hardee, the receipt said. Shipped from the *Sexy Pants Party Plan.* "Oh shit."

He leaned against the wall and slid to the floor, surrounded by foam peanuts, three packages of black fishnet stockings and a huge dildo. This was some delivery! Shipped to the hottest woman he'd ever seen.

This time his cock threatened to burst through his fly, so he eased down the zipper for more room. So much for the sweet girl next door routine.

If she needed a fourteen-inch cock, she belonged in a circus!

Man, if he thought he could get fantasy mileage out of a thirty-second conversation, this, *this,* would give him wet dreams for a month!

Not only did Kat have a great rack, but her legs went on forever. He imagined those long legs decked out in thigh-high black fishnet stockings. Oh yeah, and four-inch stilettos, the kind they say are killers for a woman's back. Not that Kat would walk around in them.

No, he'd have her legs in the air in no time flat. No walking involved.

He groaned. "Shit!" He looked at the dong again. Was this what she needed? Fourteen inches of artificial cock? And what, three inches around, he estimated. Now he could envision what he'd find at the top of her long sleek legs. A pussy open enough, wet enough to take this dong.

She'd do a wide squat over the head and place the bulbous end against her folds. With a tap on her clit her pussy would open, slick and ready. The head would disappear into her and she'd sigh with relief, close her eyes and take it deep. The image flooded his mind in living color.

He put his head in his hands, scrubbed his face to get some blood back into it because his cock had taken it all. No surprise there; even in his daydreams she made his blood run south.

After he took a shower, a very cold shower, he'd pack all this stuff up again and take it next door. Maybe he could ring the bell and leave the box for her to find without letting her know he'd left it.

Bad idea, Connors. If he didn't hand the package over to her face to face she'd think he was too embarrassed. It was bad enough that he got tongue-tied and clumsy. He refused to come across as sexually inhibited too.

No, he had to admit he opened it and let her carry the ball from there. If there was an explanation she wanted to share with him, fine. If not, he'd come home and forget the whole thing.

Yeah, like that would happen. He'd never forget a fourteen-inch dong heading straight for her wet opening.

Still, this didn't seem right. Not for Kat. He only saw her around the complex, but up to now she'd seemed like any sweet, shy woman. The Kat he chatted with was kind of quiet, studious, worked evenings so she could go to college. The typical girl next door. The kind of woman he'd like to get to know. He'd never seen a man visit. She never went out on dates.

Dare he even think that she seemed like the kind of girl he wanted to take home to his mom?

But she was a different woman than her demeanor had led

him to believe. This peek into her sexual needs disturbed and aroused him, made him wonder about her level of sexual experience.

He wasn't a monk and he didn't believe in a double standard. The morals he had worked for both men and women. Neither sex should be indiscriminate in their mating habits. That way lay disaster.

Since he was a product of that kind of disaster, he was particular about his women. He wasn't sure how he felt about dating a woman with a long—very long—string of lovers behind her. He admitted it was old fashioned, but there it was.

He wanted what he wanted. He could no more change that than change his eye color.

If he wanted an easy lay he'd have responded to his other neighbor's offers. Celia had made it plain she was available for some easy fun whenever he felt the need. But going where so many men had gone before didn't interest him.

He wanted his woman to be his. And his alone.

He stared at the double-headed dong again. Could a woman really need all this rod? He couldn't see Kat cuddling up warm and cozy with a dong. But maybe her needs were fulfilled by plastic. No male visitors and no dates did not necessarily mean she was shy and reserved.

Maybe she got along just fine with her battery-operated boyfriend.

Or maybe she never brought her dates home with her.

Who was Kat Hardee? Sexy vixen who wore black fishnet thigh highs or a sweet, shy college student trying to make ends meet?

Puzzles had always intrigued him, and this puzzle screamed to be figured out. Determined not to sound like a fool when he took her package next door, he headed into the shower to take care of a raging hard-on. No way would he be able to think straight with a woody the size of Texas.

The icy spray sluicing over him didn't do much to cool his fire. Instead, it reminded him of the night last week when he'd startled Kat into tossing water on her T-shirt. He hadn't meant to ogle her, but her breasts had peaked and the wet cotton had clung, and his brain had shut down while his blood rushed south.

Typically, she'd been adorable, flustered and shy.

Until she'd caught his look. Something hot and razor sharp had passed between them until he made the mistake of offering to finish watering the rosebush between their front doors.

His voice had startled her again and she'd handed him the watering can without a word before dashing into the house. Would a woman whose sex play included fourteen inches of plastic cock be embarrassed by hard nipples?

His cock rose into his hand as he envisioned Kat opening for him, welcoming him into her dark, wet depths. The vision and steady pump of his hand took him over the edge.

Next time he spoke to Kat Hardee, vixen or sweet girl next door, he'd be able to think.

3

Kat's doorbell rang as she bit into her peanut buttered toast. It wasn't as burnt as the smell made it seem, so she figured this was supper. She'd wasted too much time talking with Celia and now she was running late.

She should ignore the chime of the bell and hide in the kitchen until whomever it was gave up, but she peeked around the corner and saw Taye in the front door window.

With the stupid bet still fresh in her mind, she figured she shouldn't look a gift horse in the mouth. If Taye was standing at her front door, she wanted to talk with him. Hell, she'd want to talk to him even without the bet.

She waved away the smell of burnt toast as she headed for the door. Taye saw her and smiled as she approached. The man had a great smile, wide, straight. His eyes crinkled at the corners in that way good-looking people had that said they'd look good at eighty.

The man was hotter than hot, and her engines revved just looking at him. She tossed the rest of the piece of toast onto the kitchen counter, then swiped her hand across the butt of her shorts. She ignored a flicker of guilt at the way she'd agreed to pursue the man as if he had no free choice.

Of course he had choice. There was a line of single women right in this complex for him to choose from. Just because Celia had stepped up the game was no reason to scurry and hide.

The peanut butter and the burnt toast smell refused to go away but she was dead out of time. If she wanted to get to work, she had to see what Taye wanted, deal with it and do her best to flirt all at the same time.

She kicked away a pair of shoes from in front of the door and opened it.

"Hi!" she said briskly, and spied the box he'd been juggling earlier. Maybe he wanted to share the cookies his mom sent.

Or not.

He looked nervous as he swiped his fingers through his damp hair. Nervous and fabulously clean and tidy, while she stunk up the place.

Life wasn't fair sometimes. Here he was, the object of her desire, looking all good and sexy while she had a hard day of school behind her, the dregs of this morning's makeup on and her hallway stunk. Peanut butter and burnt toast notwithstanding, she pasted a welcoming smile on her face.

She straightened and patted at her hair. "Sorry I'm such a mess, I was just about to get ready for work." Something yucky caught at her hair as she pulled at a couple of strands. Peanut butter. She smoothed it, then tucked the hair behind her ear.

Unless the man had a peanut butter fetish the whole flirting idea was hopeless.

He blinked and let his gaze travel down her body. His lips lifted into a slow grin that made her wonder if she had the only peanut butter fetishist in the world living next door.

"You look great," he said, holding up the package. "Turns out this came to my place by mistake," he explained. "I, um, opened it before I read the label."

He held it out to her as if it scorched his fingers. His eyes held a feverish glint. "Sorry."

She accepted the box, brushing her fingers across his in the process. His eyes glowed at her touch while delicious flares of awareness danced through her belly. "It's for me?" She gave it a shake. Couldn't weigh more than a pound. "It's light."

She flipped it over to read the delivery label. "Oh! Now I see," she said, only vaguely aware that he shuffled his feet as she looked at the label. "They're testing a new courier company for deliveries. This should have been here yesterday."

The label was smudged in a couple places, but the guy must've been in a hurry. "My usual courier would never make a mistake like this. He's aware my livelihood depends on regular deliveries, so he takes special care of me."

She looked up at him again and caught an odd look of surprise in his eyes.

Taye nodded, then nodded again. His expression hardened and focused in a way that reminded her of the watering can incident from last week. Another shot of awareness zinged around inside.

Oh my, the man was hot.

Celia's challenge to get him naked didn't seem like a long shot now. It looked more and more like a sure thing. She forgot about the peanut butter in her hair and the wafting scent of burnt toast. "I wish I had time to invite you in and thank you properly. But—" She bit off the words.

Taye glanced back down at the package again. "You're running late," he said, his voice a deep purr of male interest. But he stared at the package as if it contained dynamite.

She tried to keep her gaze on his face, but it was impossible to miss the way his slacks filled out.

"The warehouse dispatcher said he'd tracked this down as delivered, but when I swore I didn't have it, he put a trace on it," she babbled, realized she babbled and ended with, "Thanks a ton, I really need it."

He blanched. Ran a shaky hand through his trying-to-curl hair. "Oh yes, well, I guess you do. I mean, need it, that is. We all do." His throat worked on the last words, then he swallowed hard and looked as if something was caught by his Adam's apple.

The awareness she'd been enjoying dropped like a stone into dark, anxious dread. *Oh no.* "Wait, you said you opened it?"

A sick feeling rose from her belly and she suddenly realized why he looked pale. A couple of lesbians had ordered . . . and he thought . . . and she said she needed . . .

"Oh my God! It isn't mine, I mean, I ordered it, of course, but it isn't for me. Honest. Well, the stockings are, but not the um, the um, other thing." Now it was her turn to run her fingers through her hair. Heat rose from her chest to her ears. The sound of rushing blood filled her head.

"The stockings?" His voice sounded hoarse. "Are yours?"

"Yes."

His eyes glazed with heat at her answer.

Then it hit her. Taye Connors felt the same way about her as she did about him.

Oh wow. And there was nothing, *nothing* she could do about it right now.

Her body had other ideas. Her nipples rose and points appeared under her shirt. He saw them, swallowed, but didn't speak. From the look on his face, he wasn't capable of talking.

But she had to be sure. She tightened her forearms. The resultant jut of her nipples had him widening his eyes.

"I shouldn't hold you up," he said, backing away. "You're on your way to work soon." All kinds of sorry flashed through his expression.

She felt the same way. "You can hold me up anytime." Up

against a wall, door, even a car, and she'd let him do whatever he wanted with her.

The hall clock ticked away the seconds toward the time she had to leave. She glanced at the clock face, willing the hands to stop.

"When I get home late, I hope I don't disturb you," she said, desperate for something to say to let him know how much she wanted to see him. "But sometimes your kitchen light's on. I guess you're not always asleep when I'm out here fumbling with my keys in the dark." She was so out of practice with flirting, her words sounded awkward and tight. Her chest felt awkward and tight too.

"You need to fix the light over your door," he said, just as tightly. "So you don't have to fumble in the dark." His face lit up, and her heart stopped at the sheer male beauty of his smile. "Or you could knock on my door and I could help you."

"Help me fumble?" She grinned and imagined the two of them fumbling and wrestling and finally rolling around on the front walk so hot for each other they wouldn't care that they hadn't made it inside.

"There wouldn't be any fumbling, Kat. I'd get you inside."

She let out a shattered breath. Tried to remember that time was moving on and she had a living to make.

"I don't have a stepladder, so I can't reach." She pointed to her dead overhead light. Some security-conscious builder had set the lights high enough that a burglar couldn't reach the bulbs, but it was a pain for the tenant.

"I'll do it for you," he offered. "But tonight, you could ring my bell. I'll wait up for you."

"Thanks!" She smiled and looked at him steadily while her thoughts raced straight upstairs to the bedroom. "I'll see you later."

"You bet." There was a feverishly sweet light in his eyes as he stepped around the rosebush that separated their front stoops.

"I appreciate it. And you," she said. "You're a good neighbor." She took a deep breath and held it while he tried like hell not to be seen checking out her still-jutting nipples. The nipples that tingled and weighed heavily under her tee.

She closed the door before she did something stupid like drag him into her house by the collar.

She had a party to go to. College wouldn't pay for itself.

The evening stretched before her like a silvery thread that led straight back to Taye.

She smiled and headed upstairs to shower and change. She had peanut butter to wash out of her hair. Shampooing quickly, she decided to take another five minutes to shave her legs. There was no time to wax her pubes into her favored landing strip, so she hoped he didn't mind bush.

In her room, she swapped out her sheets with fresh as quickly as she could while taking a mental inventory of her sexiest underwear. Somewhere in her drawers was a shiny silver-colored thong. One her ex-husband had never seen.

It tickled her that Taye Connors would be the first man to see her in it.

4

"So it buzzes against your clit while this other bit is inserted?" The fevered eyes of the woman sitting next to her amused Kat. They were at a dining room table, order forms in a neat stack, catalog open, toys littering the tabletop.

The demonstration had gone well, moved along by Kat's urgency to get back to Taye. With a hot man waiting, she didn't feel much like working.

She leaned in close and raised her eyebrows, not because of the woman's question but because when she moved, her silvery thong rubbed deliciously against her clit. She wondered why she'd never worn it before. "It'll rock your world," she said in response to the question about the vibrator. She added a salacious chuckle to cement the sale.

"Ooh." The mother of two squirmed. "Some nights I'm too tired to think, let alone get it on." She pouted. "Don't get me wrong, I love my husband, but I'm exhausted most of the time."

"Nap time could be fun," Kat commented in a low, evocative tone. She'd perfected the art of the soft sell. But then, it wasn't difficult to sell orgasms. Everyone wanted them.

Her customer's eyes lit up. "They nap between two and three every afternoon."

"Five minutes, tops," Kat said, reaching for her pen. She grinned. Her own thighs were sodden from thoughts of Taye, so she probably looked and sounded as turned on as all her customers. But tonight was different because she wouldn't have to go home to an empty bed.

She encouraged the woman to slide her thumb across the on/off switch to demonstrate the easy use. The hummer buzzed to life, the sound quiet and unobtrusive. "It's an excellent rush and takes you where you want to go faster than any man."

She said the last loud enough to discourage the hostess's husband from coming into the dining room from the kitchen. He assumed Kat didn't know he was there, lurking and listening to the women chatting about the party plan, the products and S E X. The vibrator thrummed and hummed in the other woman's hand. This part of the evening was private, and she didn't want a man ruining the mood.

"Hold the end to the tip of your nose," she suggested. "That will give you the closest sensation of what you'll feel on your clitoris."

"Wow, that's quite a buzz!" The woman's cheeks flushed.

Kat held up a bottle of a warming lubricant, one of her best sellers. "It goes well with our Hot Pants Lube."

"Okay, I'll take both," the woman said, reaching for her purse. Her hands actually trembled as she pulled out her wallet.

Kat took her order form and filled it out.

This was the most fun part of the evening. The demonstrations were over and she could sit quietly with each buyer and discuss their individual needs. She loved to coax the women into exploring their sexual needs honestly in a safe setting. For many of her customers this was a first.

Most times she set aside her own sexuality and focused on her customers, but not tonight. She was ready to go home, grab Taye Connors and show him her wild side. A side she'd never even shown her ex-husband.

A side she'd never suspected existed until she'd reluctantly taken this job. Normally straitlaced women full of sex-related questions, hearts pounding, cheeks flush, eyes glazed as possibilities bloomed for them was not the area of sales she'd thought to explore. But, wow, did it pay the bills.

A shadow at the kitchen doorway crossed her peripheral vision as she said good-bye to the woman. She ignored the lurker and smiled an encouraging welcome to the next customer.

Like a lot of uptight men who smirked at women showing a healthy interest in sex, the hostess's husband was probably turned on by the idea of women talking about sex. Like it was something dirty or only created for men. Guys like him were the most fun to shock, so she made it a point to imply she was into every one of the sex toys she offered for sale. After all, if she didn't use them, why would any other woman?

A heavy-chested redhead settled across from her, opened the catalog to the back pages and pointed. "Size XXL."

"Ooh," Kat crooned. "Rubber." She loved this kind of customer. They were fast, decisive and didn't quibble about prices. They knew what they wanted and were willing to pay for it.

"My man's into it," the woman said. "Lucky for me that's literal."

"How so?"

"He's the one who puts it on. I just get sweaty in the stuff, so I told him to try it one night. Turns him wild now."

Kat grinned. "Great."

"Me, I like girl-on-girl porn."

A choked sound came from the shadow lurking in the kitchen. The redhead winked at Kat. She winked back.

"I've been telling my area manager to pass it up the chain that DVDs would sell. Maybe in the next catalog."

The customer laughed. "Yeah, that's right, Chucky," she called to the hiding husband, "me and Benny are into good times."

Kat suppressed a snicker and they shared a high five.

The shadow disappeared as Chuck finally took the hint and left.

Wine flowed and the talk got more raunchy and outrageous, with the single women trying to outdo the married ones with stories of their sexual exploits.

Kat took it all with a grain of salt. If half these women did what they said they did, there would be people getting laid all over the transit system, in libraries and every other public place in the city.

Most people liked their sex behind closed doors, she thought while she completed her last order form of the night. Amid the hubbub of feminine giggles and wine-induced sexual confessions, she collected her inventory. The commission from tonight would pay for her next month's utility bills and groceries. Not bad.

Many times she'd fantasized about climbing from her bedroom window into Taye's. Usually the fantasy began at a party just like this one where uninhibited talk got her revved. She often wondered if any of the women she spoke with had similar fantasies of being the dark faceless stranger rather than submitting to one.

Climbing in Taye's window would be a fabulous way to end a night. He'd be asleep, barely stirring under the covers as she silently lifted the sheet at his feet. She could start at his toes and work her way up his legs, over his knees to his groin. Oh! The fun they'd have pretending he was being ravaged in the silent dark. By the time she reached his cock, it would be straining and full. Ready for her mouth to carry him into ecstasy. She wondered what he tasted like . . .

She blinked and forced her thoughts back to reality. The hostess had asked her a question and looked at her with amusement.

"Care for some wine? You've been talking all night, you must be dry."

Dry? Hardly. "No, thanks, I don't drink at work. Not good for you. The more I focus on booking new parties, the better for you." The easy line was a gentle way to refuse her hostess's hospitality without offense.

Besides, if she and Taye ended up in bed together, she wanted a clear head. She replayed their conversation in her mind, trying not to embellish the heat she'd seen in his gaze or the throaty way he'd said her name.

Clearly he'd been hinting at waiting for her so they could have sex. She wasn't that far removed from the man–woman push–pull thing that happened between adults that she could get his signals wrong. Surely not.

The conversations she overheard were enough to make a girl's head spin, wine or no wine. She wondered what Taye would think of them. Maybe he'd like to hear some. If they cranked her up, there was no telling what he would think.

Creative scenarios played out as a lively discussion broke out over the virtues of oral sex with a tongue piercing versus without. The conversation swirled through her head, conjuring images of Taye's head between her legs, her hands twining in his barely there curls. Needing to get home, fast, she quickly shoved the last of the toys into her sample case.

Moisture pearled into Kat's panties as she hurried her good-byes.

Behind the wheel, her nerves screamed at each red light and

stop sign. Every shift of the clutch made her pussy pulse with achy need.

Ten minutes later it started.

The doubt, the second-guessing. She groaned aloud as a chastising inner voice told her she shouldn't assume Taye wanted her on nothing more than a couple of steamy looks. All he'd done was promise to fix a lightbulb.

The fact that it was a much smaller, tighter bulb that needed screwing didn't matter. She was foolish to pin her hopes on a brief conversation where she'd all but thrown herself at him.

She hadn't given him a chance to escape, blabbing about her deliveries and whining about the dead lightbulb.

The poor man had only been placating her. Taye was kind, that's all. She was foolish to go to his door.

The clock on the dash said 11:15. Too late for the good-neighbor routine.

But if she didn't take this slim chance, she would have to listen to Celia's smug comments for weeks. She would have to wonder every day if Celia and Taye—

She couldn't go there.

She told her inner whiner to shut the hell up and stepped on the gas.

Twenty minutes later, she pulled her car into her garage and shut off the engine. With one hand on the wheel and the other on the gearshift knob she gathered her courage.

Whatever happened she would hold her head up.

She tried to conjure some of the images that had tempted and teased her all night but had no luck. The only thing she could pull into her mind was Taye's quiet smile and the way he'd gone red when he handed over the package. He'd let her know that he knew about the dong, that it was okay for her to have needs.

What she wanted, needed, craved was Taye.

Unadorned, unadulterated sex with Taye.

Taye, with his serious eyes and gentle smile. Her belly dropped with low, heavy need.

She climbed out of the car and wrestled her sample case from the backseat.

Outside, light shone from Taye's kitchen window brightening a square patch of his walkway. Juggling her purse and sample case, she was reminded of Taye trying to pick up her package from his front step with his briefcase, keys and mug in his hands.

She bet her ass didn't look nearly as good as his.

How pathetic was that?

His kitchen light spilled in a square of bright that made her own front door seem darker. She took a quick look through his mini-blinds and her heart stalled.

Holy Hannah! He was in his underwear. And nothing else.

He opened his refrigerator and leaned in, giving her another perfect view of his butt. Spectacular, she saw. He pulled out a bottle of water, turned to lean on the kitchen counter, giving her a perfect view of his chest. He drank the whole bottle at once.

Again, his hair looked damp. How many showers did the man need in a day?

And how delicious could a man look? His chest, lightly sprinkled with hair, narrowed down to a taut waist. His package swayed heavily in his boxer briefs.

He tossed the empty water bottle in the trash and glanced at the window. She stepped back quickly, with a gasp that sounded loud enough to be heard inside.

Shame took flight around her chest but she couldn't look away. Pathetic didn't begin to tell the tale, because nothing more than curly chest hair had turned her into a dry-mouthed Peeping Tom.

Suddenly he reached for the wand to turn the mini-blinds closed.

Frozen, unable to move for fear he'd catch her peeping him, her panties moistened, knees weakened and nipples thrummed to life. His gaze went sharp, as if he'd caught sight of a movement, and she sucked in her breath, hoping against hope he wouldn't see her watching from the shadows like a pervert. The fantasy of climbing in through his bedroom window was much more fun than the reality of being caught out here.

Obviously she'd have to wait a couple minutes to ring his doorbell. Hiding her voyeuristic tendencies seemed important. If he thought she was weird or kinky, he'd be put off.

And she was tired of living like a nun. Sick and tired of being alone in her bed. Alone in her body.

She closed her eyes and began to count off the time until she could safely ring his bell. With a little luck Taye might scoop her into his arms and press her against the wall, holding her wrists up over her head while he feasted on her lips, neck, sipping from the hollow between her collarbone, sliding down, open mouthed to one nipple then the other.

A gush of moisture in her channel woke her from the imagery long enough to set down her sample case. With a heavy breath, she set her finger to his buzzer.

And pressed.

"Sorry," she heard from inside the door. "I went for a run and had a shower. Let me get my jeans on."

The words *don't bother* threatened to explode out of her mouth, but the sound of Taye dashing upstairs forestalled them.

In another dash, he was down again and opening the door for her. She smiled. "Hi."

"Hi, yourself." He was buttoning his shirt without looking and had the bottom buttons askew. The man was adorable.

Giving up on the shirt, he pointed overhead. "I changed the lightbulb for you, but I couldn't turn it on from out here."

"Oh, thanks." She stood staring at him for a couple of seconds, then remembered she still hadn't unlocked her own front door. She took care of that immediately, then stepped inside to flip the switch on the wall. She set her sample case and purse down and turned toward him. "Perfect, thanks again."

Light shone down on his head, giving him a halo while casting his mouth in shadow. Moths flickered toward the light. She turned it off again and stepped back in invitation, holding the door open. The front hall was dark, but she needed the dark to hide her nerves.

For all her horny needs, she was still half-convinced she'd read his signals wrong. "Would you like to come in? I have some decaf I could brew. It's late for caffeine." She took a quick mental inventory of her wine stock. All she had was the box of white she used at parties. It was still in the trunk of her car, more than half-empty. Taye probably wouldn't like wine out of a box.

She could still smell the taint of burnt toast but Taye didn't seem to notice.

He stepped into her narrow front hall and she backed up to give him room to close the door. Firmly and with purpose, he closed it the way a man closes a door knowing it would be daybreak before he opened it again.

5

Stomach fluttering with nerves and painful need, Kat heard the loud click of the front door lock. "You've never been inside my house before," she said with a squeak. She cleared her throat and tried again. "Is the layout the same as yours?"

Her silently expectant front hall had never been so narrow, or so full of male vibrancy. He was much wider, more solid in the dark. She hoped he couldn't hear her heart pound.

She moved her hand toward the light switch, but he stopped her, his fingers hot on the back of her hand. "I like the dark," he said.

She nodded. The dark made it easy to hide her flushed cheeks and budded nipples. Stupid! Celia wouldn't hide a thing.

With a great leap of faith, Kat took the plunge and let go of the security her shyness gave her. If she continued to let shyness rule her life, she'd never get laid!

It's way past time to let your inner adventuress out to play.

Taye peeked into the kitchen, lit by a single night-light. "The floor plan's opposite. At least down here." His voice stroked her from throat to navel and she shivered in the dark, wanting to hear more.

"My bedroom's next to yours," she said softly to hide the tremor she was sure was in her voice. "We share a wall."

What would he think if she told him she wanted to climb in his window?

"Coffee sounds good," Taye said, breaking into Kat's sexual reverie. "Decaf's fine." His voice went husky, expectant. He cleared his throat and leaned in close.

He crowded her in a very un-Taye-like stance that sent thrills down her spine. "That is, unless you need to get to bed right away."

Her belly fluttered in acceptance. In approval.

In need.

She forgot what it was they were talking about. Her nerves screeched and she backed away. "Not right away, no. I'm keyed up after work. Need time to wind down."

His eyes gleamed in the dim glow from the night-light.

"I'm sorry, I burnt some toast earlier." She fought the pull of his scent, his warmth. "I think my toaster's shot." It was easier to think about letting out her inner adventuress than actually doing it.

She clenched her fist to press her nails into her palm to remind her she was supposed to be seducing the man, not complaining about small appliances.

Again, her hand went to the light switch on the wall.

Again, he stopped her. "No," he said, covering her hand with his. "This is enough light. It's dark, it's late." He brought her palm to his lips and kissed it. "It's quiet."

Her entire body buzzed from that one perfectly planted kiss.

Her sex fluttered and melted.

He slowly lowered their hands and released hers while she

stood transfixed by the change in him. Where was the geek? The nerd? The cute clumsiness she found so appealing?

"If the thermostat's gone in your toaster, it could be a fire hazard. You should toss it," he said.

What she wanted tossed was her, on a bed, with Taye following her down into the mattress. She flushed hot and pivoted the single step into her kitchen. "I'll put the coffee on." She just knew he was checking out her less-than-perfect butt.

She went to the cupboard and brought down a fresh bag of coffee beans, then remembered she needed decaf. She dug into the cupboard again and brought out a package of ground coffee. Not as good, but at this time of night she didn't think it mattered.

"Thanks." He wandered over to the counter beside her to check out the toaster. He unplugged it and his elbow brushed her arm with the movement. Zips and zings of charge sparked along her arm to her chest.

"I'll throw the toaster away right now if it's the thermostat," she said. "I don't want a kitchen fire."

"You don't? I like fire between two people in the kitchen."

"Oh," she breathed, and decided that no matter what, she would allow her inner wild woman free rein tonight. No more shy Kat, no more worries about needing commitment. It was time she grew up and went for the sex she needed.

"Yes, oh," he repeated. His smile went soft and she got lost in the gray of his eyes, going smoky as she watched. Her mouth went dry and she licked her lips. His eyes darted to the movement, and he swallowed hard.

"I'll have to wait for my next party to buy another toaster, though."

He blinked. Looked confused by the conversational turn. Confused and sweet and lip-smacking good. He was back to being Taye the good neighbor here to fix her toaster. "Party?"

His stammering response to the double-headed dong and the thigh highs he'd dropped off earlier ran through her mind. Had he spent the evening trying to put two and two together? Heaven only knew what he had come up with.

"I'm putting myself through college selling sex toys and lingerie," she told him, not just to put him out of his misery but to put his mind on lingerie and sex. "And assorted paraphernalia." She thought of the warming lube that was so popular. Not that she'd need any. She was well lubricated by juices she'd made herself.

She filled the water well in the coffeemaker with a hand that barely shook. She wrestled away her shyness and decided to let her natural inclinations take them where she figured they both wanted to go. "I hope you didn't think the double-headed dildo was mine. That thing was way too big. I prefer a more natural fit."

Even in the dimness, she could see him flush red. "I have to admit the thought crossed my mind. A cock that size might be considered a hard act to follow." The corner of his mouth lifted, and she saw his teasing side. "By a lesser man, of course."

Oh Mama, the man had a sense of humor. "Of course."

"I'm glad the courier messed up. Otherwise I might not be here right now." He slanted her a heated glance. "Paraphernalia, huh? Flesh-colored cocks and lingerie like the fishnets?"

"And merry widows, crotchless panties, warming lubes and gels. That kind of thing." She leaned against the counter and crossed her arms under her breasts, giving them a slight lift.

He noticed, and her sex went soft and open.

"You've got my interest. Although, you've had that for some time now, Kat."

Her breath fluttered out of her chest. This was really going to happen! Suddenly three years of abstinence seemed a small price to pay if sleeping with Taye was the payoff.

"Did you like the thigh highs?" She decided to go for broke. "They're comfortable and one of my best-selling items. Would you care to see them?"

He swallowed hard and shifted on his feet. Two good signs, she thought. "The thigh highs." His eyes went dark. "Stay ups, right? I'd love to see them."

"Good, I'll go get a pair."

If Kat came out of that bathroom with her long-as-forever legs in the black fishnet thigh highs he'd seen earlier, he'd come all over himself. Taye ran his fingers through his hair and tried to control his raging libido. His blood rushed and pulsed to his cock, leaving his brain blood-deprived again.

He'd always been a daydreamer, but this was too wild, even for him. He needed to focus elsewhere or he'd make a fool of himself.

Much as he tried he couldn't figure Kat out. One minute she was shyly provocative, the next she turned into a sexy vixen who made it clear what she wanted.

But always, she made him burn.

He'd promised to check out her toaster for her so he dumped a load of old crumbs from the toaster into the sink. Chunks of blackened crust fell out.

A sound behind him made him turn.

Kat stood just inside the kitchen and held a long black rope in each hand. She looked flushed and pretty and completely girl-next-door, but now he knew better. She was a vixen, out for a good time.

She was dressed as she'd been before, a sexy black sheath held up by thin straps. The material draped every curve and smooth dent her body possessed. The material shimmered and clung to all her smooth planes and pointy points.

"These come in various colors," she said, holding up the

ropes, "but I'm partial to black." She threaded one of the ropes over her hand and up her arm past her elbow. The material opened up into the mesh he was familiar with.

"Me too," he said around a thundering heart. "Although white's nice too. Virginal."

"Is that what you'd like, Taye? A virgin?" She pulled the fishnet down her arm again, slowly, like a stripper removing a long silk glove.

The image was hot, the real woman in front of him hotter.

"Because I could do that for you." Her voice went husky and offered exactly what he'd come over here to get. "Be virginal, I mean."

He turned around fully, rested his hips against the sink. Her gaze dropped to his crotch and he did nothing to prevent her bold appraisal.

She smiled and raised her eyebrows. "I see you know exactly what I mean."

"Next time," he said, "you wear white. This time, I want you in those. And I want you now." Half-crazed with lust, he couldn't believe he'd said it, and the resulting flare in her eyes said she didn't believe it either.

A storm of doubt gathered in the depth of her gaze, but just as quickly it cleared.

She distracted him by bending over. Her beautiful, fleshy breasts swayed as she reached up under her dress. She tugged, and her sheer pantyhose came down her legs and off her feet into a filmy beige pile.

The last of the coffee burbled into the maker, the scent rich and full. Forgotten.

Taye's heart pounded hard as Kat put her left foot into the toe of one thigh high. His gut sucked in and he held himself still as she smoothed and coaxed the stocking up her leg. Again, the familiar crisscross pattern emerged, adding shape and shadow to her already-curvy leg. His imagination went into overdrive as he recalled his image of that huge dong pressing into her.

He blinked to clear his mind of the dong. Soon it would be him sliding into her.

His cock thudded, blood moved through his head thick and slow as she did the same slow torture thing with her other leg.

Not sure how far he could take this without throwing Kat to the floor, he watched silently, trying to frame his next words.

What came out undid him. "Now, lift your skirt to show me."

"Wait, I need my shoes." She flitted out of the room like a fairy queen, excited and pretty and quick. Oh so quick.

She was back with her shoes on, sassy but cool at the same time. The hem of her slinky black dress swirled and caressed her knees.

"You have gorgeous legs," he said.

Her cheeks went pink at the compliment, and she blinked. He had to remember that. As much as she liked compliments he could see she didn't get enough of them.

"And fabulous breasts."

She flushed full out at that one. "I didn't think you ever noticed me."

"My fault. I should have let you know." Stupid. They could have been like this for months now instead of fumbling around each other. "Now, lift your hem. I want to see those stockings."

Her hands clasped the black material covering her thighs and began a painfully slow tug. Up, up, up the material crept, each inch heightening his desire to see everything hidden.

Everything. Everywhere.

Finally, the tops of the stockings appeared just below her pubis. She was perfectly formed, seductive and innocent. Her gaze warmed to hot and he swore he saw the same vixen peek out at him that he'd seen before. The skin of her neck and chest

bloomed a sexual flush, and she looked sweet and hot. A roar
built in his head as he made his move.

Flashes of all the dreams he'd had with Kat Hardee in the
starring role flickered behind his eyes as he crossed the small
kitchen to her.

She let go of her dress and tugged at his shoulders the second
he got close. He grabbed her delectable ass and tugged her
lower body into his erection, tight and hard.

"Kiss me, Taye, before I—"

He plowed into her open mouth with his tongue, sipping
and taking and losing himself in her taste. Her hot, wet mouth
enticed and entangled him and pulled him into her.

His hand squeezed and rubbed the fleshy mounds of her ass
as she moaned in her throat. She shifted her butt to rest on the
table edge, and he smoothly moved into place between her
thighs.

She sighed into his mouth and worked the buttons on his
shirt. Taking her cue, he smoothed the thin straps of her dress
off her shoulders and delved into her bodice. A strapless bra in-
terfered until she undid the front catch and gave him room.

He scooped her breasts free of the bra and dress. "You've
got great tits. I've wondered how they look and feel." He
weighed them, soft and heavy. He was right, the slope was
straight with the bulk of her flesh below the upturned nipples.

Full and red, her nipples were hard. His mouth watered
while he looked his fill. Finally he set his mouth to her. Hard
pearls met his tongue as he swirled and licked.

She leaned back on her elbows across the small square table
so he could move down her body to her waist. The dress refused to move lower without some major readjustment, and he
didn't want to give her time to think about what they were
doing.

If her head cleared she'd probably slap him. So he palmed
her calves, feeling the diamond pattern of her stockings under

each hand. He raised her legs, settled himself square in her cradle.

He never moved this fast with women, but he'd wanted Kat for so long, he was crazy for her.

"Do me, Taye," she panted. "Please! It's been so long." Her legs drew up his back and a flash of the stockings slammed into him.

He pressed his hard-on against her wetness, the scent of her arousing him to fever pitch. But the table height was awkward and he wanted his first slide into her to be perfect.

Her need reached out to him as she moaned and arched against his cock. He knew only one remedy for this.

Only one.

6

Taye crouched and widened Kat's cradle with his palms. A thin silver line of material bisected her pussy. A thong. A dripping, sliding strip of juicy material waited for him.

He curled his fingertips under the rubbery band at the top of each stocking and looked his fill. "You're beautiful," he murmured. "Wet and pink."

He let the beauty of the moment swirl between them as he rubbed his cheek against the soft abrasive netting of her stocking, feeling the heated softness of her thigh on the tip of his nose.

Her scent rose, aroused and needy. He released one stocking to palm her belly so she would hold still. Then, his blood racing, he set his closed mouth to her dripping lips.

She sighed at the light pressure, and her secrets popped open against his firm lips.

Then she stilled and let him scent her fully. Heaven.

He ran his chin from her entrance to her clit with a light pressure, so she'd feel the fine scraping of his bristles.

She shuddered and her clit popped out of its hood. "So pretty," he murmured. "So wet."

"If you don't finish me I'll die, right here on the table." His shy neighbor retreated in the face of raging sexual need and he loved that finally they were communicating on the most primal level.

He chuckled and knew exactly how to take her where she needed to go. He lapped at her clitoris while he slid the silver thong out of the way. Plunging two fingers into her at once, he lay the flat of his tongue against her rubbery nub.

She rocked toward him, needing more. Throaty hums and light moans rained down on him. Enjoying her response, he rotated his fingers faster and faster, while she crooned and bucked against him.

"Fuck me! Taye!" she moaned and rocked her hips while he added a third finger and gently sucked her clit.

"Oh! . . . fuck, I'm coming!" She panted as an inner tremble rose. Moisture flooded his fingers. He plunged them in again and again while she came, holding her still while he worked her clit and deepest flesh.

His balls tightened to fiery as she crashed through another pinnacle.

In. In. In.

He wanted inside her. He wanted his flesh enveloped and the sweet inner clutch of her pussy swallowing him. He nearly popped his load as he eased away from her and slid his zipper open.

Blessed relief from his clothing soon turned to agony as she lifted her head and looked at him between the bracket of her knees. Her pussy dripped, her flesh scented the air and her lively eyes looked ready for more.

"Did you bring a condom?"

He raised his face to the ceiling. Crap! "No."

"No worries," she said as she swung her foot over his head and scrambled off the table. "I've got some here," she said as she rounded the doorway into the hall. He followed and saw her bend over the case she'd brought in.

"You've got a great ass, Kat." He palmed her, smoothing his hand across her high, round cheek.

She tilted higher, and he wrestled with the temptation of sliding his cock in to the hilt as she bent over. Another time.

She rose to full height and held up a plastic square in triumph. "Hot pink!" she said with a bawdy grin. Then she reached for his hand and led him upstairs.

This was the craziest thing Kat had ever done, and she wasn't sure how she felt about it. The half of her that wanted Taye more than any other man she'd ever met loved what was happening. The half that told her sex with a hot neighbor without a word of commitment between them was wrong kept up a steady stream of complaints.

But it wouldn't be fair to say thanks for the orgasm, I got mine, too bad for you, so she waved Taye into her bedroom, told her inner whiner to shut up for the hundredth time and followed him and his rock-hard cock into the room.

Her bodice hung to her waist, the strapless bra trapped in the folds of the drooping material. She plucked it out and dropped it without ceremony to the floor.

The man was in need. His cock strained and jutted dark purple and heavy.

She'd brought him to this with her wanton offering on the kitchen table. She palmed her hot cheeks at the vision that swam in front of her mind's eye.

Her with her legs up, him with his head between them, his mouth and fingers making her come like a wild woman. Her legs still wobbled at the knees.

Her belly did a flip and settled into a low burn deep inside. She wanted more! Needed more.

Heart hammering, she stepped up to him, then wrapped her hand around his shaft.

He jerked and dragged her closer. When he kissed her she

tasted the combined salt of her pussy with the sweet taste of Taye. The combination aroused her while she used her other hand to try to undo the button of his opened fly.

Her hand shook so much he had to do it instead.

He stepped out of his cords and walked her backward to the bed. She stopped when she felt the mattress and raised the condom package to dangle between them.

With one deft move, and without looking, she tore open the foil and cheered inwardly at her panache. In a flourish she made it look easy, but three years of practice at parties had improved her skill.

She laughed when his eyes flared, and she fell backward to the soft mattress, legs wide. "Fill me, Taye. I need you."

He growled and covered his cock with the electric pink rubber and set his knees on the bed. Eyes burning with focused need, Taye grabbed her ankles and set them on his shoulders. His wide, muscular shoulders.

She caught her breath as he began a slow slide down to her. Without stopping or adjusting, he pressed his heavy-headed cock to her entrance and just kept on sliding. Straight in, straight up, straight along her inner walls, spreading her wide, wider, widest with every inch.

Filled, stretched and completed, she moaned with the heaviness of him. "This is so good. Taye, you have to let me move."

His jaw jumped with a tic as he pulled out a millimeter, then in again, and again, each time farther, harder, faster.

She surrendered to his rhythm and let him carry her over the edge. Her clit, sticky and plump, felt the tap, tap, tap of his rough possession, and each tap teased its way to her womb.

Nerve endings screamed trails that led up her spine and bloomed out of her chest. His mouth on her neck, near her ear, nibbled and kissed as he thrust into her again and again.

Tightening.

Tightening.

Tightening.

Arousal reached explosive, and she felt the tip over the edge begin. As she reached for her climax, his began with a shudder that took her up another notch.

If this was sex without commitment, then she needed more. With that thought being her last, sensation took over as she spiraled up into heaven with him.

He crooned into her ear and shuddered in her arms as she screamed with her come.

Spent, Taye rolled to her side, gathering her close. She snuggled in.

"Ready to sleep?" he asked.

"Not quite. You?"

"No." He took two slow breaths. "Want me to leave?"

"Not unless you want to go."

"No. This is good. You were fabulous." He shifted. To give him the space he seemed to need, she rolled away. He got up silently and left to go to the bathroom.

Awkward thoughts of what to expect from him ricocheted through her mind. He might want to go home. She had no experience with one-night stands. Didn't know if staying the night was expected or even wanted.

Through the closed door she heard the water run and some muted splashing sounds. He was washing up.

Taye was a tidy man and a generous lover. Her pussy twitched as she thought back over three spectacular orgasms.

She'd never had multiples before, but then her ex was always in a hurry. She should have realized how speedy he was before she married him, but she had put it down to teenage hormones.

She stuck her hands behind her head and stretched lazily.

The distant scent of the coffee came up from the kitchen. She climbed out of bed and went downstairs to bring up a tray.

Even if he didn't want to stay for more sex, he might want to stay for coffee.

* * *

The bedroom was deserted when he walked back in, and he wondered if this was Kat's way of letting him know she preferred sleeping alone.

He knew so little of her, in spite of the scorching looks and many awkward conversations they'd shared. Meaningless conversations that had told him nothing.

This was new for him. Sex before knowledge.

Generally he liked the women he slept with. He knew them well enough to know what they liked to talk about. Sometimes he knew their siblings or they had mutual friends.

But Kat had hit him so hard that he'd been consumed by lust for her and hadn't been able to do much real conversing.

Now, he was at a loss what to say. Thanks for the great lay didn't seem right, especially when he already wanted more. More sex, more talk, more time.

More Kat.

The clatter of dishes alerted him, and he looked toward the landing at the top of the stairs. Kat, balancing a tray laden with the makings for coffee.

"Cookies too?" he asked as he moved to take the heavy tray from her hands. He set it on the bedside table.

She scrambled naked to the center of the bed and patted a spot in front of her. "Let me serve you," she said, crossing her legs. He caught a glimpse of her shadowed pussy and thought of a great service she could perform.

He passed her the tray instead of making his suggestion. Plenty of time for that, he thought. Right now, she was offering him steaming coffee and chocolate chip cookies.

"Fabulous sex and delicious snacks. A good neighbor couldn't ask for more," he said.

She laughed. And lifted the coffeepot off the tray so he wouldn't topple it when he climbed onto the mattress with her.

"So, how was your party tonight?"

"Profitable," she replied as she poured cream into her mug. She added the coffee afterward so she wouldn't have to stir. "I forgot spoons."

"I take mine black anyway."

She made a check mark with her finger in the air. "Noted. He takes his coffee black."

His balls caught fire as he studied her over his mug. Her breasts swayed with every movement; the taste of her on his tongue enticed him. The dark curls that hid her pussy looked damp and tasty. He wanted to slide his hand to her and spear a finger into her hole, so she could sit there and rotate into a shattering come.

He loved to swirl the softness of a woman's G-spot and watch her eyes lose focus as he stroked her there.

His cock stirred back to life as he thought of Kat swaying with each delicate swipe along her softest inner flesh.

"Mmm, delicious," she said, but her eyes weren't on the cookie she'd bitten. They were on his rising rod.

His balls went tight as blood rushed to fill him out completely.

"So," she said, "want to hear what I heard tonight?" The grin on her lips said saucy, sexy and fun.

"What?"

"Several differing opinions on cunnilingus."

"When you say differing, do you mean there are women who don't like it?"

She giggled and covered her mouth. "Please, I was trying to swallow. No! I didn't mean there are women who don't like their pussy licked. I meant techniques."

"Did I do something wrong? Because if I did I'd be happy to give it another try." He deadpanned his features. "I mean if you want to give me instructions, I'm more than willing to learn."

Her nipples peaked into pearls as she pretended to consider

his offer. "I'm thinking this would be a win–win situation for us both."

"Indeed." He sipped his coffee, found it deliciously spiced with a hint of cinnamon. He made a check mark in the air with his finger, the way she had. "Known. Kat makes great coffee."

She looked pleased that he'd share her game.

"About those differing opinions," he led.

"Some women like the deep pointed tongue spear, others like the kind of thing you did."

"I'm not sure I have a technique. I love muff and want it all over my lips and chin. Yours in particular," he added. He made a show of licking his lips.

She stilled, and some of the humor fell under the rising heat in her gaze.

"Tell me what you liked, Kat. I need to know so I can do it again."

He thought he heard a tiny whimper she tried to cover by taking a sip from her mug. He waited patiently, then cocked an eyebrow at her when she swallowed.

"You, uh, did something on my clit with your tongue I think."

"Yes?"

"You pressed your tongue on me and let me roll my clit across it. But you used your chin too. I remember the incredible sensation of your bristles gliding across my opening."

"I wanted to gather your scent on my skin. Makes me crazy, and my balls turn to stone."

She leaned toward him then and cupped his sac. She weighed and measured and squeezed until he had to slam his mug down on the tray.

The smile she gave him would make a statue come. "Had enough coffee? Cookies?"

He slid the tray toward the end of the bed, then down to the floor.

"Then I heard a woman explain how she'd had two men at once," she said in a rush.

That stopped him. Is that what she wanted? Because he was going nowhere near there and never planned to. What if he felt a hairy, knobby knee near his Johnson, or *his* hairy, knobby knee settled next to a bristly chin. It was enough to make a man's cock make like a turtle.

Her eyes went wide when she noted his hesitation.

"Sorry," she said in a soft voice. "I'm not into that, I just thought it was . . ."

"Interesting? As a point for discussion."

She looked relieved. "Exactly."

"What else did you hear?"

"There was a woman who explained about men with split tongues."

"What?!"

She slid down to the mattress but kept her knees bent, ankles together. "She was Goth, though, so I suppose in her circle it would be easier to find a man with that kind of surgery." She opened her legs to expose her pussy. "But the more I think about it, the more I like the way your tongue works."

"I see what you mean," he said as her glistening, creamy slit opened to his view.

"You can look, but you can't touch," she said. Then she let her fingers tug lightly on the curls that hid her clit.

His balls went up in flames. The sweet, shy woman he thought he knew was gone. Replaced by a wild woman. And this wild woman planned to kill him. Right here, right now.

The medical examiner would declare him dead by spontaneous genital combustion.

7

Taye wanted to set his mouth to her pussy. Wanted to show her more ways he liked to use his tongue, but the wicked salacious gleam in her eye made him think twice.

He had a chance to show her more than the nerdy guy he must seem, so he took it. "I can look but not touch?" he repeated. "Fine by me."

Her eyes widened at the tone in his voice, and he smiled in a way that said he'd turned the tables on her. She was not giving instructions, nor would he take them. Not now.

He slid his hands under her hips and pulled her down the bed, then just as quickly climbed up her body to rest his knees on either side of her head. Her mouth opened in surprise, and he took advantage by sliding the tip of his cock between her perfect wet lips.

His breath caught at the beauty of her face framed by his knees. Her luxurious hair spread across the pillow while her kiss-roughened lips took his head.

"Take more, Kat." His voice was rough, close to a plea, but she didn't notice how much he needed, how desperate he was to feel her mouth accept him. He wanted to fuck her there, feel the wet, soft walls of her mouth. Wanted the suction, the fine scrape of her back teeth, the swirl of her wicked tongue.

His belly tightened as she opened wider, let him inch in, the wet warmth of her mouth coaxing pre-cum. The swirl of her tongue gathering the slick droplets set his teeth on edge, and he fought for control.

She softened the oh of her lips around his cock and he pulled out, then pushed in again a millimeter farther. Pulled out, pushed in, dying a little with every slide.

A groan rolled from his chest as he closed his eyes and took the sweet sensations Kat gave so generously.

The feel of her mouth set his teeth on edge, but when her tongue swirled across his head he flexed and an orgasm built at the base of his spine. "I'll come if you keep this up."

She chuckled, and the sensation inside her mouth sent his balls into another tightened flex. But her hand and devilish fingers clasped his sac and squeezed him into a spew that rocked up his back and shot sparks out the top of his skull.

He shot deep into her throat.

She took all he gave her, licking and squeezing and rolling her tongue against him.

He thought he'd been in charge. Now he saw that Kat had turned the tables again by taking what he gave and giving more back.

His heart stalled at her generosity, her giving and sweet, sweet nature. Kat Hardee was more than he'd ever hoped to find.

He lifted his still-heavy cock from her clasping lips and moved back down her body.

Her pussy streamed. The woman was a marvel. Deep pink flesh rimmed by cream welcomed his tongue as he took his cue and speared into her cunt with a firm point. She squirmed against his mouth as he used two fingers to pluck at her clit.

A wild gush and deep throaty moan signaled another orgasm as he lapped up Kat's cream.

She bucked against him with each trembling spasm. He held her there until she calmed and the thunderous rolls subsided.

Spent, he rolled to her side and gathered her close again. He smiled into the dark, marveling at how lucky he was to be in this bed, with this woman.

If he played his cards right, he'd never have to leave. "I guess this is where we talk," he said.

She went completely still against him. Even her breathing halted. "Only if you want to."

He wasn't sure he liked the tone of her voice. Something was off. She sounded hesitant and distant. No point rushing her if she wasn't ready. He didn't want to wreck a good thing before it began. "I have school tomorrow. An early meeting," he said, to give her an out. If she didn't want him to stay, she'd shift away to give him room to climb out of bed.

He waited.

Her breathing shallowed as sleep stole her away.

He smiled up at the ceiling as he prepared to settle for the night. Bonus! A whole night with her.

If he was smart and careful, the morning would bring another round of great sex to start off the day. That would set him up beautifully for spending the weekend with her. Before they left for the day they'd have their weekend plans set.

He wanted to get to know her. All of her. Everything.

She mumbled and shifted, nearly waking. The mumble got louder, more clear, until he heard her say, "Celia will be proud of me."

He wondered why she'd bring Celia into bed with them. "What for?"

"Casual sex . . . easy." She snuffled into his chest. "So freaking good. So many comes."

He grinned, figuring she was too sleepy to lie about coming.

She rolled to her back, arms loose and free of the sheet. He heard a sigh, then a girly giggle. "I won the bet."

He frowned and his gut rolled into a knot. He sat bolt upright, stared down at her. "What bet?"

The next afternoon, Taye packed up his briefcase, slamming test papers into it any way they'd fit. Monday morning his students would wonder what the hell happened. All the pages would be torn and crinkled when he returned the quizzes. He only hoped he could let his anger go long enough to mark each one fairly.

He usually marked his student's papers on Friday nights, but it wouldn't be right to try to go through them in this mood. Instead of heading home and getting this chore out of the way, he had to give himself a couple days to cool off. He'd mark everything on Sunday.

He wasn't sure how to approach the vixen that lived next door. When he drove through the gates to the housing development, Kat would most likely be at the mailbox as usual.

Looking as good as she always did.

Enticing him.

Betting on him.

He hated that his sexual prowess had been a matter of speculation among the neighbors. The single women outnumbered the single men in his townhouse complex. How many of them had been in on this bet?

He wondered how many of the other men who lived there, married and single, had been teased into bed for the women's amusement. He could only imagine how he stacked up to the other men Celia and Kat had been with.

He should have known a woman who sold sex toys would have a string of lovers and he would be just as disposable as the battery-operated kind.

The way she'd opened the condom package without looking at it got to him. How many had she opened to be that deft?

Hundreds probably.

He knew his attitude was different from a lot of men. But growing up with a bastard for a father had left a mark.

Before puberty even hit he'd promised himself he'd never take a woman's affection for granted. He'd never hurt a woman of his by using other women and laughing about it.

By the time he drove through the gates to his neighborhood, he'd calmed down enough to smile and wave at Kat if he saw her. She'd never know how he really felt about being the cock of the week. He refused to show how deeply their little game had got to him.

He'd been made a fool of by going into her bed hoping for more. Good thing he hadn't said as much. Every woman in the complex would still be laughing.

But Kat wasn't at the mailbox. Nor was she in her kitchen when he took a peek through her window. Inside the house, he tilted his head toward her living room wall. No sound of the television or music. Kat wasn't home.

He hadn't seen Celia either. They were probably out prowling for men already.

The idea of Kat doing what cats do best spiked his anger.

Last night, he'd been ready to fall asleep with Kat in his arms, snuggled up together like people who might have a future. And then she'd flustered her way through some crazy talk about betting about how he looked in his underwear and how Celia was planning to do him. Something that would never happen.

Around about then his pride kicked in and he'd slammed into his cords and headed for home. He'd been pissed off through the night and all day too.

And now that she wasn't home, his pride smarted even more, thinking of her looking for the next guy. He slammed into his fridge, grabbed a beer and drank half of it before he realized he'd downed it.

He snorted and scrubbed at his scalp in frustration, forcing himself to calm.

His day at school had opened his eyes. He'd only been teaching a couple years, so there were times some of his rowdier students threatened his authority. But today, the students who liked to test him had toed the line through every class.

He needed to remember that a teacher with his temper in check could intimidate the biggest asshole into behaving like a human being. Even a sixteen-year-old with attitude knew dealing with a lit fuse at the front of the classroom could be unpredictable.

Yes, he definitely had to remember that one. He wandered back into the living room to set his briefcase on his desk.

Bringing this kind of anger to his next meeting with Kat would be a mistake.

He still liked her. She was a good, quiet neighbor. No point ruining what was otherwise a reasonable relationship.

No matter that his pride was wounded, he still had to live here. Calmer now, he pulled the quiz papers out, stacking them neatly. Smoothing wrinkles where he could, he set a dictionary on top of the stack. It also wasn't his students' fault he'd fallen for Kat's enticements.

Any red-blooded male would have responded the way he did.

Any red-blooded male would want more. The fact that she didn't want more was what was really eating him.

And he did want more, in spite of the neighbors having a laugh at his expense.

It wasn't the same as what his old man had done. Nobody was cheating if nobody cared.

He ruminated on that for a good long time.

He wandered back out to the kitchen again, trying to avoid peering through the window to see if Kat was coming home, and failing. Still no sign of her.

Maybe judging Kat had been a mistake. Not that he didn't

think she was a vixen and that she had more men than he wanted to contemplate.

But maybe his attitude was off base. What he needed to do was re-evaluate his expectations.

So Kat wasn't the sweet woman of his dreams. But she was warm and friendly. And available.

A lot of men would settle for that. She had a spectacular body, an infectious smile when she offered it, and the sex blew his mind.

He shouldn't mess up a good thing just because it was destined to be short-lived. They could share some good times and move on, none the worse for the experience.

Grateful that he'd been too angry to say much last night, he picked up the phone to call and leave a message next door.

"Hi, Kat, it's Taye." His voice sounded hollow as Kat played his message. "Hope you're not angry that I left last night, but I had some work to get done before school this morning. I figured it would be easier to get up early from here. Sorry I had to skip out on you." Relief oozed through her.

She must have dreamed about telling him about the silly challenge Celia had thrown out at her. She must have imagined that he'd rolled out of bed, stiff shouldered and quick. That he'd slammed into his cords and left without more than a mumbled good-bye.

Whatever.

She didn't have to question her sleepy recollections any longer. He was calling and, by the tone in his voice, was happy to leave the message. She dashed upstairs for a shower, wishing she hadn't had to deliver the double-headed dildo to the lesbian partners.

If she hadn't had to tend to that bit of business she'd have been at the mailbox just like usual when Taye got home. She might be with him now.

The muffled sound of Taye's television came through the wall. He was home. Probably alone since she hadn't seen a car parked next door.

She soaped and rinsed, shaved and primped to get ready for another evening with Taye. There was a chance he wasn't interested in another evening with her, but it was a better bet that he was. People just couldn't make the kind of connection they had last night without wanting more.

Still, she needed a little insurance so she pulled out a filmy skirt and see-through blouse as if she were going to a casual party.

If Taye didn't respond to her unspoken offer, she could fall back on a white lie and say she was on her way out with friends. That way, they could both save face and neither of them would be left hanging or feeling awkward.

Most people had casual sex. Just because she usually needed more of a connection was no reason to lay her standards on Taye.

Celia was right. Her moral code was old-fashioned and B-O-R-I-N-G.

She had to learn to be more sophisticated and easygoing. More interesting and sexually stimulating. That's what men wanted these days.

Taye wouldn't want plain old Kat. Shy Kat had to die. If she wanted to keep him interested past this weekend then she'd have to be more like the Kat she pretended to be at her Sexy Pants parties.

Working at a party, she had no problem with lively sexual innuendo and telling tall tales about nonexistent sexual conquests. There was no reason she couldn't do all that with Taye.

Now was the time to walk the walk, not just talk the talk.

Her stomach knotted at the idea. Impressing Taye, being with Taye, was way more important than it should be.

She could be more interesting if she thought hard about it,

but keeping her head in her books for three years had left her boring and dull. She flapped her hands and saw her mom's nervous reaction to stress, and quickly stopped. This was no time to turn into her mother!

She slicked on a rosy lip gloss that promised kissability and smoothed her palms down her belly. She swivelled her hips in the mirror, trying for a seductive sway, but it came off wooden and jerky. Maybe if she put on thigh highs again, sheer black this time, with rhinestones shimmering at each ankle, she'd feel more like a seductress on another sexual adventure.

She dug out a fresh package, opened it, then slipped into each stocking slowly, imagining Taye's large square hands skimming up each leg.

When she got them on straight, she twisted and turned her ankles to see how well the glittery stones caught the light. Sparkly and feminine, the rhinestones danced against the black sheer stockings like fairy lights in a dark sky.

Next she stepped into a new pair of heels, liking the way the shoes and stockings seemed to add length and shape to her legs. Pleased with her appearance, she gathered her courage and headed next door before she chickened out.

At his front door her pussy tingled, moist and hot as she smoothed her skirt. She knocked and waited. *Breathe!*

The door opened and he smiled. She smiled back, heart thudding. His gaze went from her eyes, to her chest and down her legs to her feet.

Her tummy clenched, her nerves cranked to high, but her nipples gave her away.

She wanted him so much. Right now. But his expression went cold as he took in her outfit.

"You called?" she asked, convinced he wasn't interested after all. No man could look so unwelcoming and still want company.

8

_____

Kat was dressed for undressing. Beautiful and sexy. Her eyes glowed, her lips parted as she stood waiting at Taye's front door.

Waiting for him to move, to invite her inside, to do something, but it was happening again. Blood rushing south, voice gone, mind a haze of desire, he couldn't move, couldn't speak.

God, he wanted her! Any man would. But that took him to a place he didn't want to go. He couldn't think about all the other men, so he cut off this thought and swooped in.

He pulled her into his arms in a rush of kisses. He didn't want to think about her dressed like this. Looking this way. Transformed into a younger version of Celia.

But that was what she wanted. Free and easy sex whenever either of them had an itch. And Kat was obviously looking to be scratched.

He kicked the door shut and slid his tongue down to her tonsils. His cock rose as his hips pressed hers into the wall.

She moaned and shifted, giving him more room between her legs. He pinned her arms to the wall beside her head as he took her mouth again and again. The sweet taste of her, so at odds with her appearance, devastated his defenses.

She arched up and into him, offering whatever he wanted. Offering everything and nothing at the same time.

He tried like hell to drown out his conscience, wanting to stick to his decision to take what she offered until she moved on.

He clasped both wrists over her head in one hand while the other hand skimmed her upper thigh. She groaned low and hot in his ear as he found the top of her thigh high. He slipped his finger under the rubbery top that held the stocking to her leg and tracked along her skin to the inside of her thigh. "Taye," she pleaded, "touch me there. I'm wet for you."

It was the signal he wanted. Another night full of Kat. Her slick heat, her soft flesh. Her wild mouth on his.

For tonight. Just tonight. Maybe the weekend.

Then what?

Then nothing. They'd go back to polite chat and passing nods.

He wanted to slip his fingers into her wet cunt, ready her for his cock, then fuck her crazy.

If he did, he'd be so far into her he'd lose himself.

His fingers stilled a millimeter away from her wet curls. The scent of her rose to tantalize, her eyes glazed in anticipation, but he couldn't do it. He rolled away along the wall, chest heaving.

It was the hardest thing he'd ever done. He was already crazy about her, but to have her again, knowing she'd never be his the way he wanted, would kill him.

"You look ready for a party," he said. "I don't want to mess you up."

She looked confused by his backtracking, and the hesitant Kat he preferred reappeared in her gaze. He waited, fingers flexing, heart thudding, while she gathered her thoughts.

"Me? Yes, I w–was thinking about meeting up with some people." Her chest heaved.

He nodded. "Then you should go. Promises should be kept, Kat. Always."

Her eyes went wide at the comment. It killed him, but he knew himself too well to play this game. He wanted exclusive rights, and Kat wouldn't have made other plans if she was prepared to give him those rights.

It was too soon, too much to ask, but that's the way he was built. He didn't share. Not ever.

She shook her head. "I was just going out with Celia." Her eyes went dark and he read guilt.

"Clubbing? Looking to hook up?" He let his tone go sharp and hard.

"I guess so." She rubbed her arms. "I'm not sure what you want me to say." It was clear she'd say anything he wanted just to get back to where they'd been. She was turned on, ready, and he was all kinds of crazy to send her out partying in this condition.

He thought he'd be okay with the free and easy sex she offered, but he wasn't. Pride wouldn't let him ask for more if she wasn't offering.

He stepped away, opened the front door. "Then you should go. Wouldn't want you to miss out on any action."

"Oh, okay."

Celia's car pulled up to the curb in front of Taye's place. "There's your date," he said, with a nod toward the car.

When she turned to look, Taye shut his door.

Kat's head was still spinning from Taye's kisses, and her pussy buzzed with the need he'd put there. She smoothed her skirt, then checked the top of her stocking to set it right.

Somehow, she wasn't sure how, she was outside his door. To be kissed in a way that aimed her straight into the sack and then booted to the curb in the next second made her dizzy. And a little angry.

Scratch that. A lot angry. At him, and at herself.

She'd obviously come off as needy, clingy and unsophisticated again. She'd been worried she would presume too much, and she'd been right.

What a dunce!

The guy wanted an easy lay. Just the way she'd been last night. Easy. Uncomplicated sex. The kind she'd never thought she would want.

The whole sex kitten thing was nothing but a land mine. And it had blown up in her face. If she'd made it plain she liked the man and wanted a relationship, she could have avoided this whole painful mess.

She couldn't go home, because Taye would guess that she'd made up the story about going out clubbing. She clasped her hands in front of her, determined not to flap them.

Celia climbed out of her car, thunderclouds scudding across her face. She held up a hand, finger pointed to the sky. "Men," she proclaimed in woman's most common lament, "are assholes!"

"You're not kidding; what happened?" Kat walked woodenly down the walkway toward her, half-afraid of the expression on Celia's face.

"He wanted to bring his children." Then her gaze dropped from Kat's face to her dress. "What's happening here?"

"Nothing."

The look Celia gave her was accusing. "You were at Taye's front door."

"Men *are* assholes," Kat repeated in a slight wail to hide her own confusion. Much easier to blame a man, she thought, when a woman made a fool of herself.

"Give me five minutes to change and we'll hit Harry's Place. We'll arm ourselves with a couple drinks, then take a few men down with us," Celia said, marching up to her front door, dyed black hair flying behind her. She looked ready to do battle.

With Celia in an unholy rage, Kat had a feeling her evening was about to get a lot worse.

Once inside her house, Celia's rant continued as she stripped out of her skirt and blouse in the front hall. "Come on upstairs, Kat, but bring some wine. You'll find a bottle in the fridge." She headed upstairs. "I'll be getting into my come-and-get-it clothes."

True to her word, Celia kept the refrigerator stocked with several bottles of chardonnay and a couple of bottles of champagne.

Kat listened to the ranting monologue drift downstairs, punctuated by swear words even Celia's showgirl grandmother would blush at. Definitely a two-bottle crisis. She also grabbed a couple glasses on the way past the dish rack.

Whatever had happened she'd have to help her friend wind down before mentioning her unceremonious dump at Taye's front door. With the mood Celia was in there was no telling what revenge she might be in the mood for.

Celia stood in front of her closet in a soft mauve-colored thong and matching demi-cup bra. She yanked an off-the-shoulder red tunic sweater off a shelf of her closet organizer, then found a pair of new skinny leg jeans. She snipped the tags off and tugged them up her legs.

She held out her hand. "Wine."

Kat finished pouring her a glass and handed it over, watched as Celia downed it in one swallow. "More."

Kat obliged. "Better?"

Celia drank half the glass. "Thanks." Then she blinked as if she'd forgotten Kat was there.

"So? Have you figured out why a man would want to drag his kids along?"

Kat stated the obvious. "Maybe he wanted you to get to know them."

Celia looked appalled. "Why?"

"Because he likes you? And maybe he'd like you to like them and vice versa."

Celia blew a raspberry into the air before taking another drink. "No way. He should have known this would be a hot dirty weekend. If I wanted to get to know his children I'd have asked about them." She raised one hand with her finger pointed to the ceiling while she downed the last half of her second glass of chardonnay.

"I *never* ask about children."

Kat pursed her lips and took the hint. Kat didn't want to touch on a difficult subject. If Celia wanted to share her thoughts, she would. "Where did you meet this guy?"

"Jason, his name's Jason. We met at a homeless shelter where I volunteer."

"You volunteer at a shelter?" Kat couldn't keep the shock from her voice, and Celia glared at her for it.

"Sure, why wouldn't I? People need help, so I help."

Kat sipped at her wine while Celia glared. "I just never thought of you as the type of person—"

"Who would care? Is that it, Kat?" She turned and bent over as she dug through the shoes on the closet floor. She came up with a pair of stilettos and flourished them. "You ought to be careful about those assumptions of yours. They can make for errors in judgment."

"I'm sorry, it's just that you've never mentioned this shelter before."

Celia waved her hand to dismiss the topic. "It's been part of my life so long, I don't think about it. I just keep showing up on Wednesdays after work."

Wednesday was, indeed, the one weeknight when she didn't chat with Celia at the mailboxes. "And Jason?"

"He's been helping out in the kitchen for a couple of months. He's a chef at one of the five-star restaurants downtown." She stood in front of the mirror over her dresser and fluffed out her hair, then pinched her cheeks for color. But her eyes were damp and unhappy.

"All set," she said, then gave Kat a critical eye. "You look like you're dressed to party, girlfriend. We'll knock 'em dead at Harry's. I wish you'd have come out with me sooner. You're a beauty!"

Heat rose in her cheeks. No wonder Taye had jumped to the conclusion that she was ready to go out and hook up. That's what Celia saw in Kat's outfit too.

But still, he shouldn't have hustled her out onto the walkway and slammed the door in her face. What nerve! "Let's go, Celia. I suddenly need some party time."

Celia slid her arm through Kat's. "Let's go rock a few worlds, girlfriend."

Harry's wasn't as bad as Kat expected it to be. It was cozy, the music was a comfortable dance beat and it seemed full of locals.

It was Celia who surprised her. She settled in at the bar and ordered two doubles. Then drank them both.

Kat had heard the term *two-fisted drinker* but hadn't actually seen one in action before. After a couple of rounds, Celia confessed.

"This guy I walked out on. Jason." She looked bleary in the eyes, but for the most part was sitting up straight and making sense. "I thought he was the one, Kat. I really did. But when I was faced with these two sweet-faced kids, I couldn't stay. What kind of guy brings his children on a wild weekend?"

"I don't know." Kat shrugged. "Maybe a guy who likes his kids."

"They were sweet and beautiful," Celia murmured. "If I had kids, I'd want them to be just like them." She stuck her chin in her hand and sulked. "And I haven't been out in the woods since I was sent to summer camp."

"Hold it. You got invited out to the woods with a man and his children and you thought you were going for a dirty weekend?"

"What other kind is there?"

Kat laughed. "Well, there's camping dirt and then there's dirty."

Celia rolled her eyes.

"You didn't meet him in a club, Celia. He saw you as a woman who volunteers at a homeless shelter. He had a certain impression of you." She couldn't imagine what this Jason must think of Celia now.

"If you like him this much, don't give up. Maybe his kids will grow on you."

"If I was meant to be a mother, I'd be able to have children of my own." She sighed and nodded at the bartender for another drink. "But I can't, so I figured it was a sign. Some women aren't meant to be mothers, Kat. They just aren't." Her voice went so quiet, Kat could barely hear her.

The bartender hesitated and Kat shook her head at him. He moved on down the bar.

She put her arm around Celia and leaned in close to her ear. "Be careful of those assumptions, Celia. One day they'll jump up and bite your ass."

"Whaddaya mean?"

"We'll talk when you're sober."

"'kay."

"Wanna dance, Celia?" A man's voice broke them apart, relieving Kat from sob sister duty. "You look like you could use some fun."

"Always," Celia replied. She slid off her bar stool and jammed her body hard against the man who'd asked. "Hi, Jeff. What makes men such assholes?"

"I dunno, Celia. Women?" he guessed with a chuckle and led her away to the dance floor.

Left on her own at the bar, Kat wasn't sure where to look. There were men on either side of her, but neither of them interested her. The one next to Celia's empty stool must be on his way home from work, and from the woody scent of him, he worked hard at physical labor. The scent made her think of fresh-cut lumber. A carpenter, probably.

He probably cleaned up well, because he had great arms and a good strong jaw, but he was deep into complaint mode with the man next to him. No, they were a couple of guys out for a beer before heading home for the weekend.

The man on her other side was showing the bartender his wallet photos, proudly displaying his newborn son's picture. He flashed the photo at Kat and she proclaimed the baby's beauty.

Some people had all the luck. She sighed and propped her chin on her hand and settled in to watch the bartender work.

The music swelled louder after Celia shouted for more volume, and from the sound of things, more couples hit the dance floor. Kat wasn't interested enough to turn around to look.

Harry's was finally starting to rock. For everyone but her.

9

Kat didn't know what Celia was complaining about. Kat would love a man who came with two gorgeous children. That was what she used to want: a good man and a couple of kids.

She was grateful she hadn't started a family with her ex. Paying his way through college had taken all the money she earned. She'd ended up with nothing but the knowledge that she could do more alone than if she hung on another man's coattails.

In the three years since her divorce, she'd come a long way in the confidence department. Her grades were good. She was more than halfway to a degree in marketing and planned to have a business of her own someday. Her sales skills had improved tremendously through the party plan, and she knew once she settled on just the right business she could be the success she wanted to be.

All that was fine.

It was her confidence with men that suffered a blow. She'd messed up with Taye. But she wasn't exactly sure how.

She tried to put the night with Taye into perspective. A one-night stand. That's all it had been.

She'd wanted him to think she was sexually free, uninhibited. Available and ready for a casual fling. She should be pleased she'd succeeded.

Instead, she felt miserable. No more dreams of having a couple of children with a man like Taye for this girl! No way!

Hell, now she'd just be happy to find a man to provide orgasms on a regular basis. Great, big orgasms. Whenever she wanted.

So okay, she bargained. That might be a bit much, considering she'd gone years between men. She should probably adjust the dream. Maybe the man she wanted didn't have to give her great big orgasms. A little one now and then would probably do, but they had to be regular.

Definitely regular. Once a day. On that she would not compromise. She sipped the last of her wine, then caught the bartender's attention and received her third glass of the evening.

The delicious thought of orgasms swirled through her mind. The ones Taye had given her had woken her sleeping need for sex. Her pussy twitched as she thought of Taye's strong hands holding her wrists over her head. His hips had pressed against hers in need. What she couldn't figure out was why he'd pulled away.

She'd given him lots of clues that she wanted another night like last night. Quick, hard sex, with mind-blowing orgasms and no commitment.

That was what he wanted. Why hadn't he taken what she'd offered?

She glanced around the bar and watched the fluid movement of men toward women and women accepting or denying their attention.

The sexual dances people played amused her for a while, but still, she wasn't comfortable here. If she wanted to turn into a sex goddess who got laid regularly, she'd have to find another way.

Getting picked up by men in bars wasn't her thing. If she

needed liquor to make a guy look good enough to sleep with, then she was messed up more than she thought.

She went back to making her list of must-haves in a relationship and dropped her orgasm expectations to every other day.

Weekly would work, she conceded after another glass of wine. Her last glass, she decided, as she folded her drink napkin into an airplane. Any more wine and the new daddy next to her might start to look good. And that would be bad. Very bad.

She hated married people who cheated. At least her ex hadn't done that. He'd been too busy with college, but not too busy to make sure she kept up two jobs to support them.

Taye had proven to be a caring, giving and gifted lover. Damn him for setting the standard so high. Her ex had been good too. But hard and fast every time. When they were kids together, she thought that meant he wanted her so bad he couldn't stand it. As the marriage moved along, though, she saw the truth. He was selfish and wanted in and out and done.

The rare times she managed to get off was because she had a good imagination and was ready before they even got going. She definitely didn't want another man like her ex.

She wanted a man like Taye. Just like Taye. She propped her chin in her hand and smiled a *no* at a guy who asked her to dance.

"What's wrong?" he asked, looking down her scoop-necked blouse.

"I'm just here with my girlfriend for a couple drinks. She'll be back any minute." A white lie wouldn't hurt. "She just broke up with her boyfriend and she needs to let off some steam."

"Where is she? She can blow my pipes. I got steam too," he said as he scanned the crowd.

"Move along, buddy. We're here to talk not hook up," Kat said, disgusted. She didn't know how Celia could be happy in this atmosphere night after night.

Except for the volunteer nights at the shelter, Celia pretty much haunted the local bars. Always looking for . . . something.

She shuddered to think of Celia ending up with a guy like the one searching the dance floor with an avid, lustful expression. As much as Celia pretended to like a variety of men, her reaction to this Jason proved she wanted more than variety.

A whoop and holler from the floor made Kat turn to see. Celia was being passed from man to man as she twirled. Some of them were none too gentlemanly about where they put their hands when they twirled her.

Taye would never treat a woman that way. Kat had a feeling Celia's Jason wouldn't either.

That's what she wanted. A good man who knew his way around a woman's body. A man who'd keep a woman's heart safe from harm.

A hard male body slid into Celia's vacant seat. Kat looked up expecting to see the man with steam to blow off. But it was Taye instead.

"You shut your door in my face," she said briskly. "I don't want to talk to you." She stared at the bartender rather than look at Taye and say something she might regret. Yeah, something like, *Take me now!*

"I don't blame you," he said quietly.

"How did you know where to find me?" she huffed, already putting the lie to her declaration that she wouldn't talk to him. "That is, if you were looking." Oh Mama, she wanted him to have been looking.

"I opened my door to apologize when I heard Celia say you were coming here. I thought you might want to talk with her for a while. She seemed pretty upset with men in general from what I heard. Then I figured you'd hook up with someone, but it drove me nuts to think of that. I've been sitting in my car for an hour." His grin was rueful.

She perked up, straightened her spine. "You want to apologize?"

"Yes. I was wrong and jumped to a totally stupid conclusion."

"Totally stupid," she agreed. She wanted to make him suffer a moment longer so she tilted her head as if considering him. Tapped her lips with a fingertip. "Apology accepted." After all, she'd wanted him to think what he thought. She was the totally stupid one. If she'd just gone over as soon as she heard his message, none of this would have happened.

"As soon as I closed the door, I realized you'd dressed up for me. I live next door. You're not a party girl. You live a quiet life."

"Boring. A boring life." And that had to change. "What other twenty-five-year-old divorcee do you know that lives the way I do?"

He smiled and traced the side of her face, down to her jaw and along to the corner of her mouth. "Celia sounded so upset as she ranted and raved in her driveway, I figured she needed your shoulder to cry on."

"She did, but it looks like she's dealing with her disappointment in her own way."

Taye turned and frowned as he watched the men surrounding Celia. "She doesn't look like she's dealing all that well. I should go get her," he suggested.

The bartender leaned in. "You don't have to worry about Celia," he commented. "Most of those guys know her. She's the kind of woman they have fun with, but one of them will see she gets home okay. This is a friendly bar and we keep it that way."

Kat hesitated but Taye's heated glance seared straight to her heart. He nodded, apparently accepting the bartender's word.

"Come home with me, Kat. The rest of the night is ours." He leaned in to her ear. His breath tickled and warmed her neck and her body responded with sirens blaring. "I promise there won't be a boring moment."

She looked at Celia, who was doing a bump and grind with a new dance partner. She waved. Celia waved back and nodded. The smile on her face looked brittle and tired, but her bravado was firmly in place.

Whatever was going on with her friend and this Jason she'd walked out on wouldn't be resolved tonight. But for now, Celia was okay and giving her a thumbs-up to leave.

Outside in the cooling night, nerves tingled along Kat's spine. "Where did you park?"

"The lot's full so I parked there beyond the lights." He pointed out an additional gravel parking area next to the bar's well-lit parking lot.

Kat picked up the pace, grabbing Taye's hand to lead him on. "Hurry," she said, not wanting to let her pride wake up. If she thought about him closing that door on her one more time, she'd get angry again.

"I don't know if I can wait to get home," Taye said as they reached his car. He pressed her against the side door, kissing her deeply, with an urgency she loved and responded to.

Every fantasy she'd had about him seemed to be coming true. He'd held her up against the wall, now he held her against the car. What was the third one? Oh yes . . . she wanted . . .

He claimed her mouth, took every bit of her into himself and all thought ceased. The noise of the bar patrons in the parking lot fell away as Kat surrendered to Taye's kisses. She slid her hand down the front of his jeans, found the evidence of his need and stroked him.

"We don't have to wait." She reached for the back door handle.

He clicked the remote opener and she climbed in, grinning. "It's been years since I've done this," she murmured, wondering how she could make it different from the hurried sex she remembered as a teen.

Taye followed her in and grabbed her hips to lay her out as he slid over her body, warming her into lusty abandon. His aroused scent washed over her, spicy and dark, and she followed him into a deep kiss full of need and apology.

"You smell good, like flowers," he muttered between heated kisses.

His hands slid under her ass, and he cupped and squeezed her cheeks. She responded by widening her cradle so he fit the way a man wanted to.

She sighed at the rightness of it, letting him mouth her neck and suckle at the delicate skin behind her ear. He'd already learned she squirmed when he kissed her there. He chuckled and pressed his erection to her crotch in a silent demand.

Maybe not so silent, she realized as he growled his need against her throat. His chin, devilish in its curiosity, nudged the bodice of her blouse down to expose the tips of her breasts. Her barely-there bra cups were no defense against his nuzzling, and the sudden shot of cold air made her nipples flame into hard buds.

Voices from the parking lot sounded distant as people walked toward the bar. Loud raucous music spilled into the night when the door opened, but Kat was too far gone to worry. Let the party go on without her.

It was her time to rock!

She worked his straining cock free of his jeans and planted her feet on the steam slippery window of the back door, but Taye twisted to a sitting position.

"Climb on and ride me, Kat. Ride me hard."

His solid cock slid true and deep, plunging and widening every slick inch of her. She stilled as her inner muscles accepted the stretching invasion. With a shudder of utter need, she moved against him.

He groaned and cupped her bare ass. The slap of slick wet flesh punctuated each breath.

He slid his thumb to her hottest bundle of nerves and let her take charge.

Kat rocked. Kat rolled.

Kat screamed against his neck with an orgasm that pushed him into his own. Hot sudden spurts washed her insides as she closed her eyes and let the delicious final spasms ease through her.

"Hey, buddy! You gotcha some hot stuff there. Wanna share?"

"Shit!" Taye lifted her off his lap and rolled her to the far side of the seat. "I thought this was a friendly bar," he muttered.

"This is too friendly," agreed Kate, fumbling to set her clothes right, while heavy male footsteps approached the car.

A shadow appeared at the glass. A man's face cupped by a meat cleaver–sized hand pressed against the window.

"Who you got in there?" The words were slurred but the tone went conciliatory.

Taye climbed between the front seats and slammed into place behind the steering wheel. "Buckle up, sweetheart, we've got to move."

The tires spit gravel as Taye pulled the SUV out of the parking spot and headed for the lot exit.

Laughter and catcalls followed them, raining down on Kat's conscience. Catcalls! She'd behaved exactly like a cat in heat.

She should have demanded a better apology from Taye. She should have found out why he closed the door on her before she jumped his bones again. He must think she was easier than easy!

Instead of just hot for him.

The SUV veered out of the exit, rocking wildly as Taye burned rubber again. The whole incident burned a hole in her pride.

10

Taye rolled his SUV to a stop in his garage. The sound of quiet sniffs and the rustling of cloth came from the backseat. Harry's was only five minutes away and he'd made it back to their complex in two. Between the squealing tires and the rolling swerves around corners, Kat hadn't had enough time to get her clothes in order. "You okay back there?"

Her voice came out of the dark, soft and low. "I'm fine, just embarrassed by my behavior."

"I'm not." He turned and leaned around the headrest to see her. The overhead garage light produced slashes of gray, black and shadowy light in the backseat. Her eyes gleamed and her beautiful kiss-reddened mouth turned down. "I loved your behavior. I heartily approved of your behavior," he said with a grin designed to coax her lips upward.

He saw a flash of teeth as she tried not to smile. "You're being sweet. Thank you."

"Sweet nothing. All I want is to get you into the house so we can have more." He jumped out of the car and opened her door for her. She stood and looked up at him, doubt filling her eyes.

"I should go back. I never should have left Celia there alone."

"I saw her give you a thumbs-up and she knows where you are and who you're with." He opened the side door that opened onto his front walk and followed her outside. "We can call the bar to ask the bartender to keep an eye on her."

"He did say she'd be fine." Her comment proved her indecision. She wanted to stay with him, in spite of his lousy behavior earlier.

"He seemed to know his own customers." He unlocked and opened his front door, then held it open. He couldn't believe he'd shut it on her earlier.

"She'll be disappointed that I abandoned her," Kat fussed. "I'm not being much of a friend."

"I could point out that she left you sitting alone at the bar, an easy target for any guy who wanted to hit on you."

She giggled. "But to Celia that's the point of going to a bar in the first place, so she wouldn't see anything wrong with hitting the dance floor with half the men in the place."

"The only thing she's disappointed in is that you won your bet."

Still, she hesitated. "This is where I tell you that the whole bet thing happened because Celia wanted to get me to go clubbing with her. She challenged me and I stupidly agreed that if I didn't see you naked, then I'd go party with her."

"So you both won?"

She grinned. "For sure I won." She placed her palm on his cheek. "Wow, did I win."

"So, this was just between the two of you?"

"Of course. I was saying how gorgeous you were and admiring your butt, and—"

"My butt?" He interrupted with a bark of laughter. He laughed partly because of the idea two women liked what they saw enough to comment and partly from relief that he wasn't the laughingstock of the whole complex. He liked his life private. He'd suffered enough gossip and innuendo from neighbors when he was a kid.

"Spend the night, Kat. Spend the whole weekend with me." He wanted more but figured he should go slow.

Her smile lit her face and his too. "I'd like that."

He held out his hand and she took it. He tugged and she hopped into the house, face split in a grin that took his breath.

"You're all dressed up," he said, deciding the best thing to do was not rush her into bed. They'd already proven they were good there. What he wanted to show her now was that they were good outside of bed too. "Let's go out for a late dinner."

"Good idea; I didn't eat much earlier," she said on a soft breath.

There she was again, the shy young woman she first seemed. "You look so pretty and fresh," he said, sliding a tendril of hair behind her ear.

"That's hard to believe after making your SUV rock, but sweet of you to say." Her cheeks went pink and she nodded. He was way past being tongue-tied and awkward. Tonight he would finally unravel the mystery of the sexy girl next door.

Gulls squawked overhead and put on a fine show of dive-bombing some hapless tourists who'd made the mistake of offering a sleeve of take-out fries. After scattering the remaining fries as a distraction, they ran for their car, ducking and waving their hands overhead.

"Looks like a scene from that old thriller by Hitchcock," he said.

Kat chuckled and dipped a fry into a splotch of ketchup. "I love his movies. So tense, such great suspense."

"He was a master." He did another check mark in the air with his finger. "Check, she likes the same movies I do."

"So, how about Bette Davis movies?"

"Some, especially the horror thrillers she did when she got older."

"She was fearless in her roles, even when she was young and beautiful." She grinned. "Check! Remember to drag him through the classic movie section of the video store."

"You don't have to drag me anywhere. I can't think of anything better than snuggling in with you on a rainy night, with a cold beer and hot pizza watching any old movie you want to see. I'll be looking at you anyway."

She went pink in the cheeks. Her unique shade of pink. A color he grew more and more fond of seeing.

"When you blush, the color of your skin is unlike any blush I've ever seen. Instead of blotches of red, the pink is evenly distributed and makes you glow." It was the most beautiful thing about her, he decided. Keeping that glow on her face was a new desire and stacked up strongly against all the other desire she created.

"I'm glad we came here," she said, leaning her shoulder against his for a brief touch. "It's good to talk with you."

I like you was what he heard. "It's good to talk with *you*." They almost hadn't made it in time to order. The cook was about to close up when they'd arrived breathless after running along the pier in a race he let her win.

"I thought at first I should take you somewhere fancy. The kind of restaurant with prices on my menu and not yours."

She shook her head. "That's not my kind of restaurant."

"Then I thought at least a steakhouse. She deserves a sit-down meal with a good waiter and better wine."

"Then how did we end up at a fish shack on the end of a pier?" She grinned around a ketchup-covered fry.

"I've been less than my usual suave and debonair self around you."

She chuckled. "Suave?"

He looked at his feet, then speared another piece of beer-battered fish. "You make me lose my ability to walk and think at the same time. So, I figured it was time you see the real me instead of the nerd I probably look like." He chewed the fish. Swallowed. "I'm happy eating at a fish shack on a late night."

"So am I."

Relief. If she hadn't liked the real Taye, he'd have gotten out before he got in any deeper. "I'll take you out for a real meal next time. I'll get reservations and we'll have a great night. Dancing, the whole deal."

"A date? That'll be new." She dropped her plastic fork and picked another fry out of her paper sleeve with her fingers. "Dating's a foreign concept for me. I've never been on one. Not a 'pick you up at eight' date."

Hard as it was to believe that a woman who looked like Kat wasn't dating, he knew it was true. He'd been tuned to every sound from her side of their common wall for months. He apologized again for his bizarre behavior at his front door. "I don't know what I was thinking. But you just might be the scariest woman I've ever run across."

"*I* scare *you?*"

"In a way. I got tongue-tied around you for months; I still trip, fall, drop stuff. You saw me yesterday with that package and my briefcase and travel mug. I felt like a juggler on crack."

She chuckled at his description.

But he had to finish. "When I talk to you every pint of blood in my body goes south, leaving me floundering. It's the weirdest sensation." He couldn't explain it any better than that.

She patted his knee and he felt the same rush of blood he always felt at her touch. "I've only ever seen you as sweet and kind. I like that you deadhead flowers, that you still get care packages from your mom and that you teach school. A good education is the foundation for a satisfying career."

A sentiment he more than agreed with. He lived it.

Here was the last piece of the puzzle. He had the complete picture now. Kat Hardee was everything he wanted. It was even more important now that he move carefully.

"So if you didn't go on dates with your ex, what kind of time did you spend with him?"

"I was a high school bride. Mostly we roamed the streets of Bellevue looking for a party or someplace to park. Sex in the backseat of his dad's Mercury was about as close to a date as we got. And the sex wasn't even all that hot," she said, plopping her chin into her hand. "Mostly it was over way too quickly."

"Oh," he said. "Check! No more sex in the car."

She leaned her shoulder against his again and nudged him hard. "Not that *our* backseat sex wasn't hot. It was." She patted his hand.

"You don't sound bitter about your marriage or your ex." Which as a very good thing. He wasn't a guy who liked dissecting old business. Once this was out of the way, he wouldn't ask again. "What happened?"

"My husband went to college, while I worked to pay for it. He promised that when he landed a good job, it would be my turn. But by then, he was tired of being broke and didn't want to pay for me. And I wanted an education more than anything."

"He dumped you rather than give you time for college?"

"Quick as he could. We had no assets and no property to divide, so a divorce was easy. I just wanted to be free to finally go to school."

His old man went from one wife to the next, so infidelity was the first thing he thought of when it came to divorce; this was a new twist. One he'd never considered; get a good woman to pay your way then dump her. A guy like that had real class. He snorted. What a loser. "You're in college now, though."

"Thanks to sex toys!"

He laughed with her. "A lot of women would be bitter after getting the shaft like that." He was proud of her for hanging in on her own.

She was proud too. He saw it in her gaze. "Bitterness is a wasted emotion. Besides, I pushed for marriage when we were too young, convinced that sex was only supposed to happen in a committed relationship. He was too young, I was pushy. Needy, I guess." She shrugged.

"And now what do you think about sex?" The question was lighthearted until he saw her expression.

She eyed him appraisingly and he caught a glimpse of Celia lurking in her thoughts. Heaven help him! "I've had the best sex of my life with you and we're not committed to anything but this moment."

Shit.

Kat held her breath, letting the comment hang between them, foolish in her need to hear that maybe she'd guessed correctly for once in her life. Maybe Taye wanted more than some good times between them. The silence stretched while she waited, then let the hope die. She'd left herself wide open. It was her own fault if she took a hit. Again.

He glanced away, across the pier, then tossed a fry out to a scavenging gull. The bird snatched it and skittered away, gulping the fry whole.

No wonder she didn't date much. She was so rusty she creaked. She pulled her thoughts to order and gave him the out he seemed to want. "With a full load of classes and a job that keeps me out more nights than not, a steady man would be an inconvenience."

"Why are you available tonight?" His voice was definitely more cool than it had been earlier.

"Fridays aren't a good night for my kind of party. Seems as if it should be, but most people have other plans. Married women are busy with their families. Single women are on dates or out clubbing."

"You must have lean times in the year."

"January's tough. All the big parties happen before the holidays, but since it's just me, I manage."

"Tell me about the bet you made with Celia."

"It was stupid."

"Telling me about it was stupid." He must have felt betrayed knowing he was the subject of a bet.

Time to clear the air. "I never should have mentioned you to Celia in the first place. Once she saw I was interested in you she wouldn't let up. Made me think you were hers for the picking." And that had forced her hand.

He snorted. "Not likely. I'll never be attracted to Celia. She's not my kind of woman."

"I'm glad." She popped her last fry into her mouth while he chewed his last piece of fish. "So what kind of woman do you like?"

"Faithful ones. I want a woman who sees life the same way I do. My old man was a son of a bitch and flaunted his affairs. Took my mom too long to walk away."

"That must have been rough." Did he equate Celia's easygoing sexuality with the women his father ran around with?

"For a long time I thought I'd be just like him, but eventually I realized what I want."

Her heart stilled while she held her breath. "And what's that?"

"Mostly I want peace. The kind of peace in a family that comes from fidelity and trust. The dramas I grew up with are behind me and that's where they'll stay." He spoke firmly and with conviction. He'd put a great deal of thought into his answer. He cleared his throat.

"Peace sounds like a good thing to want," she said. Without

prompting, she went on to explain her own dreams. "I want my education, a career, my own business someday. But I'd like a stable family life too. I want someone I can depend on."

The fish shack cook slammed the wooden flaps down over his order window as he shut down for the night. The noise made Kat jump and the encroaching gulls take a few steps back.

Taye wiped at his mouth with a paper napkin and stood. He held out a hand for her.

"Greasy," she said, wiping her mouth with a paper napkin. "But delicious."

Taye looked about to speak when her cell phone rang. He frowned at the interruption. "It's late for a call. Could it be business?"

"Not at this time of night." She dug the phone out of her purse and answered it. "Hello? Kat Hardee speaking."

"Hi, Kat, could you come get me?" The feminine voice was shaky rather than slurred.

"Celia? Where are you?" There was no music in the background, just a lot of yelling and metallic clattering sounds. It wasn't the bar, but she couldn't place the noises.

"I'm in the hospital emergency department. I'm in no shape to drive and I don't have my purse so I can't call a cab."

"What happened?" Then she realized she was wasting time with questions. "Never mind. I'll be right there."

Taye watched, a concerned expression flitting over his features. He'd take her wherever she needed to go. She could count on him.

"You hang on," she said into the phone. "We're not far away." She flipped the phone closed and dumped her trash in the bin. "We've got to hurry," she said, and broke into a run back down the pier.

Taye ran beside her. "What happened, did she say?"

"No. She needs me to pick her up from Emergency. She's

got no money and she can't drive." She looked at him. "If something awful's happened to her I'll never forgive myself."

"She was drinking, that's why she can't drive. She can't be seriously hurt. We saw her two hours ago."

But anything could happen in two hours, she thought. She felt a tug on her arm and he slowed them both to a walk. "If she'd been involved in anything serious there's no way a hospital would release her this quickly. So logic says whatever happened is minor."

She calmed a little, but her heart still thudded. "You're right. I panicked. I always panic with hospitals."

"You'll feel better when you see her for yourself."

Grateful for his calm and reason, she steadied her nerves. "All she needs is a lift home," she said as her pulse returned to a more normal pace. "That's all she asked for."

In spite of what he'd said, all kinds of scenarios raced through Taye's head as he hurried to the hospital. Kat sat tense and silent beside him. Blessedly, she hadn't started pointing fingers at him. Yet.

He'd been the one to separate the women tonight. If she didn't blame him already, she would soon. "I'm sorry, Kat. You were right, we should have stayed at Harry's or got Celia out of there."

"We shouldn't have left her alone. What if?" Her eyes, when they turned to his, were moist and tearful. "What if the wrong type of guy got hold of her?"

"She'd kick his ass. Besides Celia's too smart to be in the wrong place with the wrong guy." He hoped, but one of the rowdies she'd been dancing and flirting with might have got the idea she was up for anything. Even rough sex. But what did he know? Celia might like all kinds of rough.

Still, two hours was too damn short a time to be heading home if anything serious had happened. But then, if it hadn't been serious she'd still be waiting for someone to attend to her.

THIGH HIGH / 183

"Any chance she's fine and she took someone else in for attention?"

"I don't think so. She doesn't have her purse with her," Kat said, turning her face to the side passenger window. "She may have been mugged in the parking lot."

"I doubt it. There were a lot of people coming and going, and the bartender said the regulars were a good bunch. There are lots of reasons she'd be at a hospital without her purse."

Kat nodded and lapsed into silence again. A too-short silence. "I should have asked more questions, but the clattering and banging made it hard to hear. Celia's voice was low. She sounded tired. I didn't want to aggravate her."

"There's the hospital, I'll let you out at the emergency entrance, then go park."

"Thanks." She jumped out as soon as he pulled to a stop.

By the time Taye parked and found the women, he'd calmed down again.

Celia sat in the waiting area with a square white dressing on her forehead near her scalp line. She was holding her head. Kat squatted on her haunches, hand on her friend's shoulder. A blood-spattered shoulder.

Taye jogged over. "What happened? How are you?" She looked like a truck had run over her face.

Kat looked up at him while Celia covered her head with her hands to hide the bandage along her hairline. In spite of looking like an accident victim, she was still vain enough to worry what he'd think. "She tripped getting into a car, split her scalp open on the door and got dropped off here. Her purse must still be where she dropped it."

"Where's the guy she was with? Did he go back for her purse?"

"Married," Celia said. She shook her head. "Ow! Remind me not to do that, will you?"

A married man. Figured. It wasn't enough that she was free and easy with her body, she had to mess with marriages too.

"Don't look at her that way, Taye; the guy wasn't looking to hook up, he was just seeing her home safely. She sent him away as soon as she could." Kat's expression was defensive.

He backed down and schooled his features into bland disinterest. He'd had enough of people of both sexes who felt marriage was only a stepping stone to be trampled in their pursuit of selfish pleasure. "Can you stand and walk? Or should I get a wheelchair?" he asked Celia, his voice flat with impatient displeasure.

He was stuck with the situation for now.

"I can walk, it's just a few stitches."

Kat clucked and supported Celia on one side as they shuffled out of the hospital.

On the way home, he swung into the parking lot at Harry's and dashed inside to check with the bartender.

"Anyone turn in Celia's purse? She lost it in the parking lot," he said. Then he took a few more minutes to explain what happened.

The bartender shook his head. "Celia isn't too fussy about who she goes home with. She's a good sport, but not always aware of collateral damage."

Exactly as Taye suspected. "You told me you had a good bunch of regulars here, that Celia would be fine."

"She was fine when she walked out. It wasn't the first time she left with the guy. He's married, got a couple kids. That's a lot to lose for a woman like Celia. Can't say as I blame him for leaving her to her own devices."

Taye nodded. "She wants her purse back, so call if anyone turns it in."

"Sure thing." The bartender went back to serving.

"Your purse wasn't turned in," he said when he climbed back in behind the wheel. Both women were in the backseat to allow Celia to lean on Kat.

Kat spoke. "You'll stay with me tonight," she offered with a glance at Taye in the rearview mirror.

He nodded and focused on getting everyone home. "She may need to be woken at regular intervals," he said to Kat.

"No," Celia interjected. "There's no concussion. I didn't black out, not for a moment. This is just a gash. If it weren't on my scalp it would hardly count."

"Scalp wounds are ferocious bleeders," he conceded. She must have looked god-awful when she walked into the hospital.

Kat fussed some more, but when Taye left her at her front door, she fumed at him. "You shouldn't think the worst of people, Taye."

"Right."

Next morning Celia, sporting two black eyes, slid into the kitchen chair across from Kat. "You look horrible," she said after assessing the discoloration.

"Thanks, sugar. I wanted to faint when I looked in the mirror and saw my face. The doctor warned me I'd probably wake up like this, but still, it's a shock."

"I was thinking maybe the guy you were with knows where your purse is."

She shrugged. "It's possible that it fell into the car instead of outside when I planted my face."

"Can you call him?"

"And say what to his wife? I was thinking of doing your husband last night, but I fell on the way into your car. Have you seen my purse?" Celia rolled her eyes. "That's almost as bad as asking if she found my panties."

Kat tried not to sound like the prude Celia thought she was, but it was damned difficult. "You said he was giving you a lift home, that's all." To hell with worrying how she sounded. "You wouldn't have actually . . . ?"

"Wouldn't I? I haven't slept with a married man yet, at least not to my knowledge, but that doesn't mean I wouldn't. I was still pretty angry about Jason. So I'm not sure what would have happened." She shifted in her seat, but her gaze was bold and unflinchingly honest.

"So you're not sure if being angry with Jason would drive you to sleep with a married man." There were issues here that went beyond her experience. She reconsidered. "Were you angry with Jason or yourself?"

Celia rolled her eyes. "Here we go with the analysis." She sipped her coffee, defiance in her gaze. "Look, I shouldn't have fallen for a guy with kids. He wants a different woman. His kids *need* a different woman." Finally, a crack in the tough-girl front. Celia cared deeply for this Jason.

"Why do you feel like you're not the kind of woman he and his children need?" Insecurity could play out in a million ways. For Kat, it meant awkward shyness with Taye, a man she wanted more than anything. A man she was so desperate to have she even pretended to be someone she wasn't just to have him for a short time.

"I'm not nice in the way you are, Kat. I'm different. We're not destined for the same things." Her hand trembled as she lifted her coffee mug. She set it back down.

"You think you're not good enough for Jason. Or good enough to mother his children." That's why she'd reacted the way she had. Why she'd carried on so wildly in the bar. To prove she wasn't worthy.

"At least I know who I really am," Celia said. "I'm not fooling anyone, or pretending to be something I'm not."

The flare of accusation and anger in her friend's gaze made Kat back off. "What are you going to do when you see Jason at the shelter on Wednesday?"

"I don't know."

"He'll see the bruises around your eyes and you'll still have stitches."

"So? If he sees the truth, maybe he'll back off and understand I'm not the Goody Two-shoes he thinks I am." She rested her head in her hands. "Remind me not to meet guys anywhere but in bars. The men elsewhere are dangerous."

Kat chuckled. "Are you sure you don't want me to stay home with you today? I'd want company if I were you." She had deliveries to make, but she'd left her friend alone last night and look what happened.

"That's another way we're different," Celia said. "If you were in my situation, I wouldn't offer to help you. I'd be selfish with my Saturday." Celia patted her hand. She grinned and shook her head without wincing, which was an improvement.

They were different, and the idea of trying to be more like Celia, more freewheeling with her heart and body, suddenly seemed stupid.

"As much as I appreciate your offer, I have a lot to do. You'd just get in the way with your fussing." Celia finished her coffee. "I need the landlord to get me into my place and get a new lock. I also have to call in about my lost credit cards and identification. I'll spend all day either on the phone or waiting for someone."

"Well"—Kat still hesitated—"if you're sure. I feel awful that I left you last night. I feel as if I've broken the code by putting a man before my girlfriend's safety."

Celia frowned and gave her a derisive look. "Oh puhleeze, I'd have left you in a New York minute if Taye Connors had come into Harry's looking for *me*."

She believed it. Now.

"I'd have trampled over you to get to him, but he's never given me a second look. He's yours, Kat. All you need to do is reel him in."

"You think?"

"I've never had a chance with Taye. He made that clear right after he moved in and got a good look at you. He's been lovestruck for weeks."

Her heart rate kicked up a notch. Hope grew. "Last night we were really talking for the first time, and when you called, it interrupted things."

11

Taye wasn't home when Kat got back from delivering her party orders. Nor did he come home all evening. It was close to midnight by the time she heard him arrive. Too late to go to her door to catch him on the way in. Instead, she rolled over to her side, pulled the sheet over her head and tried to sleep.

She heard the muted sounds of water running while he prepared for bed. He wasn't usually gone all day Saturday, so she couldn't help wondering where he'd been. Or who he'd been with. She wanted it to be her.

All the time.

The expression on his face when he'd thought Celia was planning to sleep with a married guy shouldn't have surprised Kat as much as it did. With his father's infidelity so fresh on his mind, his expression had said he couldn't stand the sight of Celia.

Last night, she'd believed that Celia had only accepted a lift home, but now she knew different. Even Celia wasn't sure how far things would have gone with the married man. Kat's stomach twisted at the thought and she wanted to talk to Taye. To tell him he'd been right to be suspicious of Celia's behavior.

Who was she kidding? She just wanted Taye. To talk to, to sleep with, to have. Celia's comment about Taye being love-struck and his own admission about being tongue-tied around her made her think Taye felt the same way she did.

Hmm. What to do, what to do.

After climbing out of bed, she put her ear to the wall and listened until the water stopped running. He'd be about ready to climb into bed now, she thought.

She'd fantasized deliciously about being the mysterious stranger who climbed in his window.

One more wild escapade called to her. Then she was through with wild. Really.

She went to her bedroom window, opened it and stepped out onto the shingled overhang that projected across the front stoops. Taye's window was only five feet away. She clung to the window ledge as she inched her way across the scratchy shingles.

Cool air gusted up to her ass under her filmy nightie, while the shingles tingled under her bare feet. Her fingers turned to claws as she held on for dear life.

But she felt more alive, more daring than she'd ever felt in her life. Her heart thudded in her ears, moisture pooled inside her, slick and needy.

The shy woman she used to be would never actually do this. But the Kat she was today was brave enough, adventurous enough to try anything to get to Taye.

She tried to lift his window from the outside, but the landlord had been security conscious on the second floor as well. She had no choice but to tap on the glass, holding her breath that he'd hear her.

A dark shadow loomed in the room. "Kat! What the hell?"

He opened the window and clasped both her wrists. He pulled and shifted and tried to get her inside any which way he could.

His worried concern was not part of her fantasy.

The window was supposed to open silently to allow her to creep in. "Shhh!" she hushed. "I'm a mysterious stranger bent on seduction."

"Have you lost your mind?"

"No. Well, maybe. A little." Her heart. She'd lost her heart but couldn't tell him that. It was crazy!

Her foot caught on the window frame and she tumbled into him. His hands grabbed her forearms. Then he dragged her into his chest and kissed her hard.

"Good God, what were you thinking climbing around out there?"

"I've wanted to climb in your window for months. Climb in and have my way with you."

"You want to have your way with me?" He sounded amused but it was dark so she couldn't see his expression. It was kind of hot to imagine his eyes filling with male focus. "You could have knocked on my door or called me on the phone."

"That's not nearly as much fun. You probably think I'm quite the adventuress but I'm not." Her eyes were adjusted now and she could make out his mouth and the dark gleam in his eyes.

"Adventuress?"

"That's right. You think I'm sexy and bold, but in reality, I'm quiet." It was such a relief to admit the truth.

"Shy?"

"That too."

He held her close. "Okay, Kat, what's going on? Did Celia put you up to this?" He peered out the window, suspicion clouding his words.

"Of course not. It's time we cleared the air."

"About what?"

She bit her lip and plunged in, worries be damned. "About what you think of me, who I am, and who and what I've been pretending to be."

"Okay." He looked bemused again, but willing to listen.

"I'm not a wild woman." She blinked. "In spite of climbing through your window." He was still listening. "I'm not promiscuous and I don't engage in casual sex. In fact, you're the first casual encounter I've ever had."

He tilted his head, and his lips twitched. "Why do you say it was casual?"

That took her aback. "Well, wasn't it? For you, I mean."

He reached for her shoulders. The heat of his wide palms filled her. "No, sex is never casual for me. I like commitment, Kat. In fact, that's what I'm looking for."

"I was afraid to let you see how much I liked you and wanted a relationship because I made that mistake before, with my ex. I put too much emphasis on marriage and ended up divorced. If I'd only just gone with the flow, enjoyed the sex, and then moved on the way most first loves do, I wouldn't be divorced today. I pushed for more than he was willing to give because I didn't want sex to be a—a—bodily function!"

"Where did you get that idea?"

"From Celia. That's what she calls sex. A bodily function."

"Come here." He dragged her into his arms and kissed her deeply. "Sex with you is serious, Kat. And that's exactly what I love about you."

She sighed against his lips. "Stop talking now and kiss me again."

He did. For a long luscious moment their mouths touched, tongues tangled, lips sought. His hand cupped her breast and she moaned for more.

His cock rose hard against the flat plane of her belly and she pressed to feel more of him against her. "You love this about me?"

"I love that you believe sex belongs in a relationship. That it's important to you that you share your body with a man you care for, who cares for you. I feel the same way."

"You looked so upset with Celia when you heard it was a married guy who took her into the hospital."

"My father treated my mother like a convenience while he ran around on her. I want more from relationships than sex, Kat. But I wanted you so bad I was willing to bury my doubts and let lust take over."

"That's how I felt too. Willing to set aside my better judgment just to be with you."

He frowned and growled. "Climbing out onto the roof certainly constitutes lack of judgment."

"I won't do it again. Promise. Still, there was something exciting about it."

He tilted his head back to search her gaze. His eyes lit with desire. "Now that I've got you safe in my arms, I'll admit you looked damned cute tapping on the glass. Your hair was being tossed in the wind and your nightie was fluttering around your thighs. Tell me more about this fantasy of yours."

"Okay." She heated. "I climb in the window silently and find you asleep on the bed."

"Like this?" He climbed into bed and pulled the covers up to his chin.

"Silly, you're not supposed to be facedown. You have to be faceup for this to work." While he rolled to his back, she moved to the foot of the bed. Her lowest belly tingled with need.

The sheet tented at his crotch. Her mouth watered.

"Now what?" he asked, his voice low and intimate with sexual need.

"I start at your toes and work my way up to your knees with my tongue. Eventually, I'll get to your cock. Take it in my mouth—"

He sat up, cutting her off. "That won't work."

She sighed, exasperated. "Why not?"

"My feet are so ticklish I'll probably kick you in the face."

"Check! No tickling." She grabbed both his feet and gave them a strong squeeze. He jerked. "This is my fantasy and I want it," she demanded.

"Far be it from me to ruin a good fantasy."

"When we're done with mine, you can have one of yours."

"The only one I have is of you, marrying me."

Her breath caught, but she held onto his feet and squeezed again. "Like I said, I get my fantasy, you get yours." She whooped when he slid to the end of the bed and grabbed her. Rolling her to her back, he settled between her thighs.

His cock nudged into her wet warmth. "Let me love you, Kat, the way I want to. Forever."

PARLOR GAMES

*To Ann Roth, whose kindness and generosity helped find
the setting for Perdition House.
My deepest appreciation.*

1

The line of cabs moved slowly toward the mansion's wrought iron gates. Matt Crewe tapped his knee in impatience as each car ahead of his inched along in turn as, one by one, they disappeared up a driveway covered over by pine boughs. Without warning the cab ahead of his stopped three cars back from the gates and the rear passenger door opened to allow a woman to exit.

She paid her fare at her driver's open window. Highlighted in the headlights, she was fine featured and dressed for comfort. Her movements were briskly efficient as she handed over some bills and waved away the change. Walking shoes and blue jeans topped by a bright red fleece surprised him. He'd expected to see women dressed in silk and satin designed to tease and entice.

But then it wasn't the women who would be on the auction block, now was it, he noted with a bitter smile. It would be men. And Matt was one of them.

He tapped his driver on the shoulder. "She's got the right idea. It'll be faster if I walk," he said. The woman picked up a laptop case and an overnight bag and made for the gates on foot. If he was lucky he'd catch up to her before she reached the mansion. Whoever she was, he wanted to talk to her.

As he cleared the gates and took his first step onto the grounds of Perdition House, the enormity of what he planned grabbed him by the cock.

Selling himself. A sex-filled weekend with a woman he'd never met. Would never see again. Desire rose at the thought, hot and insistent. A slight breeze kicked up, snatching at his hair, pressing his jeans against his legs.

The woman he trailed stopped about twenty feet ahead, then dropped her overnight bag to the ground at her feet. The laptop case went next, but she was more careful of it. Then she stretched her arms out in front of her and shook her hands as if to get the blood flowing again. She rubbed her arms from shoulders to wrists, even stamped her feet into the soft pine needles that cushioned the driveway.

She was foot-stomping cold while he was fine. More than fine if his hardening cock was any indication. He hurried to catch up to her.

More cabs arrived, inching along beside him toward the house. If not for the headlights the driveway would be pitch black.

Ten feet to go and the breeze turned cold, drove hard right through his leather jacket and jeans, leaving him numb but strangely alive. As if every sense he had was on high alert. The woman suddenly wrapped her arms around her waist in the age-old gesture that signaled a need for warmth. God he wanted to wrap her up and hold her. The thought came from nowhere, and everywhere.

His own arms tingled from shoulders to fingertips, and all he wanted was to reach her, enfold her in his arms and share whatever body heat she needed. Then he wanted to lay her out and take her. Heat her up to boiling.

The impulse to drag her into the bushes and get her jeans off came sudden and hard. Hot damn he was horny. Randy as a teenager. Must be the woman. Either that or the purpose of the weekend was getting to him.

He tugged at his collar to release some of his pent-up heat, but it didn't help. He hurried the last few steps, happy to get the weekend off to a good start.

"Hello," he said as he reached her side.

She was startled but smiled back at him. "Hello. Are you the talent?" Her tone was bold as a shore-leave sailor's. She assessed him while she flapped her arms around her middle.

"Apparently. One of them anyway. You're here to bid?"

"Yes." Her glance heated as she let her gaze travel from his face down to his hikers.

What he saw when she looked back into his eyes was approval.

A small worry drifted away. He'd done everything in his power to be included on the auction block this weekend and it looked like he passed muster.

"Matt Crewe," he said, "very pleased to meet you."

"Carrie MacLean," she said with a nod and smile. "Sorry about the talent comment, it was rude. I'm not sure what came over me, but as soon as I walked through the gates . . ." She looked back at them, but the entrance to the driveway was obscured by pine boughs.

"Cold?" he asked.

She released her arms. She unzipped her fleece to mid-chest, then loosened her collar the way he had. "No, I was freezing a moment ago, but now I'm hot as can be."

"You can say that again," he muttered as he bent to pick up her overnight bag. "I'll carry this for you," he offered.

"Thanks!"

The cabs spread ahead and behind them as people arrived at an orderly pace. She watched every car that went past with interest. "Do you see the optical illusion?"

"You mean the boughs swaying away from the noses of the cars?"

"Yes. It's odd. I don't think I've ever seen anything like it."

He shrugged. "Like you said, it's just an illusion." But his sexual arousal was real as real could get. His cock strained behind his fly.

She glanced up at him, her eyes catching reflected light as it bounced off the tree limbs. "Yes, an illusion. Have you been here before, Matt?"

"No, this is my first time."

"Me too."

"Virgins, then."

She chuckled. "In a manner of speaking." There was just enough room at the side of the driveway for them to walk side by side. They took it.

He wanted to understand the colors at play in her hair, see the smoothness of her cheeks, how straight her teeth were, the level of intelligence in her gaze, but the on-again, off-again lighting only allowed for glimpses.

No matter, he'd see her soon enough. See her and know her in ways he could barely fathom. He wasn't prone to fanciful thoughts, but he did know gut reaction, and his gut was screaming full speed ahead with her.

Lights from the house began to appear between the trees ahead, and they rounded one more curve. The driveway curved directly in front of a three-story Victorian mansion aglow with welcome. She caught her breath at the sight, and he wondered what she'd sound like in the throes of passion. He was determined to find out.

"Perdition House," she said. "A weekend of rest and relaxation awaits us both."

"You could call it that." He called it a sex club, pure and simple. But if she wanted to keep to her own illusions she was welcome to them. "This is where we part company, Carrie

MacLean. The hired help is expected to enter through a side entrance."

"See you later?"

"Yes, you will."

She put her hand on his sleeve and looked up at him. He felt a punch of desire to his gut he fully accepted. "I'm already looking forward to it," she said. She licked her lips, and the power of the simple gesture undid him.

He headed across the drive before he dragged her into the well-tended rosebushes.

An hour and a half later, Matt slid the bow tie through the collar around his neck and tied it perfectly on his first attempt. He took stock in the mirror. His face had been shaved to baby ass smooth. "Not bad," he muttered, skimming his gel-slicked hair.

The guy next to him snorted as he also checked his reflection. In the mirror he flashed Matt an apologetic grin as he stuffed a sock down the front of his tuxedo pants. "Gotta advertise, man, that's the name of the game."

Matt shrugged. "What the hell." Then he shifted his cock and balls to show them to the best advantage too. He shot his cuffs and adjusted his collar with a sideways glance at the sock.

Then he looked at his own package again. He bulged behind his fly, hard since he stepped through the gates. If he was honest, the blood started to gather the minute he saw Carrie climb out of the cab ahead of him. No idea why, because he wasn't here for the sex. He was here for the truth. But still, he had more to offer than sock man.

From the looks Carrie had given him, she was just as interested in Matt as he was in her. Convenient since he planned to fuck her senseless all weekend.

A bell over the door chimed a warning, and Matt turned toward the door with the rest of the men. Twelve in all. Mostly randy college kids but for a couple of guys who looked like pros. The pros were older, jaded and cool, ready to serve. To a man, they were tall, muscular, good looking, with granite jaws and perfect teeth.

And all for sale. Even him. He'd sold himself for the truth. And if he had to, he'd lie himself to hell to get it.

He waited his turn to leave the library-cum-dressing room and felt his years. He was just as buff but noticeably older than the randy college boys. He couldn't gauge what the pros were thinking stacked up against this kind of competition. At twenty-eight, he shouldn't feel old, but a wall of jocks in their early twenties could remind a man of his unfulfilled ambitions.

In his yearlong hunt for sex clubs, Perdition House was the only one he'd found that catered exclusively to heterosexual women. He'd been damn lucky to find it too. A maze of misinformation existed even though the place was relatively new. Someone had covered their tracks from the very beginning, and covered them well.

As for being the *talent,* as Carrie had called him, he'd had to go through hoops to secure his spot. Having a clear criminal record was just the beginning. Strict guidelines and criteria weeded out sexually inferior male specimens.

Only the best men found their way onto the auction block. References were checked, health certificates required and even a psychological test was given to screen out potentially violent men.

The women who paid top dollar for these weekend sex marathons expected the best. The best was exactly what the owner of Perdition House, Faye Grantham, gave her clients. That the weekends occurred under the guise of charity auctions was beside the point to him.

Aside from his need to research the place, Matt was pumped that he'd been selected.

Which went a long way to easing him past his most recent

failure with The G Spot, the only club he hadn't managed to in-filtrate. Lesbians didn't want him nosing around. Go figure.

Eventually, he would deal with that minor problem, but right now he had to get through this weekend. In all the other clubs he'd found, he'd been an observer.

But not this time. The only way he could get in was in the guise of a full participant. He would stand on an auction block and be purchased for a weekend of hot sex with a woman he would never see again.

He'd never been turned on by the whole sex slave fantasy, so his arousal and interest surprised him. But there was no other reason for his hard-on since coming through the gates.

If his luck held, he'd be Carrie MacLean's sex slave. He rubbed his smooth jaw and thought about her giving him orders. Maybe he should rethink his stand on bondage.

He imagined himself on his knees wearing a heavy black collar being told to lick Carrie's boots. He chuckled at the vision of her walking shoes as she'd stamped them into a bed of pine needles. Nah, not his bag. He'd break out into laughter and wreck the mood.

Whatever the weekend held, he would be matched up with a woman with similar sexual predilections. The quiz on preferences had pretty much covered every sexual situation known to man.

For Matt, sex was about mutual enjoyment. Equal pleasure for each partner. He liked wild, raunchy, fast and hard. Raw was good. Hard was great. Fast had to be mutual. But slow? Slow was best.

Having a boot on his throat? Being strapped down? Not so much.

He wasn't the kind of guy to be at anyone's beck and call. Ever. For anything. That's why he'd been given red silk boxer briefs for the actual bidding. No dog collars or leather for him. Wasn't his style.

204 / Bonnie Edwards

The tuxedos were to be worn during the cocktail party mixer so the women had a chance to talk with the men. But the auction was where the real truth came out. Some of these guys would be dressed dominant. Some would show themselves as submissive. Blue bikinis meant multiples welcome.

As far as he knew the red boxer briefs he'd be wearing indicated he liked his sex straight, one on one, and often.

Worked for him.

He slanted a glance at sock man. False advertising wasn't his style either.

Carrie was his style, with her sensible shoes and practical fleece. She was not the kind of woman he'd expected to find here. A spike of need rose through his belly to his chest at the thought of what the weekend with Carrie would bring.

The men around him quieted into an expectant silence. Some checked out the books on the shelves while a couple others sat at a games table set up with chessmen. Matt leaned against the dark oak wainscoting and settled in to wait.

A cold draft seeped through the wall where his shoulder touched, then traced down his body with icy fingers. Those fingers settled south of his belt and his cock responded with a full-blooded howl of delight. He closed his eyes to better enjoy the sudden sensation. His balls tightened, chest heaved, blood rushed and pumped. Full-out arousal made him sensitive to everything around him.

He tugged at his collar for air, then adjusted his slacks to hide his raging woody. If any of the men in the room thought it was for them, he was doomed.

He hoped Carrie bid for him, but he wasn't sure it mattered. His cock filled out to rock hard and his heart pumped fast and furious. The cold fingers stroked his lower back, slid down between the cheeks of his ass and cupped his sac. How could he feel so hot when the hand stroking him was arctic?

2

Silky strokes on his cock continued as Matt gritted his teeth against coming. The guy ahead of him started to move with a slow shuffle toward the door. Sweat broke out on his neck. He wasn't the only man fully cocked and loaded. *What the hell?*

He broke away from the wall. The hold on his cock and balls eased and drifted away. He took a couple of steps, then looked back at the age-darkened oak where he'd been. Nothing but the patina of time and the luster of wax marked where he'd leaned.

The idea of being auctioned off as a sex slave turned him on? Fuck that.

It was Perdition House itself. Something weird had been happening to him ever since he walked through the gates.

The atmosphere oozed sex and sensuality and made him randy as a teenager. The whole mansion teemed with sexual imagery. Statuary of lusty satyrs, the paintings of lush nudes, even the old wallpaper looked sexual. Overblown flowers, their petals were folded open. Bulbous stamen sought entrance. The obvious sexual aura was enough to get most men's libidos cranked up.

Wherever this led, his sex-addled brain decided to go along. He'd sort it out in the morning. Surely by then he'd be spent and his brain would kick back in. Til then, he planned to enjoy himself and one Carrie MacLean if he could.

As he followed the rest of the men into the hall, he glanced up to the soaring ceiling. A mural caught his eye, and in the flickering shadowed light from a hall chandelier, he thought he saw the figures move. He blinked, but the light tricked his vision into seeing sex acts.

His blood boiled again as he stared harder, trying to discern exactly what he saw.

Naked circus performers. Trapeze artists, mostly, but he saw a couple of jugglers too. The light and shadows kept up a steady ebb and flow of imagined movement among the painted figures. In shock, he nudged the guy next to him and pointed to the mural three floors above.

Sock man tracked his gaze. "Wow, look at that," he said, voice hollow with shock.

The college boy on his other side looked too. A low whistle from him drew more attention. Soon the entire group of men was staring straight up.

The painted figures continued to move and writhe, the naked bodies bending and jutting toward each other.

Matt broke out into a sweat as he zeroed in on one couple. She faced away from the man behind her, her arms looped up around the back of his head, making her breasts jut up and out toward a woman's open mouth. The woman with the open mouth dangled upside down from a trapeze swing, while a man had his face buried in her pussy. Matt could swear he saw the guy's head move as he ate her.

The man behind the first woman clasped her ass in his hand

and squeezed in a subtle demand for her to open to accept him. The woman on the swing had a man licking her clit while her mouth worked the first woman's nipple. A regular round robin.

Matt blinked. Blinked again. He must have been mistaken because now the tip of the woman's breast was inside the trapeze artist's mouth while the man behind thrust deep into her pussy. Her own hands were now sliding over her clit while her face looked ecstatic with sexual release.

"What the fuck?" sock man muttered. "I swear there's a guy up there getting the best blow job I've ever seen."

"Where?" Matt couldn't see anything of the sort. He was caught in the whole swinging girl, pussy-eating, tit-licking, doggy sex round. "You see the girl on the swing?"

"No. Mine's a juggler getting deep-throated."

"Fuck."

"No shit."

The whole room heated up as guys all around Matt hitched at their slacks.

Every man there was a walking hard-on.

Faye Grantham, the mansion's owner, cleared her throat, getting their attention. Not that anything she did would go unnoticed.

"I'd like a crack at her," came a rumbling voice from somewhere in the crowd. A shuffle of agreement went through the group. Matt tried to remember he was there for research, but his throbbing cock told him otherwise.

Faye Grantham was sex kitten hot. Platinum blond hair that looked natural framed an exquisitely pretty face. Wide blue eyes and a pouty red-tinted mouth that invited deep kisses added to her allure. Smooth round shoulders framed a great rack, while a trim waist flared into hips a man could hold on to.

Like a screen siren of the fifties, she oozed sexuality and licentious need. She touched the elbow of the man nearest her.

At her touch he came out of his stupor. "Please, come into my parlor."

Said the spider to the fly. The strange thought flit through his head like a razor through shaving foam. Then he heard a light female giggle. Matt shook his head to clear it.

The man next to Faye followed her with dutiful steps through a double pocket door that seemed to slide open without her touching it.

A womanly groan of sexual release floated around his head, but he refused to look up at the mural again as he followed the rest of the addled men.

Carrie watched carefully as the bachelors entered the parlor, a group of agile, virile guys who all looked like models. Athletic models. Most were younger than Carrie, but some looked to be in their midtwenties, like her. Like Matt, the one she'd met outside.

She watched for him particularly, but he hadn't come through the door yet.

Every one of the men sported a woody, making the whispering women closest to her go quiet. Except for the one who leaned in to the woman next to her and remarked in a stage whisper, "Looks like lunch, girlfriend."

They snickered, heads together, but the other women around them nodded in lascivious agreement, including Carrie. If she belonged here among the moneyed, hard-working female CEOs, lawyers and bankers, she'd be just as quick to get excited.

She was probably the only woman in the place who didn't want to get laid. But still, being a red-blooded woman with needs that hadn't been met in too long, she looked her fill.

She dismissed as an aberration the embarrassing lust that had overtaken her on the driveway the minute she laid eyes on Matt. Her weekend was not about indulging in sexcapades. Not with Matt or any of these other gorgeous ready men.

She went back to cataloguing the new arrivals, keeping a professional eye sharply tuned for a likely target for an interview. The one with threads of silver at his temples looked bored, as if he'd been doing this too long. She pegged him for thirty or so and too jaded to be free and easy with what he said. He looked most likely to see through her facade, so she dismissed him.

She didn't want to lie about why she was here, or even about who she was, but she had no choice. Telling the truth under these circumstances would get her kicked out.

Bidding on one of the younger men was the way to go. Someone eager to please. Someone who wasn't Matt. She couldn't trust her reaction to him, not after she'd wanted him to throw her into the rosebushes and take her like an animal.

No way could she bid on a man who made her feel like that!

Three or four likely candidates showed up as the men trailed in. Young, randy, hot. A couple looked feverish with arousal. She doubted either of them would give her time to ask one question, let alone several.

But still, the frat boys who needed tuition money would be the easiest to get information from. She'd need documents to back up her story, and from the scraps of information she'd gleaned, she knew there had been questionnaires filled out and health certificates required. These young men with their cocks at full attention would be so anxious to get their rocks off, they wouldn't notice Carrie's questions. Maybe they would even provide her with the documentation she needed.

Until she'd walked through the mansion's gates, sex had been the furthest thing from her mind. Right now, sex was front and center. Her pussy twitched. Her breasts felt heavy and warm. A familiar drumbeat of need pounded below her waist. Her panties moistened with a slick release, and she tightened her thighs in response.

"Whoo," she said to no one in particular, "it's warm in here."

The woman beside her nodded. "The heat always cranks up when the men arrive," she said with a salacious grin. She looked ready to pounce.

"You've been here before?" Carrie whispered.

"Three times. Best sex I've ever had. These men are ready, willing and able." She sighed dramatically. "There's mine now." She nodded in the direction of the men filing in, and Carrie noted the man. Tall, with olive skin and shoulders the width of Texas, the man wasn't Matt. She gave silent thanks. But it was easy to see why the woman was salivating over the guy. The other woman shifted forward, blocking Carrie's view.

To see around her, Carrie stepped back to lean against the wall to watch and wait for Matt's arrival. She shouldn't want to see him again, but she was only human and he was gorgeous. Even the odd glare and shifting shadows created by the moving headlights on the driveway hadn't been able to hide that fact.

Heavy velvet drapes cushioned her back, but a cool draft nipped at her ankles from beneath the material. She turned to check and found the source of the draft was a bow window behind the draperies. She should move toward the fireplace across the room, but the thought vanished as quickly as it entered her mind.

Besides, a cluster of women already stood by the fire taking up all the room. Oddly, most of them had their hands on the mantel. Their faces looked dreamy and needful.

A low heavy weight pooled in her belly, bringing another gush of sticky moisture. The drumbeat of need rose in tempo to a tattoo. Insistent. Thudding. Dangerous.

The parade of men continued. The women around her gauged each of them on their physical attributes. The tattoo of arousal rose to crescendo inside her.

Frantic thoughts dashed through her head. One of these men would do. *Any of these men would do,* her fretful mind whispered. She glanced over her shoulder at the vague thought. Silly. Nothing there.

She shifted and reminded herself that she, Carrie MacLean, soon-to-be hard-hitting investigative journalist, was hot on the trail of a big story. This weekend was all about getting the goods on the so-called bachelor auctions being held by Perdition House's owner, Faye Grantham.

Grantham thought herself clever hiring a combination of financially strapped and perennially horny college students and male escorts for weekends in her family mansion. Under the guise of contributing to charity, the wealthy women who came out to the mansion paid highly to use the men for their pleasure.

She held on to that thought before it, too, winged away. She dredged up more of her plan, desperate to remember why she was here. This article would take her out of the bush league world of fluff and entertainment pieces and into the big leagues of journalism.

As heat coursed through her and she moistened again, she sucked in a deep breath. This weekend was not about getting laid! It was about getting to the truth and exposing it. Her editor had promised her story would go above the front page fold. Placement there would get her noticed. She tried to fill her mind with dreams of the *New York Post* and *USA Today,* but failed.

Sexual need took over and drowned out her plans for the story. Her ambitions were swallowed by a tidal wave of lust.

All she could conjure was an image of herself spread eagle on a bed with this gorgeous parade of men feathering their fingertips down her arms, her breasts, across her belly to the tops of her thighs. Cold, firm fingers delved into her slick pussy making her hot and needy. What an odd sensation. Cold making her so damn hot!

She squirmed and closed her eyes because the fantasy invaded her entire body. She fought to open her eyes but sank back, enveloped by the heavy velvet drapery folds.

She no longer cared about being watchful or how the parading men looked as her fantasy sprang to life behind her eyelids. The sensation of fingertips, feather light, dusted along her arms, circled the sensitive flesh on her inner elbow. Oh God, that felt good. Sexy and sensual, the fingers moved down to her palms and traced more lines there, making her hands clench in resistance. In need.

To touch and be touched. Like this, cool and warm, cold and hot and oh-so-right. Carrie had never experienced slow and steady touches and temptations. Fast, bucking sex was more what she was used to.

Fast and hard . . . and not particularly good for her.

But this! This felt incredible.

And all from her own mind.

But it didn't matter; the endless brushing of fingers continued, all over her body. Inside and out. She reacted with a shiver as several light touches brushed down her back to the tip of her tailbone. Her ass cheeks warmed under the gentle swirling sensations.

Her pussy moistened, her clit plumped, her outer lips softened in readiness for a man. She tried once more to open her eyes, but her lids were too heavy. She moaned lightly, swept up in the wildness of her imagination.

3

The images Carrie created swirled again and suddenly the men were naked. So was she. Naked on a soft warm platform, arms and legs stretched wide but not bound. Open and vulnerable, she understood all the men surrounding the platform were at her command. Cocks hard and glistening with drops of pre-cum under dim candlelight, they waited for her instructions.

She couldn't see their faces, just their lips and jaws, square and handsome. Their hands, large, competent, continued the swirling patterns around her body, coming close to her areas of need but never touching. Except for the cold, deeply entrenched fingers she felt inside. Hot on the outside, cold on the inside, she shivered.

Her nipples beaded hard, her pussy dripped onto the soft, padded platform. Mouths and lips and tongues roamed so close, gently swirling, tasting, tempting. . . .

She felt tracers of heat across her mons, in the curved hollows at the top of her thighs. Her outer lips opened, her inner lips bloomed, her heart pounded and her ears thudded as her blood rushed. Still the fingers traced and teased. The cold inside was gone now, leaving her empty and open.

Oh God . . . so open. Empty. A hollow woman, unfilled and unfulfilled, she wanted to weep with the realization.

Her life stretched behind and ahead of her, with nothing but her career in sight. She shuddered at the vast emptiness and knew she had to get out of this fantasy turned ugly.

But the mouths suckled and licked and took her places she'd never been.

If she didn't pull out of this now, she might embarrass herself, cry out or moan like a cat in heat. She pulled her shoulders away from the wall to stand upright, away from the cloying heaviness of the curtains. They dropped away from her and she could open her eyes again.

She looked quickly behind her, uncertain what she'd see. Arms in the draperies that held her there? Hands that slicked along her secret crevices to bring desire to life? Fingers that entered her slick and cold?

Nonsense. She was tired, needed a moment to collect her thoughts, had got turned on by the sight of so many buff men in tuxedos. And she'd had a glass or two of wine. She couldn't be sure how much she'd had because waitstaff wandered around with a bottle and topped off her wine with each pass.

She set her flute down on an occasional table and smoothed her palms down her thighs. Oh, she was turned on. Electric with need.

She wasn't certain how long she'd been in the grip of her fantasy, but the parade of men was now over. She'd missed Matt's arrival. All the men were now circling the women, weaving in and out of cliques and groups, chatting with some, patting the arms of others. One woman smoothed her palm across a man's butt. He had his hand on her waist. Old acquaintances, she guessed.

Finally! Matt at four o'clock. She pivoted toward him and sighed her way into a welcoming smile. Older than the college men, younger than the jaded pros, he was perfect in every way. All the desire she'd felt for him in the driveway rushed back.

Intelligent gaze, broad shoulders, great hands that looked honest and capable rather than manicured and pretty. The man looked real all over. Real and hot and ready. Yes, a glance at his crotch told her. He was definitely ready.

Her mouth watered as he approached, deep-set eyes poring over her hair, face, mouth. Taking inventory. Liking what he saw. Wanting what she had.

And she wanted to give it to him. At this moment, in this house, she'd give him everything and anything he wanted.

Her need grew as each step brought him nearer. He dodged other women who sent him admiring glances, sidestepped a waiter who suddenly moved across his field of vision, nodded to one of the other men who changed direction when it looked as if he, too, was making for Carrie.

She thrilled at the focus in his eyes, at the way he ate her with his gaze.

By the time he stood kiss-close, she was ready to lay herself out and hand him the key.

Oh, baby, drive me. Drive me hard.

He looked deep into her eyes, set a fingertip to her cheek and traced a line down the side of her face. His eyelids drooped in sexual invitation as he tracked a feather-light line along her jaw. Unable to deny him, the delicate skim ended at the hollow at the base of her throat. She melted into her panties in a flood of heat and feminine need.

No college boy could interest her after this.

His eyes heated and glazed with desire. She leaned in close to catch a scent of hot need rising from the skin of his neck.

"Hello, Carrie," he said, with a tilt to his head and a focused stare at her mouth that said he wanted to taste it.

She shivered in feminine response. "Hello, Matt," she said, when what she wanted to say was *Do me. Do me now.*

Something told her he heard her loud and clear.

Carrie let his name fill her mind, finally accepting what her body had known all along. He was the one she needed. Matt was perfect. If she could read anything, she could read horny. He looked so fucking randy, he was barely able to think.

His crotch was deliciously tented, his lips hard. His eyes carried that male focus that centered a man on a woman and wouldn't let go.

She was a professional journalist, he was a professional escort. She shouldn't be locked on him this way. And he should be getting busy with the most wealthy woman here. She looked far from wealthy with her department store silk and bargain brand shoes. He'd even seen her in her jeans and fleece!

But in spite of all the reasons he shouldn't have zeroed in on her, he was locked on like a heat-seeking missile. If she were smart, and she'd always thought of herself that way, she'd take advantage of his sex-addled mind and get some answers, but for the life of her she couldn't remember a single question.

Whatever questions she'd wanted to ask were gone like mist in the sun. She found nothing in her mind but a need that matched his. Which in itself screamed questions.

Neither of them should be in this condition. Not under normal circumstances. Had the wine been spiked?

She glanced around. The room swirled in a kaleidoscope of impressions, so she tried to focus on the people within a few feet. That much she could manage. The frat boys had the too-horny-to-wait look, but she put that down to hormones.

The older men, the jaded ones, seemed relaxed and comfortable. They stood with a couple of women who had much the same attitude. They all looked prepared to enjoy themselves and each other in due time, while she and Matt were ready to devour each other.

Matt. She looked at him again. Her plan had been to get one

of these guys alone and arouse him to fever pitch before she asked a few subtle questions. If she could remember what her questions were, she'd be fine, but she was just as aroused as Matt. And just as befuddled.

He hovered close, his mouth an inch from hers. Oh, the strain of not meeting his lips could kill her where she stood. The women nearby were pairing off with men they were interested in, so why couldn't she? She wanted to blend in, be one of the crowd. It made sense to cut one of these guys out of the herd for herself.

"Are you, umm, feeling all right, Matt?" she asked, almost afraid of his reply.

"I'm—" He shook his head, looking confused. He frowned, pulled himself back. "Sorry, no, I don't feel right. I'm pumped, primed, ready to pop. It's as if I've been slipped a—"

"Me too," she said quietly, interrupting him.

He slid his lips next to her ear. His breath stirred tendrils of hair at her neck sending sensation overload down her neck, and spine. The hair he disturbed tickled her flesh and even her hair follicles screamed *Do it!*

"Do they have a pill for women?" he whispered.

"For performance enhancement? Not yet. At least, I don't think so. Not one with this effect."

His eyes flared and his voice went deep. "And what effect is that? Tell me." His breath smelled of mint and good scotch, and she wanted to taste his mouth. To know the feel of his lips and tongue. Heat bloomed deep in her recesses.

The spice of telling him what her body was going through enticed her. Maybe if they talked about it, the incredible need would ease. She set one palm on his upper arm to steady herself while she leaned up to his ear. He tilted his head down toward her. His arm felt hard and muscular under her testing hand.

"My nipples are hard," she whispered, feeling them tighten

more with each word. "And it feels as if my skin's on fire. Like I'm screaming inside. I've never been so turned on in my life."

He nodded. "My blood's running hot, like coals banked before bursting into flame."

She let her eyelids droop so she could better imagine what he described. "And?"

"My balls are so tight I could howl."

She already knew he was fully erect. Her thigh kept swaying toward contact, but she managed to hold back. She dropped her hand from his arm. "If I touch you again, we're done for."

"If you *don't* touch me again, I'll die." He glanced around the crowd. No one else seemed as intent for each other as she and Matt. "The others aren't warmed up enough to enjoy a live sex show, and while I'm willing to be auctioned off, I have my limits."

Auction. She needed to focus on the auction. The bachelor auction for charity. Right. "I was told these things make a lot of money," she said.

"Do they?"

"For the charity, I mean."

"Right. The charity." His mouth dropped close to hers again. "I want to touch you. Taste you. In private, where I can caress and lick all I want." His eyes burned bright as flame, and his skin glowed with a sexual flush she responded to immediately.

His voice went deeper, huskier. "I need to kiss you."

She backed up a step, fighting with her inner fire all the while. The draperies caressed her back, warming it, heating her.

"What else is happening to your body?" he demanded. "Tell me more."

His gaze pulled at her, sucked her in, tore her away from her surroundings so that they were alone in the crowd. She didn't know him, didn't trust him, didn't think he was in control of himself. But then, neither was she.

"I'm wet," she whispered so quietly she doubted he heard. "Down there." As she spoke more moisture built in her channel and seeped ever so slowly into her panties. Inside, she trembled.

"Are you dripping right now? Into your underwear?"

She nodded.

His jaw clenched and a muscle jumped. "Are your lips hot and full?"

"Yes."

"Your clit plump and rubbery?"

"Oh yes."

"I'd love to taste you, dip my tongue into you."

"Ahh." Her whimper leaked out between her pursed lips. She couldn't hold in the tremble any longer.

"You're shaking."

She nodded, nipples throbbing.

"I want to roar and rampage around the room, strip off your clothes and eat my way from your pussy to your mouth. Then back again."

"Oh my God." Blood rushed south of her waist, making her lightheaded with achy need. She backed away from him, desperate to regain control of her body, her own thoughts! The draperies enfolded her. The arms she'd fancied before enveloped her, tugged her deeper into the folds.

Matt followed and leaned in close, trapping her in the reams of heavy material. She was caught, unable to move. Didn't want to move. *Do me! Do me!*

He swirled the draperies around them, cocooning her. He turned again and suddenly they were through the drapes and in the half moon of a good-sized bow window.

The party continued on without them.

The area cried out for a window seat, but she was relieved to see nothing but an ancient wicker rocking chair with shortened rockers. A person wouldn't be able to rock much. More like gentle rolls.

The idea caught hold, and images of wild sex on the chair whizzed through her mind. A man on the seat, a woman, gloriously naked, straddling him. Speared by his cock, she rolled her hips while the chair moved, heightening the experience.

The musk of sex scented the air in the small space. The images faded, leaving her mind clear and her body humming.

Matt stared hard at the chair, as if he'd seen the couple too. Then he turned to her, his nostrils flared.

"May I touch you?" Matt asked on a husky plea. The sounds of the party were distant, muffled by the velvet. Light came in through the window, weak and secretive.

"Yes, please," she whispered.

"I'll apologize now, because once we start, I won't stop."

She tilted up, and finally his mouth did what it had been threatening to do.

It took. Demanded. Ravaged.

Hot, hard, his lips crushed hers, his hands clasped her forearms and held her tight. She struggled against them, but not to escape, to move closer. She needed full body contact, mouth to mouth, chest to chest, hips aligned and pressed close.

The bulge at his crotch scorched as she reached for his fly and unzipped it. She felt bold, wild. So needy.

His hands skimmed up her legs, paused at her garters, then moved on to heat her naked thighs. She shuddered in anticipation of his touch at her center. *Get on with it.*

"I'm glad you changed out of your jeans. This is much easier." She widened her stance to give him room. He took it and palmed her through her wet panties.

She found heaven in his fly and sprung him free with a quick jerk.

He groaned at her touch and incredibly seemed to grow even larger in her hand. She swirled her thumb across the tiny slit at his tip and smeared the slick bead she found. "Oh, you're so hard, I want—"

He cut her off with a deep kiss that stole her mind and raged through her body. His tongue, like a devilish imp, seduced hers, coaxed and invaded, heated and laved.

His fingers tapped insistently against her, and she pressed her pussy against them. Muscles deep under her flesh clenched and released as need made her reckless. Her clit pulsed with each gentle tap.

The party sounds were gone now, replaced by their hard breathing and hushed moans.

"Let me take off my panties."

"Too late," he said. The pop of tearing cloth punctuated Matt's words, sounding loud in the quiet of the bow window. Carrie thought she heard a cheer go up at Matt's rough and ready actions.

4

Matt's fingers slicked across Carrie's slit. She melted, slippery with honey, as she sagged with relief at his touch. His thumb—oh!—his thumb found her clit and smeared her juices in tantalizing circles while she slid her hand up and down his cock.

If she dropped to her knees to taste him, he wouldn't be able to continue the magic he was making with his hand. Frustration rode her hard as she reached for release.

Suddenly taken by two fingers at once, she crooned into his mouth in acceptance. "Oh yes, do it. Make me come."

He turned her back to the wall and pressed close while his fingers danced in and out of her. Her pussy felt swollen and needy, her clit full and ready. Tension curled and rolled and grew, gathering strength against his onslaught of rippling sensation.

She crooned and came with a gush and spasm that shook her.

Matt's cock jerked as she moaned again. With a strong flex, he buried his face in her neck and locked on. His teeth against her pulsing neck, the rush of knowing she could make him come in mere seconds, snapped his control. He flexed again and spurted with a low moan.

She gushed and rolled against his questing thumb grinding her achy clit into orgasm. "Unh . . ."

His hold on her neck eased, her legs trembled, her arms felt lifeless as the last pulses faded.

"More," he said against her ear. "I already want more." His breath sent shivers down her spine.

She pulled her head back to look up into his face. He looked as stupefied as she felt. She nodded. Unbelievable as it was she had to admit, "Me too."

"Bid for me?"

"Yes."

He smiled, loose and easy. The flash of his white teeth and intelligence in his eyes dazzled her. It was as if she'd looked at him through a veil of sexual need and seen nothing but a hard mouth and jutting cock. But there was a man behind the desire. A person of worth and intelligence.

She smiled back at him, fully engaged in her moment of discovery. Was he seeing her for the first time too?

"Wow, you're a knockout when you do that."

And she had her answer. Her face warmed with pleasure, and it didn't matter that they'd been crazed by sexual torment, because they'd found each other now.

He leaned in to her ear again. "Sorry about the panties."

A clock in the parlor struck the hour and the party noise from the other side of the curtain went from muted to loud. The babble and murmur of voices became suddenly clear.

Odd.

A woman's voice called, "Time, gentlemen. We need you to retreat to the dressing room. When you return, the bidding will start."

"You've been paged," Carrie said. He pecked her cheek and

tugged at the curtain to leave their private cocoon, but he turned back to her before stepping into the parlor.

He dropped the curtain, set both palms on either side of her face and kissed her fully on the lips, drawing her desire up from her depths again.

By the time she opened her eyes and the world stopped spinning he was gone.

"Shit, woman, get a grip," she muttered. She smoothed a palm down her belly and wondered if her editor would spring for the amount of money she was willing to spend for one weekend with Matt Crewe.

By the time Carrie stepped out from behind the draperies, the men had left the parlor. She checked her watch. She'd been with Matt for a full thirty minutes. Which made no sense. Once they touched, it had taken no time before they were coming together. She'd had orgasms before, but that one was spectacular.

Utterly spectacular when all they'd done was grope each other. She couldn't figure out where the time had gone. She'd never had full-out sex last for thirty minutes. In her experience most men were damn quick on the draw. She'd learned early that she had to rev herself up plenty with her superb imagination way before the main event if she wanted to get anywhere.

But Matt was different. Something about him called to her. She flexed her inner thighs in memory. He'd torn her panties open in his need.

A cool breath of air tickled the hair on the back of her neck, and she shuddered. She swiped her hand across the chilled flesh and thought she heard a giggle from behind her.

A woman two feet away rubbed her arms in an unconscious effort to warm herself. Another was reaching for her wrap, another stood in front of the fire, hands on the mantel, expression rapturous.

As Carrie watched, the woman threw her head back and let

out a hushed sigh. With a shudder that worked her from her hips up to her shoulders, the woman looked to be in the throes of a nifty orgasm. Carrie decided to check out the mantel.

If she'd seen a couple on the rocking chair and felt those chilly hands in the drapery folds, maybe she wasn't the only one seeing and feeling . . . things.

With a nonchalant attitude that belied her inner thoughts, she moved over to the other side of the parlor to inspect the fireplace. The mantel was carved with buxom women and heavily aroused men enjoying sixty-nines all the way up from the floor to the center of the mantel.

The woman who'd been shuddering in climax suddenly popped open her eyes, licked her lips, then smoothed her skirt before turning away.

Carrie reached out to tap the woman on the shoulder to ask what had just happened, when another server stuck a fresh wine flute in her hand.

Yes, a drink. That's what she needed, and the question she'd been about to ask the orgasmic woman flitted away, out of her head.

Feminine chatter rose to the ceiling as the women's groups moved and flowed one to the other. She allowed herself to be carried along, picking up bits and pieces of information.

"Faye's man is gorgeous," she heard one woman say in an undertone to another.

"A lawyer," came the response. "Liam Watson. They say he's hung like a bull."

"Who's 'they'?" The woman took a drink of her wine. Her glance flew around the room seeking out the identity of the lucky woman in the know.

Carrie froze in place, straining to hear.

"Word is, he worked in skin flicks in law school. Very hush-hush."

"Really?" The woman wriggled her hips and stared unabashedly across the room at the hostess and her escort, a man dressed in loafers and cords, topped by a T-shirt under a suede sport coat. Underdressed for the occasion, but man enough not to care, Faye's lover exuded friendly but watchful possessiveness over his woman.

Faye didn't seem to mind; in fact, she trailed her fingers across his flat belly when she thought no one was looking. Every time she did, he leaned in close to her ear and said something that heated her cheeks.

Carrie returned focus to the overheard conversation. "No hard core. I doubt he'd have been able to get away with that. I believe it was simulated sex. But still, a man would have to possess some impressive attributes to get into the business."

"Impressive," the friend repeated with a sigh. "Did you meet anyone of interest?"

"An art student this time. I checked him out. His attributes were . . . interesting." She chuckled suggestively.

"You know what they say, more than a mouthful's a waste."

They laughed together and moved on to join another group of women. The hugs and air kisses Carrie witnessed told her they knew the other women well.

Her research had shown these auctions had been going on for a year or so. The first weekends must have been kept ultra-secret, because she couldn't find a definite date for the first one. It seemed incredible that in such a short time, the information she gathered was foggy. There were signs of misrepresentation and red herrings during her search for information.

The pocket doors opened with a quiet whoosh, getting everyone's attention. She waved away another drink, needing to keep a clearer head. Her thoughts were jumbling up and over each other for prime position. She couldn't keep anything straight.

Not that it mattered, because the auction was about to start. Sexual need rolled like thunder through her veins. It was easy to blame her behavior with Matt on too much wine, so she decided not to drink another drop.

That resolve lasted until the men walked in again. Heat rushed through her from the floor up to her scalp at first sight of them. She swiped a wine flute off a tray and tipped two fingers into the cool liquid. She patted her neck with the wine in a desperate bid to cool off.

Matt was the third man through the door, and she downed the wine in three gulps. Gorgeously seductive in a bright red pair of silk boxer briefs, he sported sculpted muscles, long legs, and a sexy sprinkling of chest hair that made him stand out from the bulky, hairless other men.

Matt was seduction personified.

His eyes scanned the room, obviously seeking someone. He made eye contact with her and her breath held as she read his signals. The man wanted her as much as she wanted him.

Hallelujah.

The parade of men strolled across the front of the fireplace to stand for inspection.

Murmurs of approval rose around her as Carrie studied the lineup. She needed to watch carefully so she could jot notes in her room later. She wished for her digital camera but try as she might she hadn't been able to get it to work. Even her backup disposable had died. Both had tested fine before she left home.

Matt flashed her so many heated looks she wondered how she'd find time for notes.

Some of the underwear the men wore boggled her mind. There were body slings made of slinky nylon with elastic-looking straps over the shoulders. See-through mesh pouches on a couple of the men left nothing to the imagination. The hunks wearing them swayed with each step, their packages outlined by the black netting. Some of the men wore leather, and some even had on studded collars. She shivered, thinking there may be some code in the clothing she wasn't privy to.

The men gleamed in their male beauty. The lighting cast them in perfectly delicious colors of chocolate, beige and bronze. Each one carried himself with the sure knowledge of sexual prowess and virility.

She scanned the line of men as they continued to flow into the room, every one looking like sex kings. They shone with slick oil, the planes and rounded muscles of their pecs and taut abs perfection.

Matt was the only one without a tan. The others had obviously been on tanning beds for weeks. Matt's color was light buff, tinged with the powerful tint of sexual arousal. His nostrils flared, his belly tightened with each breath and his eyes burned into hers. She melted and decided that even if her editor balked at paying, she would add money of her own. She did a quick mental calculation of her bank account.

Troubling as hell was the fact she wasn't the only woman to notice him. A voice from behind her crooned in a sexy purr about the man in the red boxer briefs.

"He's looking right at me," Carrie heard from over her left shoulder, and she wanted to turn and tell the bitch to back off, but she couldn't draw that kind of attention. Blending in was the only way to stay for the weekend.

She gritted her teeth and ignored the woman, in spite of the low-pitched growl and seductive hiss she kept up.

The bidding started and a few women around Carrie dug deep to buy the men they'd marked for their weekend of pleasure. The sexual temperature in the room rose by several degrees as each man stepped up to the front of the line to display himself to the best advantage.

What should have been an upsetting, distasteful display of

flesh peddling took on an aura of sexual expectancy for everyone in the parlor, men included.

Faye Grantham's voice softened to a purr as each man moved through poses designed to heighten the women's awareness. Hips gyrated slowly, hands slid along thighs to outline and cup their organs. Each man got hard before the women's eyes. Their cocks rose up their bellies, burgeoning and jutting, thick and full. Some of them peeked out the top of their varied underwear. All of them made the women's mouths water.

Carrie was no exception. The women around her shifted where they stood, their thighs squeezed and released, their nipples beaded and obvious under their clothes. The air warmed to unbearable.

To her left, a woman sighed and moaned lightly. Carrie turned to see and watched a hand slide from a belly to a crotch and brush lightly. But the crush of the crowd prevented her from seeing the face of the woman who sounded way past control. All Carrie saw was French-manicured fingernails clenching black silk. That description worked for most of the women in the room, including her.

It had to be the house. There could be no other explanation for everyone's behavior. Hers. Matt's. The woman who'd had an orgasm by touching the mantelpiece.

Her article took an amazing shift as she considered the ramifications of all she'd seen and experienced.

She faced the front of the parlor and found Faye Grantham's gaze locked on her. The other woman's full red lips kicked up at the corner, and a tilt of her head made Carrie's heart race.

Ambition. The motivator drove Carrie hard. And Faye was the answer to a prayer. There was an incredible story going on at Perdition House, and she would get it. She wasn't sure what was happening yet, but this story would carry her to the top of her profession. All she had to do was get rock-solid evidence.

She couldn't get any photos tonight, but she should be able to track some of these men and get photos later. Maybe one of them had brought a camera. Or maybe even video. A lot of people seemed to enjoy taping themselves. Hollywood was full of phony sex-tape scandals engineered by publicity-hungry celebrities.

But the women are here because they want privacy.

Right. She'd forgotten that. Careers could be damaged, not to mention corporate profits, if stories of this house's real purpose came to light.

If someone had known about her cameras they could have messed them up while she was in the shower earlier.

There was no way the women would talk about the auction. Maybe Matt could shed some light on the whole process from his side.

He was up next, and her receptors went on high alert. His attitude, his body, his searing focus on her and the memory of his kisses, the way his hands had taken her over the edge, called to her.

"Bid for me?" he'd asked.

Without a doubt!

Faye Grantham shifted her shoulder toward Matt, smiled at him with a comment only he could hear and the bidding began. Instead of posing the way the other men had, Matt simply stood and stared at Carrie with clear intent.

The bottom dropped out of her belly.

Barely aware of shuffles all around her, Carrie realized the women had tracked Matt's gaze to her. The spotlight of attention was now hers. It was clear she was a first timer and no one knew her.

Some of the women tossed her looks that made it plain they didn't want her scoring such a juicy looker as Matt her first time out.

The bids rose quickly and higher than any for the other men

so far. Tongue-tied, Carrie watched her chance to be with Matt slip away as her editor's contribution was surpassed.

She raised her hand at that point and wiped out her savings. If this article helped her career, she'd be able to replace that money soon. She hoped.

With the bids finally topping out at over two thousand dollars, she waited with her breath held as an expectant hush fell over the room.

"Twenty-five hundred dollars," came a voice from behind her. It was the same woman who'd commented on Matt's red briefs. Carrie turned but couldn't tell which of the avidly attentive women had outbid her.

Too much. Twenty-five hundred was too much. She couldn't swing another five hundred dollars, and she gave Matt a silent apology.

Faye repeated the amount once, twice, and suddenly Matt stepped up to Faye and lightly clasped her forearm to stay the final announcement.

"Three thousand," he said.

"This is highly irregular, Matt," Faye responded, although sultry humor laced her words.

"I pay, I choose."

Faye smiled enigmatically. "Yes, I suppose you do."

"The bid stands."

The murmuring around Carrie rose high as the ceiling. Apparently this result was unprecedented and Matt's desirability rose along with the voices. Clearly he had his sights set on Carrie, so there were no more bids.

The moment the bidding for Matt closed, he made his way to her.

Matt Crewe belonged to Carrie MacLean for one weekend.

All thought of ambition fled, overtaken by sheer thrilling lust.

A weekend full of Matt and sex. A girl couldn't ask for more.

5

Getting through dinner was a bitch. Never mind the meal itself, just getting to the dining room had been a challenge. After messing up the bidding process and throwing out all chance of being one of the guys, Matt had failed at getting Carrie upstairs to her room. She had insisted on blending in and eating dinner just like everyone else.

But Matt had a gut feeling he and Carrie weren't like everyone else. They were marked somehow. Different. And this weekend would change them both.

The ideas were fanciful, but he couldn't deny them. He still couldn't wrap his head around the idea that he'd paid three grand just to sleep with a woman. And he hadn't even paid *her* for the privilege!

Where had his objectivity gone? His cool observance of the proceedings had disappeared the moment he'd stepped through the gates of Perdition. He'd been attracted to Carrie on sight, but one step onto the grounds had his version of horny hitting sky high. In spite of knowing something was wrong with this house, all he could focus on was Carrie. He could not keep his mind on track.

At least for now Carrie was beside him, eating as if her mother were at her shoulder telling her to clean her plate. She didn't smile or engage anyone in conversation. Carrie focused entirely on the food and service, as if to stop eating would bring disaster.

The disaster was that he was sitting here in a pair of briefs with the hottest woman in the room keeping both hands public.

He slid his right hand to her thigh, while he reached for his crystal wine goblet with the other. She froze, her hands poised elegantly over her plate, her knife and fork still.

A shudder wracked her as he traced light figure eights along the flesh above her knee. He slid the silk of her black skirt higher up her thigh, fingers unerringly aimed for the sweetest spot on her body.

She looked at him then, and her gaze flayed him where he sat. Hot and needful, she opened her lips to speak but no sound came out. Her eyes went wide and pleading.

To stop? He wasn't sure he could. He leaned in close to her ear. "I want to touch you. Let me."

Her eyelids drooped in a way that said she wanted it too. "Not here, in front of all these people."

He glanced around the table. Aside from Liam, Faye's lover, he was the only man with a hand out of sight. "As soon as it's polite, we're heading upstairs. Do you have a room yet?"

"On the right at the top of the stairs," she said. "Four-poster bed."

"I want you in it."

Another shudder went through her.

Gooseflesh rose on her arms. "Feel that draft?" she asked, with a quick glance behind her.

"No, I'm on fire." Good thing, considering he was next to nude. Still, she shivered as if she'd been tossed into a blizzard naked.

As hostess, Faye kept the dinner conversation moving, but Matt couldn't track any of it. His attention wandered to Carrie and locked on. Course after course arrived in front of him, but all he could do was pick at the food. His hunger was for the woman at his side, stoic in her silent, mechanical response to the meal.

The food smelled good, looked fantastic. The labels on the wine told him this was the best he'd ever had. Italian. French. Lusty and bold. Not a flavor was murky, not a scent undiscerned, but all he could feel, smell and see was Carrie. He pulled the taste of her into his mouth from memory and conjured it on his tongue throughout the meal.

He probably shouldn't have messed with the auction. The whole idea behind his research was to experience the clubs the way they were, without embellishment or personal bias. He needed to be objective. Skewing the bidding to have Carrie for the weekend was a huge mistake.

Fuck that. He wanted her, she wanted him. They were in a strange situation in an even stranger house. Besides, he had a pretty good handle on how this particular club worked anyway.

You don't need to focus on Perdition. The thought came from nowhere but he had to agree. Perdition House was a fine place. A woman's home, a family legacy. He wasn't out to ruin Faye Grantham's good name. Nor did he want the auctions to stop.

His book was about the why of sex clubs. The need for people to congregate for sex for whatever reason. Like minds, like tastes, like fetishes. Whatever.

So bringing up the name of the house wasn't necessary. He

decided to make reference to the idea of a club for heterosexual women. That was all he would write.

If his editor wanted details, he'd provide them. Otherwise, he'd leave the place in peace. He liked it here. The grandness of the old mansion, the heavy furnishings and wall coverings, all spoke of a bygone era. Perdition House operated as a haven away from the rat race of modern life. He wouldn't ruin it with unwanted publicity.

On that thought, he glanced to the head of the table and caught Faye's appraising gaze. She smiled happily as if privy to his decision. She raised her glass of wine to him and tilted her chin in a silent thank-you. Then she leaned toward her lover's ear and whispered to him.

Liam Watson's gaze shot down the table to his. A curt nod of thanks and he went back to moving his hand under the table, while Faye's eyes drifted close and her ruby lips parted.

Carrie's fingers on his naked thigh speared into his attention. Heated pinpoints tracked from his knee to his groin as she turned her body toward his. Her eyes glittered in the light from the flames of the candelabra in the center of the table. Her nipples went hard as he watched.

Christ, she was hot. Ready. Wet, he guessed. Wet and open. He already knew the scent of her aroused flesh and wanted to taste her again.

"It's warm in here," she said softly, flesh rosy in the candlelight.

"Then why do I feel a chill at my back?" He turned to see, but the pocket doors to the hall were closed. There shouldn't be a chill. And hadn't they just said this in reverse? Now he was the chilly one and she was too warm.

"This is a drafty house. And from the oddest places too. Solid walls, the draperies. The chill just seems to move around."

"Yes," he said, focused more on her touch than her words.

"So, Matt," she said brightly, "how did you find Perdition House? The auction and . . . everything." Her voice slowed when she noticed him staring at the hair that curled by her ear. He wanted to lean in and nibble her there, and he figured she knew it.

The feel of her deft fingers on his thigh tantalized and enticed him to lean close. "Slide your fingers up my leg, Carrie."

She did. To within an inch of his raging package.

"Go to the tip, Carrie. I want to feel you." With their heads nearly touching and their eyes locked on each other, the other diners disappeared behind a fog. The sound of the quiet conversation around the table muted and the clatter of dishes and cutlery disappeared.

Finally her hand slid across the cool silk of his briefs to his waist. She hooked the waistband of his briefs down to rim the head of his cock. Her fingertip crossed the tip. Heat flashed through his belly at the contact. He jerked in his seat, the movement tugging at the fine linen that dangled into his lap.

Her knife slid off the table and she ducked to pick it up. The witch tipped her tongue across his cock head as she made a show of fumbling for the knife on the floor.

He sat bolt upright as she licked him in a wicked tease designed to fire all cylinders. Needing to stop her, but needing more of the incredible sensation of her mouth, he palmed her head and leaned forward to give her some privacy while she plunged her mouth to his base and held still.

For a long moment, he just closed his eyes and *felt*. Her heated mouth, her silken flesh inside it. The wetness as she held him, still and silent.

Just as he thought he might be able to bear the torture, she moved her tongue against his shaft. He jerked again and his cock throbbed as she flicked him once more.

Then she swallowed. Each slick, tiny muscle in her mouth worked him. Sweet heaven!

She released him as suddenly as she'd latched on and came up smiling. The knife gleamed in her hand while his heart pounded so hard it hurt. She set the knife on the table beside her plate, and a server replaced it with brisk efficiency.

She smiled her thanks and sliced her next piece of meat as if nothing had happened.

This woman blew his mind and she was his for the whole weekend. A man couldn't ask for more.

6

The bedroom at the front of the house had seemed cold and spare when Carrie had arrived. Without much thought to her surroundings, she'd dumped her suitcase and laptop on the bed, then headed downstairs to watch the other women arrive five minutes apart. Not ten, not fifteen, but exactly five minutes went by between arrivals, just enough time for each guest to register.

She'd returned to the room to shower and prepare for the evening. Lots of time for someone to mess with both cameras. So much for being clever enough to bring two.

Alone for a few minutes while Matt collected his bag, Carrie noticed the room seemed different than it had earlier. It drew her in with a cozy atmosphere. The drapes had been drawn and an artificial log burned in the tiny fireplace. Dappled shadows and light danced across the Persian rug. She thought of naked bodies twining and writhing in the glow from the fire. A bow window sat directly over the spot where Matt and she had trampled each other to take care of their mutual need.

Her laptop was where she left it on the bed, and the sight of it reminded her that she should make notes. On what though?

The draperies in the parlor holding her in their icy grip came to mind. She could imagine her editor's response to an article based on her wild imaginings. No one would believe she was held helpless while cold fingers played her pussy.

Momentarily stumped, she thought harder. Her article needed a different slant. Besides, she wasn't about to tell the world about her sudden attack of hormones and the way she'd behaved with Matt.

Her cheeks heated and she palmed them, disbelief at her own behavior rampant within her. She had to pull herself together. Her sudden sexual appetite was more a cause for dismay than celebration.

But it was celebration she wanted. More than anything. To dance, to sing, to enjoy sexual fulfillment. Joy rose at the idea of an entire weekend celebrating the most intimate actions of man and woman.

Her outrageous act at the dinner table still rattled her. But, oh, the sexiness of licking his cock, taking the chance on being seen, of getting caught, still made her pussy weep. The spice of her daring actions had the power to make her want to do more outrageous things.

As soon as Matt arrived, she would ask him some questions about the auctions. How the selection process worked and if he'd saved a copy of whatever questionnaires he'd filled out.

Then she'd fuck his brains out.

She giggled in the quiet of the room and felt a hominess surround her. Delighted with her plan, she felt the heaviness in her lowest belly grow. She was up for an all-nighter if Matt could manage it. From what she'd seen he would have no problem.

Salacious need coursed through her.

To tamp it back, she opened her laptop and booted up, praying that the computer still worked properly. If she didn't get her notes typed up now, while her mind was relatively clear, she may forget something important.

She made notes on her sexual arousal, starting with the way she'd responded to Matt at first sight in the driveway. From there, she noted the wall had gone cold at her back. Then she moved on to the way the draperies had felt around her.

Things got fuzzy after that, because that was when Matt had walked into the parlor. Once their gazes locked, her memory nearly deserted her. The chronology of events was gone, replaced by sensate memory. She remembered his scent, the way he felt under her fingers, the taste of his kisses, his flesh, but nothing of how they'd actually decided to step behind the draperies into the bow of the window.

A chair was about all she could recall that didn't involve a sex act. An odd rocking chair, with shortened rockers. Wicker back, no arms and very low to the ground. She'd seen . . . something . . . but the images escaped her for the moment. She left a couple question marks in the notes to remind her to come back to that section later.

Some of the time behind the draperies was blank, but the orgasm she'd had on Matt's hand had been indelibly marked by her brain. Certain she would be able to conjure the sensation again for at least a decade, she grinned as she typed her notes on it. Grinned and flushed and heated as her fingers flew over the compact keyboard.

Her pussy twitched as if that part of her body wanted to relive the whole experience. She moaned as the physical memory of her release shook through her.

Matt opened the door and stepped inside with a duffel bag in his hand. He turned away as he closed the door, then gave the key a slow, certain turn to lock the door. His profile was sharp in the golden light cast by a single soft white bulb in a bedside lamp. His shadow against the wall looked misshapen and distorted.

He studied the doorknob and key lock, in no hurry to face her. Next, he closed the door to the bathroom, making sure that too was locked.

Expectant silence stretched as he squared his shoulders. A hiss rose from the fire as if rain had dropped from the chimney. But the sound only proved the silence between them.

He finally swung to face her. "Hi," he said, his voice intense and deep. The front of his boxers tented and a chill shot from his corner of the room straight through her.

She gulped at the sudden icy feel, her stomach and chest flexed as the shaft of cold moved from front to back. When it passed, she settled the laptop on the floor away from the bed, then moved across the room to him.

He watched as she approached. His fine sculpted chest rose and fell with each breath. The nearer she got, the more she heard his breath until the sound of each one filled her and pulled her toward him.

Invisible strings stretched out and coaxed her near. She followed, unable to stop or think as she approached him.

He was so beautiful. Strong, intelligent and sexy as hell.

Nothing called to a woman more than a man who wanted her. Not just any woman, but her.

Matt Crewe wanted Carrie MacLean, and she would not deny him.

Could not deny him.

Like a preordained cataclysm they came together in a sudden rush of seeking mouths and grasping hands.

She had far too many clothes on, she realized as he made short work of them.

They landed on the Persian rug in a heap, hands roaming. His neck felt hot, so hot under her lips. She nipped him in her eagerness and he bit back.

Her shoulders shook when he finally opened her bra and swept the cups apart. Wet heat enveloped her nipple while his tongue twirled and flattened the rosy bud in turn.

She slid her hand into his briefs to cup and squeeze him lightly. He groaned and his balls tightened into hard nuts.

"You paid for me," she said.

"There isn't another woman anywhere that could make me as hot as you do. Carrie, I can't get enough."

She responded to every lick, nip and deep kiss he offered, thrilling at the attention and deep affection behind every move. It was too much, too soon to think of this as making love, but that's how she felt.

"Oh, I want this. You. I want you." She said it over and over, coaxing him out of his briefs.

Finally naked and able to see each other in the pretty firelight, they looked their fill.

"I love your breasts," he said, molding each one in turn. He swept his hand down the flat plane of her belly to cup her mons. "I love how wet you get." His fingertip rolled her clit side to side, creating a tidal wave inside her. His other hand skimmed her cheek, then tipped her nose. "I like your nose. It's perfect. The most perfect nose I've ever seen."

She laughed. "You, Mr. Crewe, are a little off the wall."

But she loved that he commented on her nose.

"In a room full of smart women, you stood out, Carrie. When I stepped into the parlor, it was your watchfulness that caught my eye. You were cataloguing every man and woman in the place, and it was clear how intelligent you are. And how much you thought you didn't belong. But you're head and shoulders above every woman in the house in the smarts department."

Her belly fluttered at the compliment. It was good to know this wasn't all about tits and pussy. "There was no way you could tell any of that from our conversation outside. I was a hag to call you the talent."

He snorted. "I knew even then that if I didn't get to you, some other man would, and I couldn't let that happen."

"You felt that way at first sight?"

"At first sight," he confirmed. "I was in a cab directly behind yours and I followed you on foot." Then he tilted down to kiss her and she lost all semblance of intelligence and let sensation take over.

With a quick flip that surprised her, Matt knelt between her knees, then set her ankles on his shoulders. He snugged her ass up close to his thighs and slid a condom on.

"If I don't get inside soon, I'm going to bust. Okay?"

"Thank you. I'm way past needing foreplay. Slide on in, big man." Empty, oh, she was empty. *Do me. Now.*

He chuckled and pressed the head of his cock between her folds. With a straight push he entered her, filled her, caressed her from the inside.

They stilled in the moment and waited while they each felt the other. The heat, the clasp of muscles, the slick heady balance of woman to man.

Slowly then, with a reverence that took her breath, Matt moved. Slightly at first, with utmost consideration for her comfort, his cock tantalized her inner walls. As she adjusted, he moved faster, harder, with urgency riding them both hard.

Sensation took her quickly to the peak where she hung for a long moment before toppling over the crest.

Her orgasm built in her channel, creating havoc along her nerve endings, up her back to her chest, where it exploded and she flew apart.

Unaware of anything but the incredible release, she held on to Matt, desperate to ride it out. As the world came back to intrude, she felt his cock flex deep inside as he pressed and held her ass still for him.

He groaned and growled with his spew and took her back into release again. One on top of the other, it was a first for her. She'd never come twice before. She'd never come apart in a man's arms before either.

"This is all new to me, Matt. You're incredible." Talented, the man was so damn talented.

The firelight flickered and flamed across them, still entwined but sated. They rested together shoulder to shoulder as they watched the light dance along the high ceiling.

The next morning, sweaty and satisfied for now, Matt stretched out on the four poster beside Carrie. She settled her head on his chest and draped a leg across his. Her skin felt smooth, enticing in its softness, and she fit against him perfectly. The musk of sex rose all around them, the sheets were in a hell of a state, but none of that bothered him because all he could feel was her.

Carrie, warm and sated next to him.

He smoothed his palm in a rhythmic sweep up and down her arm while she breathed in the scent of his skin. "You're wonderful, Carrie. This is fast turning into one of those unforgettable nights."

"Now that I can think again, can you tell me why you bid at the auction?"

"I wanted you and only you. Seems straightforward enough to me." Now wasn't the time to mention his book or the fact that he'd probably made a mistake by messing with the auction. No woman wanted to be considered a mistake.

"We both know these auctions aren't about charity, Matt." She raised her head and looked at him. Her lips still glistened from his kisses, his cock was still semihard and her head had turned toward questions lightning quick. If he didn't know better, he'd think she was questioning him for a reason.

"So, what are they about?" he asked.

She grinned. "Most of the younger men are still in college. That much was obvious. The older men looked jaded enough to be pros, but you don't seem to fit either category. I'm just curious."

"Curious." He repeated to give him time to come up with a suitable response. If she guessed he was doing research for a book, it would be game over. She'd tell Faye and he'd be kicked out.

*But you decided to give the charity auctions only a passing
mention. You promised no specific details about Perdition House
would be published.*

"I needed the money," he said. "I'm between jobs and I
heard about this gig." He shrugged. "I sure didn't expect to
find someone like you."

"If you're between jobs, can you afford to pay the three
grand? Because I could kick in some." She grinned and ran curious fingers down his belly.

"It's my privilege to spend this time with you. I'd already
like it to be longer than a weekend."

"Me too."

"Do you live nearby?"

"Tacoma. You?"

"Near the Canadian border." Which wasn't a complete lie.
He couldn't tell her the truth, that he'd flown in from upper
New York State, so he kissed her, hard and fast. A thrill raced
to his cock as she responded exactly the way he needed her to.
"Let me take you to the bath. Did you see the tub in there?"

She nodded, her eyes glazed with desire as he lifted her easily into his arms. "Near the border, huh? That's pretty far from
Tacoma."

"Yes, it is," he said, keeping his tone noncommittal.

The bathtub was already filled and the water temperature
perfect, as were the rose petals floating on the surface. He knelt
beside the tub and she slid into the water without a sound.

He settled on his haunches and gazed at her, his chest tight,
his cock and balls swinging freely between his legs. She was
slick and rosy; her breasts bobbed on the water's surface, and
her perfect legs stretched to the end of the extra long tub.
"You're so beautiful." His voice held the surprising hush of awe.

She turned her lovely face to his and frowned. "Aren't you
coming in too? There's room." She drew her legs up to her
chest to prove it.

"I'd like to bathe you. Run my hands all over your wet skin and slide the soap everywhere." This was new for him. Quiet and sensual wasn't his thing. But with Carrie, sex felt brand new. Undiscovered territory and adventure waited for them. He might as well enjoy it while it lasted. With her life in Tacoma and his on the other side of the country, when they left the house, they'd leave each other behind.

But for the time they had together, he'd pretend things were different. He'd pretend he wasn't lying about why he was here and who he was. He'd pretend they had a shot at something more.

She blushed prettily and he got caught by the assessing intelligence in her eyes. So many of his thoughts didn't seem to belong to him, he wondered if she guessed what he was thinking.

"I could get used to this," she said, relaxing her neck to rest her head on the tub rim. Her eyelids drifted shut while he took a bar of red glycerine soap in one hand and a soft cotton cloth in the other.

He lathered up the cloth and began at her neck, paying close attention to the flesh under her ears. He'd found the spot with his teeth earlier, and her soft moan now confirmed her enjoyment of the attention there. She rolled her head as he massaged. "This is so nice, Matt. Incredible."

Next he swept down to her bobbing breasts and slid the terry cloth back and forth across her hardening nipples one after the other. Her knees fell open under the water as her breath caught on a sigh of satisfaction.

As he moved, the splash of water muted to soft quiet. His cock stiffened as he watched her lips part in sensual enjoyment. He bent and took one nipple into his mouth and sucked strongly.

"Oh, that's good! So good . . ." She rose out of the water with the suckling, offering more. He took it, swirling his tongue around her crested breast.

She arched up and her eyes flew open. "Touch me, Matt, I need your hand."

He obliged and slid one hand behind her back to hold her for his lips, while the other hand sought the wet heat of her.

Even in the water, she felt hotter, wetter in her slick center.

He speared her with two fingers at once and she arched higher and groaned. Her hips undulated on his fingers, while his thumb found her clitoris.

Stroked.

Rubbed.

Rolled.

She panted and bucked against him. The water sloshed and waves threatened her open mouth as she reached for another orgasm.

"Let go, Carrie. Come on my hand. Come the way I know you want to." His cock stood at full attention now and his balls tightened into rocks as he watched her full-out orgasm. Her inner muscles clenched around his fingers and her clit plumped to a firm pearl under his thumb.

As she took what he freely offered, his heart opened up only to be filled with the essence of Carrie. Yes, for as long as he could, he'd pretend they could have a life together after Perdition.

7

"A buffet breakfast is served in the dining room." Matt was shaving, so Carrie read aloud from the service card, letting her voice carry through to him. The scent of roses still perfumed the steamy air from the bathroom.

"I'm starved," Matt responded. He hummed while he shaved, the sound distorted by the movement of his disposable razor and his jaw contortions. She grinned at the mental image of him in front of the antique sink and mirror, removing all the stubble from his jaw. For her. He'd scraped the side of her inner thigh with his bristles this morning.

She contracted her thighs in memory. Then palmed her soft belly, thinking of the kisses he'd planted on her navel. Mmm. Slipping lower, she tapped at her clit.

Nice. She was so responsive, so very . . . aware. Of her skin, her nerve endings. Even her hair follicles seemed more sensitive. She combed through her curls and tugged.

If she wasn't careful she'd be in need again. Matt would definitely be up for it; the man's stamina was nothing less than astounding, but she was sore.

Her stomach growled, reminding her they both needed food if this hot sex was going to continue. And she badly wanted it to continue. His comment last night about wanting more than the weekend resonated with her.

Too bad he lived so far from Tacoma. She envisioned a few weekend visits, but the distance would eventually become burdensome. Whatever heat they shared would cool, leaving them friends.

Could be worse, she thought.

"The coffee service was great," he called, referring to the silver tray left outside their door an hour before, "but a man needs sustenance if he plans to pleasure a woman all day."

She chuckled. "I was just thinking that myself," she admitted with another tap to her clit. Moisture gathered in her channel as she rubbed experimentally. Her legs fell open while she wondered if she had time to get herself off before he came back into the room.

But then, so what if he did see her? She was supposedly here for a sexually liberal weekend. Pleasure was the name of the game.

A very enjoyable game.

She heated and thrilled to her toes. Pleasure was hardly the word she would use. Ecstasy was more like it. And not the phony drug variety of ecstasy. Pure, unadulterated, sexually charged sensory overload had been with her all night.

And it looked to be around for the rest of the day too.

Suddenly hot and aroused to the point of not caring what he saw, she threw the covers off and plunged two fingers into her dripping pussy.

She used her other hand on her clit, rubbing harder and faster. *Harder. Faster.* The thought came again as she swirled. Tension built and speared up from her pussy to her womb as delicious clenches rolled along her inner muscles.

Release was sweet and rolled through her like an incoming tide. Legs splayed wide, she threw her head back and rode it out, feeling wanton and sated.

The sound from the bathroom changed from a hum to a whistle. She plunged her fingers in again to coax the last of the trembles to completion.

Matt gave a low whistle from the bathroom doorway. His eyes focused hungrily on her. The sight of him, fresh and clean and shaved, made her feel dirty, sweaty and very naughty.

She pulled her fingers out of her slickness, then slid them across her mouth. "Want a taste?"

Apparently he did. His eyes flared and his cock twitched to life. She smiled and crooked her finger at him.

He crossed to her and sat on the bedside. Grasping her wrist, he nibbled and licked at her pussy-wet fingers, sliding his tongue deep into the apex. She melted as he made love to her sensitive flesh.

The man was incredible. Warm, kind and oh-so-sexy. He clasped her hips and pulled her down the bed. He climbed on top of her, then growled and twisted around so his cock speared toward her mouth, while he nuzzled at the juncture of her thighs.

Enthusiastic in his tongue work, Matt nibbled and licked his way from her clit to her trench. Once he found the source of her creamy liquid, he scooped into her with his tongue and drank her essence.

With a squeal of delighted abandon, Carrie locked her heels around his head and opened her mouth to take his cock in a long deep suckling that made him groan.

She opened her throat and let him set the pace and the depth while she worked him.

His chin played her clit while his lips nibbled and took, driving her into a frenzy of rising need. No longer able to give him control, she set her heels into the mattress and arched up to his mouth, demanding he take her over the top.

He obliged, driving fingers into her and using the flat of his tongue to hold her clit while she rocked against him.

She crested and crooned, deepening her hold on his cock while she gushed into his mouth.

After he held her at the peak for as long as he could, he set her hips free again and stilled while she swirled her tongue around the head of his cock. Pre-cum leaked into her mouth, tasting slick and salty good.

She pressed his balls in a gentle squeeze until they tightened. With a wild groan, he pulled out of her mouth and spilled across her tits, spewing cum with a roar of release. He smoothed his hot semen around her breasts, massaging it into her nipples and down to her smooth belly.

He rolled off her and they lay together, head to toe. "Fuck, that was good, Carrie. You're so hot, I don't know how you manage to live without getting laid by every man who walks by."

She laughed and kissed his big toe. "I rarely get laid," she confessed. "Maybe that's why I'm making up for lost time."

"Maybe. But I find it hard to believe you'd have to come here to pay for a weekend of sex."

The lie she'd told ate at her, making her feel small. She wished she could tell him the truth about her note taking and the article, but she couldn't. Not yet, at least.

Matt rolled off the bed and walked to the closet. His back view was as perfect to Carrie as his front.

His ass was high and hard, his legs perfectly formed. The shoulders she'd clung to were broad while the muscles in his back were defined. He pulled out a thick velour robe with the Perdition House crest embroidered on the lapel. The navy blue made his skin glow with vibrant health, and he took her breath away when he slipped it on.

He didn't bother with the house slippers, preferring bare feet. "I'll bring you back a plate of food from the dining room. Eggs? Toast? Bacon?"

Her stomach growled. "Yes, yes and yes. I think you've given me one hell of a cardio workout." Then she patted her butt muscles and gave them a deep rub. "My hips are done for too," but she gave him a teasing smile when he frowned and looked concerned.

Then he grinned at her tease. Deeply engaged eye contact warmed her.

"Miss me," he said as he pulled open the door and stepped into the hall.

The nutty thing was, she probably would miss him.

And that was worth noting. She found her laptop under the bed and dragged it out. There was no wireless connection at the house so she couldn't check her e-mail in-box, but she could type up more notes.

Her plans to interrogate Matt had gone awry. The only thing she'd established was her own seemingly insatiable desire for sex. Need for Matt and the sensual pleasure he gave her had outstripped her ambition by far.

And while that should terrify her, she couldn't drum up enough interest to care. The man devastated her on too many levels to count.

She was busy keyboarding when Matt returned laden with a serving tray and food that smelled delicious. She put the finishing touches to notes on her freshly discovered masturbation techniques and some of the thoughts that had driven her when she'd been doing it. Some of those thoughts didn't even seem like her own, she now realized.

She saved the file and closed the lid of her laptop as Matt kicked closed the door.

"Hey, you need to give that thing a rest," he said with a nod to her laptop. "This is a weekend dedicated to R & R, remember?" He set the round waiter's tray of food on an octagonal marble-top occasional table set in the bow window. Set to each side were low, velvet brocade chairs in classic Victorian style.

She grinned at him. "You're right. I need to stop obsessing on work."

"You haven't told me what you do that needs all this attention."

"I'm a fact checker for a syndicated television news show."

"That sounds interesting. You must know a lot of trivia."

"I know how to find trivia, do research, that kind of thing. It's pretty boring mostly." She'd thrown in the bit about television because she thought he'd believe she made enough money for a weekend like this one. The food saved her from more lies, as the smell of bacon rose through the room.

"This smells great!" Something she couldn't say for her own body. Instead of being practical and showering while Matt was downstairs, she'd wasted time typing notes that didn't mean anything. She shook her head. Her notes meant the beginning of the article that would land her a better job.

And she was dangerously close to forgetting that fact.

"Are your thoughts wandering?" she asked. "I can't seem to keep mine on track. Whenever I think of work, I get fuzzy headed."

"Me too. So I've stopped thinking about work. It's easier. Go with the flow, Carrie. The weekend's about you and me, nothing else. Even if I wanted to think of something else, I can't get you out of my mind. The way you smell, taste, kiss. It's all I think about."

She warmed, surprised at how easily he confessed his fascination.

"Just now, in the dining room," he said as he tore a piece of toast in two, "a pile of hash browns reminded me of your pretty pink pussy. The length and shape, I mean. I stared at them for a full minute trying to clear the image, but I couldn't. It was like I was up close and personal, ready to stick my tongue between your lips and eat you out. Suck you dry. Took all my willpower just to use the serving spoon. Felt like desecration or something. And then, all I wanted was to be upstairs in the room again, to see that you were all right."

"And you found me working." She grinned. Not that she could remember anything about what she'd typed.

"Yes. You were working when I wanted you to be thinking of me too."

She chuckled. "I promise to think of you and nothing else for the rest of the day."

"And night." A feverish light filled his gaze.

"All weekend. We're together all weekend." Bought and paid for, just the way the auction promised. Only in their case the buying had been his choice. There wasn't another woman here he wanted to be with.

Matt Crewe was all hers.

And she was his.

"Breakfast is served," he said, tucking into his eggs.

"This would be lovely and formal if I weren't naked and you weren't in a robe." She should have showered. Her notes could have been done at any time. They weren't important.

Matt was important.

This weekend with him was important. A new job wasn't.

She shook her head, rattled by the turn of her thoughts.

He dropped his robe to the floor and eased into his seat. "Now we're even."

She chuckled and tried to recall what questions she needed to ask him. But it wasn't easy. Her normally incisive mind went foggy. She couldn't even remember what she'd just been typing. No matter. It was either notes for a story or an e-mail. Or something equally boring.

She set her chin on her hand and drank in the sight of Matt, her meal forgotten. He was gorgeous. "In this light, your hair catches the sunlight and it looks like sparkly bubbles. Like the ones in a glass of good beer."

He grinned tidily around a mouthful of scrambled eggs. "You need to eat, Carrie. The nutrition deprived are targets for mind control."

She giggled, feeling light and free. "Mind control." There was something she needed to ask him. Questions. Answers, questions, answers. What the hell, none of it mattered. What mattered was that her boobs were hot.

She looked down at them. The steam from her eggs wafted across her nipples. She giggled again.

"Carrie, eat." His voice was a teensy bit more stern.

"You're cute when you're concerned." She picked up her fork and did as she was told. "These are good," she muttered as she polished off her eggs. She carefully scraped the side of her fork across the plate, scooping every last bit of egg. Then she wadded three strips of bacon into her mouth with her fingers. She chewed around another giggle.

"Do you have a health thing I should know about?" He stared in shock at her, making her giggle again. "Are you diabetic? Or, I don't know, something." He looked way past concerned now. He seemed downright worried.

"You look so anxious. Which is funny because . . . hmmm, I don't know why it's funny, it just is. And no, I don't have any health issues." She was healthy. Always had been. "So . . . if you wanna go bareback that's fine with me. Would you like that? Feeling all that wet pussy on your cock when you're inside? Warm, wet pussy." That was really hysterical. "Warm, wet." She repeated the words in her head, emphasizing the T sound on *wet*.

"We're practically strangers and you want bareback? No way." He poured her more coffee and lifted the cup so she'd take it.

She did and drank the whole cup at once. "Did I just suggest we forgo condoms?" Horrified, she stared at the empty cup and couldn't remember drinking it.

He snapped his fingers three inches from her face. "Track my fingers." He moved them left to right and back again. She followed them and focused as hard as she could. "And yes, you asked if I wanted bareback."

"That's crazy." She looked at her plate. Scraped clean. She never ate that much breakfast. She'd had enough food on her plate to feed a lumberjack.

She ran a hand across her belly. "I can't believe I finished my plate." She leaned back in her chair and took stock of how she felt. Stomach full, pulse normal, fog lifting from her mind. She smiled. "I'm fine now. Maybe you were right about me being nutrition deprived. I got lightheaded." Crazy was more like it.

"Yes, that must be it."

"Did many people eat in the dining room?" At least she hadn't made a public fool of herself. With Matt she could be anything. Foolish or smart, sexy or not, sharp minded or foggy. He seemed to like her every mood.

As much as she liked his.

Like the one he was in now for instance. Concerned but happy. Conscious of her every thought and word. But aware, too, of her need. Always aware.

"None of the women were there, just the men. Everyone must have decided to eat in their rooms."

"At the same time," she said, wondering at the coincidence. "And only the men went for the food?"

He nodded. "Not a woman in sight. You'd expect at least a couple of them would want to choose their own breakfast." He frowned, obviously thinking as hard as she was about the oddity.

"Especially if they're used to running companies and managing departments," she added. "Do you think they feel as foggy headed as we do sometimes?"

He shrugged. "Who cares? I want to focus on us today. What would you like to do now?"

She let the questions go, uncertain that she cared enough to pursue them. Matt didn't care, she shouldn't either.

"Mind if we go for a walk around the grounds?" Movement would help digest the lumberjack special.

"A walk would be great." He reached out and moved a tendril of hair from beside her eye. "There are several acres to explore. Woods ring the grounds and there's a gazebo in the side yard at the foot of the lawn."

"Give me fifteen minutes," she said, scooting into the bathroom to shower.

The sting of water on her face cleared her thoughts again. Something weird was going on with her. Matt was right. She should see her doctor. First thing Monday, she'd make an appointment.

Offering Matt bareback was insane. Gobbling her food like a robot was off the wall. But when she thought about it, she'd had the same reaction to her dinner last night.

The meal had been perfect, served impeccably. But she couldn't recall tasting any of the courses or the wine.

She had to be slipping a couple of mental gears. The question was, why? How? Was there some drug in the food?

Doubtful, she realized. Drugs were created for serious health concerns. No pharmaceutical company spent money just to muddle up your head. Matt had the right idea. She should focus on the weekend and spending this time with him.

So what if it took her years to find another breakout story. She tried to like the idea of plodding from dog shows and theme-decorated houses to mall openings.

No, no, no! She would not let her career stagnate. She had to stay focused. She scrubbed her face with both hands, trying to shake her brain cells back into the correct configuration. If only it were that easy.

She thought back over the notes she'd typed, reminded herself of the questions she still needed to ask.

Right now, as the hot water streamed over her, she knew what she needed to do.

Talk with Faye Grantham. Openly and candidly. A chat with Liam Watson would get her answers as well.

An engaging conversation, a few remarks deftly woven through an easygoing chat would get her started. Yes, that would work.

She'd try to set something up for later.

She shut the water off and stepped out of the shower. Matt waited, fully dressed, with a heavy heated towel for her. The guests of Perdition House were afforded every luxury.

She smiled at Matt. And promptly forgot what it was that had seemed so important just a moment ago.

"Thank you," she said, and raised her face to his to kiss the tip of his nose.

Bemused and amused, he followed her into the bedroom and watched as she dressed.

By the time they got to the bottom of the stairs, they realized they were in the middle of a stampede of people. Everyone who had been at the auction the night before was in the front hall. "What is this?" Matt said, more to himself than to Carrie.

"Curiouser and curiouser," she muttered, leaning up to his ear. "It's like a cattle drive. Did we all get the same idea at the same time again?" Like sending the men to get breakfast and eating it in their rooms. "Was everyone having sex at the same time too?"

"I don't know, but I'm not heading out the door with everyone else," he said. Then he grabbed her by the hand and tugged her along behind him as he skirted through the crowd to the dining room.

The room was blessedly empty. All evidence of breakfast had disappeared. Not a serving tray remained; all the dishes were cleared. Not even the scent of bacon remained in the room. She hardly had time to register the lack of scent when, without stopping, he pushed through the swinging door.

"You can admire the kitchen later," Matt said as he led Carrie through the swinging door from the dining room. "We've got to get outside." Where he could think. Carrie wasn't the only one with thoughts that led nowhere. Maybe outdoors he'd be away from whatever the hell influenced them inside the house.

He tightened his grip on her hand, determined to keep her moving when she stalled to stare open-mouthed at the kitchen. It was like stepping back through decades, but he couldn't afford to stop and admire.

Urgency to get outside rode him hard. He passed a pantry door on the left, barely registering the bottles of preserves that still lined the shelves.

"Wow," Carrie said from behind him. "Look at all this stuff." Her voice had the faraway sound in it that told him she'd gone foggy again.

Through the window in the top half of the door he saw a couple of high-backed wicker chairs. Obviously a side porch.

All he had to do was step outside and Carrie's head would clear. If he could just keep her moving, they'd be fine.

He opened the door and heard low voices coming from his right. A man and a woman. The man's feet rested on a low wicker table.

"Someone's out there," he whispered to Carrie, holding her behind him, hesitating. He wasn't sure he wanted to be seen, but the need to escape the house overrode his caution.

"So?"

"So, nothing. Let's go."

He opened the door and stepped out onto the side porch, keeping Carrie close behind him.

"Good morning, Matt. Ms. MacLean," Faye Grantham said

with a merry smile and nod of greeting. "Care to join us?" She waved an elegant hand to encompass the high-backed wicker chairs.

"How lovely!" Carrie said and took a seat. Her face lit up happily.

The urgency to flee the house winked out and he slid into the chair beside Carrie. She was different from Faye. Faye was sexy, beautiful, and he could see why Liam Watson had fallen for her. But to Matt, she was just a lovely woman, not a woman to be desired.

He saved all that for Carrie. Odd how right that felt already, but there it was. He couldn't see himself with any other woman.

Faye's lush curves were draped in dark pink satin. Delicate lace trailed from her elbow to her wrists. The nightgown and matching robe were like something out of a thirties movie, sleek and clingy. The setting, the clothes, even her swept-up hairstyle, made Faye elegant. In a lot of ways she looked like she belonged in another time. The perfect hostess for Perdition House because the mansion *was* from another time.

Beside him sat Carrie, dressed in jeans and a fleece with a well-worn pair of sneakers on her feet. He'd rather be alone with Carrie, but she looked more interested in chatting with Faye and Liam for the moment.

Two extra coffee mugs sat on the tray beside Liam Watson. "Did you expect us?"

"Of course; we often have people drop by here. This side of the house is more private. And our guests always seek privacy." She assessed them both with a critical eye. "You seem quite refreshed this morning. Enjoying yourselves?"

"Very much," Carrie said, reaching for the coffee mug Faye offered.

Matt accepted a mug as well, keeping a sharp eye on Carrie

for any befuddled behavior. Maybe the earlier silliness had been lightheadedness from hunger, but he had his doubts.

"So, Faye," Carrie said quickly. Her eyes looked bright and inquisitive. She seemed fine. As sharp minded as he'd ever seen her. "Have you always lived here?"

"No, I haven't. I inherited Perdition from a great aunt."

"It's beautiful. You're lucky to live here."

"Luck has nothing to do with it," Faye remarked. "It's difficult to keep up, expensive to maintain and I'm forever fielding the temptation to sell it to developers." She glanced pointedly off to the right, as if addressing someone else.

Liam cleared his throat. "What about you, Matt? What is it you do when you're not . . ."

"Selling myself?" Matt smiled to let the other man know there were no hard feelings. "I'm a writer working on a screenplay," he lied.

Carrie took a sharp breath and stared at him. "A writer?" she said, clearly shocked. "You didn't tell me that."

"I dabble," he admitted, and sipped at his coffee watching Faye's reaction. He couldn't recall what phony career he'd created on his questionnaire.

While Liam gave a light cough of surprise, Faye smiled enigmatically. "Good luck," she said. "I hear selling a screenplay is tough. Perhaps you should stop into my store, TimeStop, and talk with Kim, my manager at the Fremont location. She's got a lot of contacts in Hollywood."

"TimeStop? That's an interesting name," Carrie said. "What do you sell?"

"Hollywood castoffs mostly. I used to specialize in clothing from the heyday of Hollywood." She waved a hand down the bodice of her gown to indicate the decades-old style. "But lately we've been doing a brisk business in more contemporary pieces."

"Your peignoir is beyond beautiful," Carrie gushed, and reached out to fondle the lace that trailed from Faye's wrist.

Faye indulged her feminine response to lovely material with a pleased smile. "Thank you. It was worn in a musical in 1936." She fluttered the sleeves, and Carrie gave a sigh of appreciation. The women lapsed into a conversation sprinkled with words like *ruche* and *bias cut* and *rhinestones,* and both men tuned them out with a shared grin.

"Interesting architecture here," Matt said.

"I could show you around some," Liam offered. "There have been several additions, all of them in the same style, all of them at least seventy-five years old. The original building is coming up to a century."

"Let's go," Matt responded, and stood.

They left the women chatting. Matt had a feeling that once out of earshot, their conversation would change. Carrie's questions had taken a turn to more recent times. He heard the word *auction* come up just as he and Liam walked around the corner out of earshot.

Carrie caught a glimpse of the men as they rounded the front turret, deep in conversation about the foundation. Liam pointed to something by the wall. Matt looked interested and walked up to examine the brick and mortar. He really did have a nice butt.

She turned back to Faye and went in for the kill. "So, how did you come up with the idea for the bachelor auctions, Faye?"

"It seemed a good way to launch a business. Promotional dollars being at a premium, and the house being my biggest asset, it seemed a good match. Perdition House has a reputation for providing the ultimate in accommodations."

She'd just bet. "It's odd, but before I arrived I thought I'd look up whatever information I could find on the house itself.

The architectural history, the historical archives, that kind of thing. There's no mention anywhere. Hard to believe a home of this size, with grounds like this still in existence, would be ignored by so many people who've been painstaking in their drive to protect and preserve places just like this."

"I've never checked archives. But I dare say not many people want my family home listed on any historical documents." She leaned forward and dropped her voice to a conspiratorial whisper. "Seems it was used as a house of pleasure for too many years. Right up until the mid-1960s, in fact."

She glanced to the right of Carrie's shoulder, then winked.

Perdition was still a house of pleasure, she thought. Sexual heat spiked from her lowest belly to her heart and she broke out into a light sweat.

8

Carrie's nerves screeched as she shifted her eyes enough to catch sight of a shadow beside her. It blinked out. Gone, definitely gone, along with the chill it had radiated. She ran her palm along the back of her upper arm. "What was that?"

"Excuse me?" Faye looked wide-eyed with surprise. Phony as hell.

"Someone was right there, next to me. I know it." She peered around the wing of the chair trying to figure out what she'd seen. "And so do you."

"I know nothing of the sort." Faye sipped her coffee calmly.

"Perdition House has secrets, and I aim to dig them out and expose them."

"Even if you find what you think you're looking for, no one will believe you. I fear someone's put strange thoughts in your head."

"I've been taking notes, Faye. This house is not as simple as it appears." But it was also so much more complex than anything she'd ever experienced. No mere article in a local newspaper could do this place justice. The enormity of her foolish declaration swamped her.

Her hostess looked unperturbed by the threat of exposure, confirming Carrie's defeat. In fact, Faye looked downright relaxed. "Speaking of notes, if you'd like to check your e-mail while you're here, please feel free to use my office. You're more than welcome to plug into my Internet connection."

If the woman had something to hide, she'd be kicking Carrie to the curb by now. "Thank you, I will," Carrie responded. Either that or she knew how futile it would be for Carrie to pursue the matter further.

"We haven't gone wireless at Perdition because we see the place as an oasis away from worldly pressures. Our guests badly need downtime, and we've found complete avoidance is the best way to get that kind of rest."

Somehow control of the conversation had been taken from her and she had no way to get it back because the men returned. Matt looked into her gaze and smiled warmly.

Deep affection sparked between them and she let go of her notion to interrogate Faye further. It was clear the woman was too smart to release any information by mistake.

Matt held out his hand to her and she responded with sexual need. "Let's enjoy the grounds, before the rain comes."

She checked the sky. Sure enough, clouds hung low over the horizon, threatening rain for the afternoon. She warmed at the idea of getting cozy with Matt under the thick down duvet in their room. She loved listening to rain on the windows while she was snuggled under cover.

And snuggling with Matt seemed to dominate her thoughts. He held her gaze, mentally wrapping his wide heavy arms around her, and she soaked up the heat.

She put her hand in his and rose, without so much as a nod in farewell to the other couple.

Matt. This weekend was all about Matt. The questions she'd thought were so important to ask Faye drifted away like smoke on the wind.

They held hands, hers warm and snug in his larger one, and crossed the lawn to the cliffs overlooking Shilshole Bay. "Liam told me there used to be a set of stairs around here somewhere, but they got shaky and some decades ago they collapsed. He told me he heard a great story about one of the women who lived here racing down the stairs stark naked."

"Hope it was midsummer." She shivered as a cold gust of wind clawed her back. In spite of the fleece and jeans she wore, the bite of cold went through to her bones. She leaned into Matt's warmth. His arm came up around her shoulders as they edged closer to the cliff. "I can't imagine running headlong down this vertical drop. I'd get dizzy."

The push of cold behind her made her turn her head sharply, and for a split second she caught sight of bare flesh and long, streaming hair as another gust went through her. The image disappeared down the cliff.

A second later, Matt lurched and steadied again.

A darker shadow emerged through Matt's chest and headed down the cliff too.

As if . . .

As if . . .

No, it was just the shadow of the incoming clouds. Had to be.

"Did you feel that rush of cold? We should head back. It's too windy out here. I don't want you too close to the edge if the rain comes in hard. Could get slippery." He stepped back and urged her away.

"Thanks. Maybe we should head for the gazebo to see it while we still can." The clouds gathered, grays deepening to a threat.

"Did you see shadows a moment ago?" he asked.

"I thought I did, but then, I've seen a lot of strange shadows since I came in through the gates."

"Me too."

They turned and headed for the gazebo, still dappled with sunny light. The eight-sided structure had white pickets with a green roof. Faye obviously spent a lot of time in it because the benches were covered with happy yellow gingham seat cushions and pillows in contrasting bold colors. The effect made Carrie think of continual summertime.

As they got closer, she heard a tinny music play. "Can you see speakers anywhere?"

"No, but then, speakers can be minuscule these days. They may be in the trees that ring the lawns."

"I wonder how deep that ring of trees is."

"Let's go find out. But I believe there's at least an acre between the lawns and the fence line."

They bypassed the gazebo and turned left toward the trees. "Lions and tigers and bears . . ." chanted Carrie.

Matt laughed, stopped walking and turned toward Perdition House. "Heaven only knows what we'll see in these woods, Carrie. You feel adventurous?"

"With you? Yes." The slash of his grin was all the reassurance she needed.

They stepped into the cool shade of the trees and the world fell silent. No birds sang, no sounds of the surf, even the tinny waltz music disappeared.

"Guess we'll never find where that music's coming from."

"It doesn't matter where the speakers are," said Matt, and she agreed. Right now, this minute, all she wanted to hear was her own breathing.

And Matt's, in her ear, trailing down her neck, past her chest, her navel and into the melting spot between her legs.

Need raced and ping-ponged around and through her. His

eyes heated and his cock rose against her hip. "Do you feel that? This heat? Different from the cold down by the cliff edge."

She nodded, unsure if her voice would work.

She checked over her shoulder and saw another couple dancing in the gazebo. "Look, do you see them too?"

"Yes," he responded without looking. He was focused on running his palm up and down her arm. She pulled away from him.

"No, look. Really look at them. Do you recognize them from last night?"

The woman was tall, slender, with burnished copper hair, and the man wore a navy peacoat with a captain's hat. They danced beautifully, perfectly in tune and in step with each other.

"No, he's not one of the men."

And she knew.

Accepted and understood.

"The biggest secret of Perdition House is the ghosts." She shuddered, surprised she wasn't more fearful.

He nodded. "You okay with that?"

"Say good-bye to my hard-hitting news career. It's back to fluff and the family pages for me." No other paper in the country would hire her even if she did manage to get her story printed.

"You're a journalist?"

"Obviously not a very good one." She looked up at him. "I got involved in my story. In fact, I'm so involved I can't remain objective enough to report what I've learned about these sex-for-sale phoney charity auctions." She nearly said the weekend was a waste, but she knew better. It might not make her career, but her love life had spiked into the stratosphere.

"A journalist," he repeated. "Not a fact checker?"

"Mad at me?"

He shook his head. "I'm not mad. In fact I'm relieved. I haven't exactly been honest either."

"What do you mean?" Her belly flopped. If he said he was a gigolo she'd eat her hat. She really really really didn't want Matt Crewe to be a pro. She held her breath and braced for the ugly truth.

"I'm writing a book on sex clubs. Not an expose like your article. But a nonfiction book on why sex clubs exist in today's sexually free society. No matter how free we say we are, sexuality is still frowned upon in a lot of circles. And any sexuality that veers from the straight and narrow definition of one man and one woman is generally kept private."

"Like in clubs."

"Exactly. Now, are you disappointed I wasn't honest with you?"

She rolled her eyes. "I'm no hypocrite." She sighed. "From a career standpoint the time here was wasted, but I'll just have to go back to searching for my big story. I'll find one someday."

"Will you still report on the auctions and expose Faye's sideline?"

"I have to think about it. Present company and myself excepted, I don't like people who cheat and lie. Never have. It's one of the reasons I want to move into investigative journalism."

"You lied to me." But his eyebrows rose and lips twitched in humor as he said it.

She pursed her lips. "You lied first. You pretended to be a pro, you took me behind those draperies and made sure I got a good taste of you so I'd bid on you."

He flushed the most gorgeous manly shade of red. "What would you say if I told you I think the spirits made me do it?"

"You mean they messed with your head too?" She remembered all too vividly the feel of heavy velvet hands in the draperies, the writhing people on the fireplace mantel. "The whole building is a sexual portal for what? For whom?"

"The spirits of dead hookers? Their johns?" He echoed her own conclusion.

She looked through the trees to the dancing couple in the gazebo. Their expressions shone with love, their body language took them to an exquisite place of yearning and connectedness she could only hope to experience. "These are more than hookers and johns, Matt. Look at their expressions."

"I see."

The spirits of Perdition were lovers, friends, confidants and mates. Eternal mates. Love glowed around the dancing couple, sparkled as they twirled in each other's arms.

The vision of the pair winked out suddenly, and the gazebo was empty and still. "Matt, we're being given a message."

He nodded. "You're right. But I never thought, never imagined my research would find me wanting so much. Needing this much." He turned her to face him and his eyes glowed with deep affection and caring.

She wanted him to ravish her, to tear off her clothes and drill his cock into her on the leaf litter at their feet, but he didn't.

Instead, he stole her heart. And gave her his.

Cupping her head in his palms, he blessed her forehead with a kiss, moved his lips lovingly across her brows, her nose, lips and chin. When he tilted his head back to see her, he smoothed her cheeks with his thumbs.

She melted into a puddle as he finally tipped his mouth to hers in a kiss that rattled its way into her chest.

"What's happening to us?" she breathed.

"I don't know, but I like it."

A bird twittered overhead and Carrie caught a flash of color in the leaves. A finch. Pretty and yellow, the bird tilted its head this way and that, then took off.

"That's the first bird I've seen here," she said, and followed the erratic flight as the finch flew deeper into the trees. A few yards in, she spied the bird on another tree branch in a tiny clearing. Well out of view of the lawns stood a huge maple tree. The trunk was wide, the branches sturdy, the leaves big as the span of two hands. The finch's yellow head blended into the autumn color of the leaves.

Hanging from one of the sturdiest branches was a swing. The seat was covered in delicate silk and rounded.

Matt lifted the seat to inspect it. "This isn't wood, it's like a padded bottom, rounded to be comfortable." He lifted the seat to face height and peered through a hole at her. He waggled his eyebrows at her through the hole. "You don't suppose?"

"This was used for sex?" she breathed, hopeful that they'd discovered the exact purpose. But she was already melting into her panties at the idea of sex in the woods.

Matt looked to the sky. Brilliant sunshine beamed down on him. The clearing warmed and went softly silent as the moment stretched between them.

"I'll never get another chance like this again," she said, and stripped off her jeans.

He laughed, delighted with her readiness, and stepped out of his jeans too. He was cocked and loaded and Carrie salivated at the sight of all that beautiful jutting flesh. All for her.

For all time. The thought wasn't hers, she was sure of it, but she wished it was.

9

Carrie dropped her fleece to the ground but left her T-shirt on. Even though the sun shone on the clearing, it was still late September. Besides, Matt looked more interested in her body below the waist for the moment.

His gaze bored into hers as she settled her behind into the slinglike swing. Instantly, the seat molded to her bottom, the hole in perfect position to expose her secret flesh. Matt chuckled deep and throaty as he clasped her hips and rocked her to and fro in the swing.

"Put your legs up," he said.

She tilted back and lifted her legs. He grasped her ankles and set her heels into padded stirrups. She gasped at the sensation. Cool air tickled her pussy as Matt made certain she was comfortable in the odd position.

She soon felt completely at ease as her weight settled into the sling. Whoever had designed the swing had thought of comfort and ease of movement.

"I've been to some clubs where swings were in use, but I

didn't see anything like this. What a great design," he said with admiration in his voice. He inspected the stirrups again. Ran his hands from her heels, down her legs past her knees to her buttocks. "You're comfortable?"

"I'm wet and wide open and horny as hell. Now get busy!" Her frustration with the whole setup had her edgy. She needed filling and she needed it now. She wasn't sure how long she could stay in this position and she didn't have time for a male's interest in mechanics.

He chuckled and ran an experimental finger along her open outer lips. She jerked at his touch, inflamed all over again.

Fire, she felt fire on his finger. Fire that traced her from her clit to her ass button, skirting the deeper, moister flesh she needed touched the most.

"You're so lovely. Pink and wet and open. For me, Carrie. Just for me." His voice firmed on the last words and all she could do was nod yes. "Say it," he demanded.

"Just for you, Matt Crewe, just for you."

His eyes narrowed. "Now, I'm going to lick you the way I want to."

"Please." She wriggled in the seat, wanting him to just get to it!

He knelt and she sighed with anticipation when his large hands cupped her bottom. He tilted her to his mouth like a chalice and drank from her.

The fire that had toyed with her flesh exploded into a conflagration the instant his mouth settled on her. She cried out, startling the finch out of the tree, as Matt suckled her clit gently, unerringly coaxing the small bud to reveal itself.

Carrie bucked against his mouth as best she could, but the position made movement next to impossible. She felt completely at his mercy, which didn't bother her in the least.

Matt was a kind, benevolent lover and attended to her needs

with gentleness. She relaxed and let him lick and please her and himself. The swing moved gently as he worked her sensitive flesh.

Finally she came in a rush of sensation so intense she imploded, her pussy drenching his mouth and chin with a mad gush. He lapped at the flowing juices and settled her with a firm palm on her lower belly to hold her. Mad with orgasm, she crooned and howled as Matt coaxed her and held her on the peak for as long as he dared.

The blood drained out of her legs as her orgasm waned and she felt lightheaded.

"Get me down," she gasped as her inner pulses ebbed.

He worked quickly and silently to release her heels. Her legs felt rubbery and out of control as she set her feet on the leaf-strewn ground.

Matt helped her stand, holding her in one arm while he unhooked the seat of the swing. It fell open, revealing the truth. In an intricate series of folds, the swing had a dual purpose. When open, it made a thick quilted blanket. When folded correctly, the quilt formed the swing seat.

"Ingenious," he said. Then he flapped the quilt out and settled it on the ground at Carrie's feet. She slid onto it in a heap, grateful to whoever had designed it.

She settled back on the quilt, and response rose at the sight of his unrelieved erection. The splendid purple head of his cock speared the air, so stiff it reached his navel. Wide, perfect, the shaft was roped with heavy veins, the root nestled in a patch of curls. Her mouth watered, but her legs were still wobbly and she couldn't trust they'd even let her crouch over him.

"Bring your cock up here." She patted her lips.

With an eager grin, Matt knelt beside her. With a worm's view of his cock and balls, she did a slow slide with her tongue from his tight hard sac up the heaviest vein to the weeping head.

He tasted sweet, salty, hot and ready. He shifted to give her room to set her head between his legs. She grinned up into his handsome face while she took each hard nut into her mouth. She sucked gently on each ball in turn, loving the shivers that ran through him.

He groaned at the wet contact of her mouth, the tickle of her tongue as it swirled and darted from one side of his sac to the other.

She played and cajoled and chuckled, sending shock waves up his body.

"Move up," he pleaded. "I need to feel your mouth all over."

That was the cue she'd wanted to hear. Rising to her elbow, she opened her throat and slid down his cock as far as she could go, drenching him. She rolled her tongue in swirls around him while her fingers played against his sac.

He roared his approval in a rain of love words that coaxed and seduced her.

With another wild groan, he pulled out of her mouth, slid on protection and mounted her in a deep spearing motion that took the breath out of her lungs.

Heaven! The heavy push–pull of his cock along her walls dragged her into another come immediately. Her clit, sticky and full, accepted each press and release as she tensed around him just before tipping over the precipice.

Her orgasm triggered his, and he reared up on his haunches, pulling her up with him. He surged deep into her and held her still while he spewed.

"Oh, Carrie, you're . . . love you . . ." he groaned, the rest of his words lost to her.

They collapsed together on the quilt, too sated to speak for a moment. Matt reached for the edge of the quilt and pulled it up over her gently. Then he tucked her head under his chin and rested in the quiet.

The sky above was still clear and she wondered where the

dark clouds had gone. Surely they'd have hit landfall by now. But the blue overhead seemed to go on for miles.

Matt's heart thudded under her ear, and contentment rose from her belly into her heart.

"What was that you mentioned about clubs?" Her journalist mind kicked in.

Matt looked rueful. "I've been researching sex clubs all across the country."

This was interesting. "Learn anything?"

"Just that I'll never wear a dog collar or get off giving orders." He grimaced.

"Leather hot pants might be cute," she teased. "I wouldn't mind seeing you in those." A hard edge of jealousy spiked at the idea of how many other women he'd had in these clubs. Experienced women. Wild women. Women who knew more about pleasing a man than she did. "So, how, ah, how many women did you do in these clubs?"

Great. Now her insecurity was out there where he couldn't miss it.

He snorted. "None. I was there to observe." His gaze went serious. "I haven't met anyone like you, Carrie. Not anywhere, not any time."

"So, I started out as a research subject? Just another woman who frequented a sex club."

"For all of thirty seconds. As soon as I got close to you, my mind went foggy and all I knew was that I had to have you." She remembered the intense focus he brought to her. It was like nothing she'd ever seen before.

"I had much the same reaction, but I fought it hard. My ambition's been all-consuming these last couple of months."

"Which is probably why you've gone in and out of the fog. You had a lot riding on staying sharp, so you fought harder than I did."

She shuddered. "Falling in and out of mental alertness was disquieting from my side of things," she said. "But I'm relieved I'm not dealing with a permanent chemical or nutritional imbalance. So, do you think once we leave we'll be back in charge of ourselves?" This incredible urge for sex might be gone too. "Will I feel the same way about you when I leave?"

He gathered her close. "I hope so, because I'm crazy about you, Carrie." He winced.

"Crazy might be the operative word, Matt." She pulled out of his arms. "I'm in over my head with this stuff. How can we trust what we're feeling if we slide in and out of our minds?"

"I don't know. Maybe we should ask Faye. Or Liam. He's pretty cool with what goes on here, but he lives away from the house, so he's got a clearer perspective."

"Good idea. What will you write about the house?"

"Not much. I won't divulge the name. The idea of the bachelor auctions deserves to be explained, but I'm not out to destroy Faye or the house. Especially not now." He took a quick glance around the clearing.

"Why not now?"

He picked up her other leg and started another massage. He had marvelous hands, strong but gentle. She settled in to enjoy the sensation of being served. "When I spoke with Liam, I got the lowdown on the mansion. The reasons for Faye's decision to run the auctions make it difficult to mess things up for her."

"You like her."

"So do you."

She bit her lip. He was right. There was something forthright about a woman who understood the difficulty of businesswomen having any kind of private sex life and doing something about it. Not everyone would approve. Not everyone would see the need for a place of respite and relaxation for powerful, career-oriented women. And certainly not many people would be able to provide a place like Perdition House.

"You have to admire a woman with a head for business like Faye Grantham."

"Yes, well." He cleared his throat. "Maybe it isn't Faye's business sense that we're admiring."

"What do you mean?" Her belly dropped because she wasn't sure she was ready to learn everything he knew.

"She's getting advice from a great aunt. An aunt named Belle Grantham."

"So?"

"Belle Grantham isn't exactly . . ." He trailed off and went red. Shook his head as if he couldn't believe what he was about to say. "She built the house. Back in 1911."

1911. The waltz music in the gazebo, the clothes the dancing couple wore. . . . Her belly dropped again.

"She isn't exactly alive, is she? That's what you're leading up to." She couldn't believe she'd said it, but the relief on his face made her breath catch. "Oh no!" She scrambled backward out of his grasp. He caught her ankles easily and dragged her back, worry etched into his features.

She sat up to face him. "It's more than shadows and images twirling in the breeze." More than the figures carved into the fireplace mantel and icy fingers in the draperies.

He enveloped her in his arms, rocked her side to side in a comforting gesture. "This mansion is full of spirits who don't know what will happen if the house is bulldozed." His voice rushed through her head as if he was afraid to stop speaking. As if he had to get it all out at once. She shivered and accepted his comfort, afraid her heart would pound out of her chest.

He tilted his head so he could look at her. She calmed. If Matt could handle this, she could too.

"If Faye can't afford to keep the house," he said, "she'll have to sell. These bachelor auctions provide enough money to keep the place going. But she's on a shoestring until her other business gets established. That will take awhile."

"Her second store location." TimeStop, a fitting name for a business selling vintage clothes to support the home of a bunch of sex-starved dead hookers and johns *from the last century!*

"Yes. That's why I decided not to mention the house by name."

Hardly sex starved, came a miffed feminine voice inside her head. *Now that we have all this fun with visitors, we do quite nicely in the orgasm department.* Crap! That sounded like a reasonable bit of conversation. Her world tilted and Carrie fought a faint. She put her head down, felt her blood rush. "I just heard a voice responding directly to my thoughts." This was too creepy for words.

"Take a few deep breaths," Matt coaxed.

Exhale. Inhale. Hold. Release.

Better. The blood stopped rushing and her heart returned to a more normal pace.

"And you've all figured out that I'm here to expose the secret," she said, talking to the voice in her head and to Matt at the same time.

"They probably knew before you arrived," Matt said.

That sent a chill to her bones. A chill that came from inside her, not from some unseen spirit lurking around them.

Her head stopped spinning and she chanced a look up at him. He smiled and palmed her shoulders. "I wanted to expose the bogus charity auction," she said. "Making these women think the money they spend is for charity is deceitful."

Check with Faye. See the books.

"I want to talk to Faye," she said. "I have questions."

"Of course you do. Any good journalist would."

She smiled at that. Matt smiled back and retrieved their clothes. They dressed quickly. The clouds finally darkened the clearing.

"In a weird way, I'll be sorry to leave the mansion," he said as they picked their way through the trees. "I found something here I never expected."

"What's that?"

"You."

10

Carrie closed the accounting program Faye used. She'd been surprised by the easygoing response to her request to see it. But then, Faye had good reason for wanting to share.

The mansion was doing a roaring business on lodging, but the actual auction money was going to different charities. Each charity was in some way involved with the welfare of women, children and families in need.

But there was one thing in the books that didn't jive with her own experience at the mansion.

"I don't see enough food supply bills on here to account for the five-star dining." She tapped her index nail on the desktop. Her suspicions proved correct when Faye went pink in the cheeks.

"That's because the guests are—how shall I put this?—encouraged to think they've eaten more and better than they have."

The spirits could make people think they'd eaten when they hadn't. A chill ran down her spine.

"So, what did we eat at dinner last night?" She recalled a

uous meal of five or six courses. A meal she'd eaten mechanically and couldn't remember chewing.

"Soup du jour and a nice array of deli sandwiches. Everyone ate. No one could make a guest think they'd eaten when they hadn't."

"Nice that you uphold such strict principles."

Faye flushed a deeper shade of red. "Thank you. If you noticed the lack of invoices for food, you'll also see that meals are included in the cost of the room."

The books showed the money bid for the bachelors was going to charity, while the income from the lodgings provided went to Perdition House.

A loophole perhaps, but a good one. For all intents and purposes, the auction seemed like any other bachelor auction. What happened after the bidding took place was a private matter between the bachelors and the women who bid for them. Around for years, these auctions were fun and an easy way to raise funds.

Carrie set her chin on her hand and looked at Faye.

"Yes, they buy sex," Faye admitted. "But the women who visit us need the quiet, restful atmosphere of Perdition House just as much. The sex is the best they'll probably ever have because they're relaxed. They're not squeezing time for sex out of busy schedules while they're here."

"You must have a lot of regulars."

Faye smiled. "We do. Will I give you a list of their names? Not on your life."

"I wouldn't expect you to. And I wouldn't ask. The women who attend these auctions were never my target. I never wanted to expose their secrets."

"Just mine." Faye nodded. "And now that you know the truth, what will you do?"

"Tell me about them, Faye. Why did the ghosts or spirits or

demons allow me to come if they already knew why I was coming?"

"Don't dare call them demons. They're lost souls, looking for their mates." She pursed her lips. "They brought you here because they've decided you need help."

"Help with what?"

"Your love life. You need help finding love, and since Matt was coming here anyway . . ."

The horror on her face must have been plain, because Faye's voice trailed away.

Carrie's hackles rose. "My love life? I don't need—"

The blond beauty raised her hand to cut off the protest. "Understand, this isn't me. I've been meddled with myself. Tortured in a way. My sex drive was tweaked to beyond bearable. I walked away from a wedding, had to choose between two new lovers, was driven to distraction by a practical joker who thought it was fun to have me fuck my brains out with a man I'd just met."

"Liam?"

She nodded.

"But he's a wonderful man."

"Exactly." She shrugged. "And then there was my landscape designer. She arrived and met a man my Aunt Belle had called in from Florida no less."

"And?"

"More meddling." Faye rolled her eyes. "I don't know how they do it, but they seem to know who needs help and who doesn't. But not everyone who comes to Perdition is receptive to the girls."

"The girls?"

"That's what I call them. But I suspect we've got a couple of men around too. I haven't met them all yet."

Carrie let the rest of her questions go. She had enough to digest for now. Like the idea that the story she'd hoped would get her out of the fluff pages wasn't even her own idea! How awful was that?

Defeated by the knowledge that she wasn't half as bright, or as dedicated as she thought she was, she slumped into the office chair.

"Why so dejected?" Faye asked.

She sighed and responded to the kind regard in the other woman's eyes. "Six months ago I was happy writing articles about the local scene. Dog shows were fun. I found a local author's book launch inspiring. During the holidays I even reported on craft fairs and found a way to enjoy it. But then, I soured on the whole thing. Needed to be harder hitting, sharper. I thought I'd come up with my breakout story on Perdition House myself. Now I find the idea was a ruse to get me here."

Faye nodded. "Your ambition made you set aside your dreams of love. That's probably when the girls picked up on you."

Carrie rolled her eyes. "Whoever heard of a bunch of hookers giving a rat's ass about love?"

"Hookers who found it themselves." The softness in Faye's tone touched a chord.

"One more question, if you don't mind."

"What is it?"

"Have these girls of yours been messing with Matt and me all along? Every time we made love?"

Faye considered. "Sometimes you can tell right away. Outrageous behavior outside the norm is a good sign they've given your sex drive a crank. But if you feel normal in your desire, it's likely all you. At least, that's what's been happening so far."

"Are they in my head during sex?" Or in her body?

Faye shrugged. "Probably not." Then she wrinkled her nose. "But they do like to feel orgasms."

"What?!"

"They leech off them." She held up her hand to silence her. "Maybe even enhance them. It's the only physical sensation they still have, so part of this is because they want to feel something again and the other part is about them helping you find love."

"Love." She considered how her feelings for Matt had developed so quickly. "So Matt needed help too?"

"You may not have met him otherwise. If the old saying is true that there's someone for everyone, why not Matt?"

Indeed. And since that first spectacular session with him during the pre-auction cocktail party, the sex had leveled out. The swing in the woods had been private, fun and interesting, but not out-and-out bizarre for her. With a caring lover a little adventure that pushed her sexual limitations was reasonable. Everything with Matt felt right for a start to a relationship. Everyone knew that in the beginning the sex was hot and plentiful, that the urge to get down and dirty helped a couple focus and commit to each other.

It relieved her to know that once they hooked up, the spirits had pretty much left them to their own devices. She'd felt no barriers with Matt, no awkwardness in how they made love. The fact that she thought of it as lovemaking should have been a clue.

If this weekend had just been about sex and retreating from a hectic world, she would have kept some defenses in place. As it was, she'd let Matt take her heart without a fight.

Faye studied her while she thought. "Carrie, may I ask when you'll know how much you plan to reveal about Perdition House in your article?"

"I'm not sure what I'll say." She'd begged to do the article, and now she wasn't sure she could deliver. But she needed to give it a shot, and Faye's question was fair. She hedged with a question of her own. "Why?"

"The girls are concerned. Rightfully so because the financial balancing act for the mansion is delicate. If your article impacts the auctions in a negative way, I'll have the devil's own time trying to replace that income. I'd hate to displace the spirits before they've had a chance to reunite with their loved ones."

"Matt told me something about this."

Faye nodded. "Once their true love story has been told, the girls move on to wherever they're going. Love is not just for this plane, after all. It lasts into eternity if given a chance. That's all they need. A chance. For some reason the spirits of Perdition House hang around until they're reunited. Rather romantic, don't you think?"

And a lot of souls to be responsible for. Not to mention their everlasting happiness. She looked at Faye with new eyes and saw the burden she carried. "That's a lot of responsibility. I'm not sure I want to be the one who ruins their chance for eternal love."

Faye looked relieved. "I'm glad you understand."

"I do understand your concerns. And theirs," she added as an afterthought with a glance around the room. She couldn't be sure she and Faye were alone.

She needed to talk to Matt. "No worries, Faye, I'll get back to you soon. I have to turn in an article, but it won't be the one I planned. I won't expose the sex-for-hire side of the auctions." With one more glance around the room for any lurking shadows, she headed out into the hall, where Liam told her Matt had gone up to the room.

She hoped he had the bed warm. She needed some downtime with him. Then she'd be able to think clearly. They could toss ideas around for the article, maybe come up with a fresh slant her editor would like.

But when she found Matt, he was packing his duffel bag, with his head tipped to one side. Between his ear and his shoulder sat a cell phone.

"Talk to you in a few days, after I make arrangements." The phone slid onto the bed as he shoved a sweater into the bag. The phone bounced once, then he snatched it up and flipped it closed.

"I'd hoped we could spend some more time . . ." Her voice trailed off, getting smaller and smaller as fear gripped her throat. He was leaving, trying to get away from her without a word of good-bye. No soft promises of tomorrow, not even an exchange of telephone numbers.

He was ditching her.

He turned and his face lit. "Did you see Faye?"

"Yes. Did you talk to Liam?"

"I did. Pack your bags—we're out of here."

Then she saw her laptop case, zipped closed and propped against the bed. Her bag lay open on top, ready to be filled. She moved toward it. "Where are we going? And why?"

He stepped to the dresser drawer she'd used and opened it. "Grab everything and come with me."

Feeling his urgency from across the room, she obliged by scooping out her lingerie and change of clothes. She hadn't brought much, so it didn't take long.

By the time she'd stuffed an armload of clothing into her case, he'd gone into the bathroom. He rattled around so she went to the doorway to look in on him. He gathered his toothbrush and other toiletries. "She talked you out of doing the article, didn't she?"

"Not exactly. What's going on, Matt?"

He raised his head and stared at her. "Not here," he mouthed. Then he spoke out loud. "We've got to go. Now!" But his voice sounded stretched out like audio in slow mo. The spirits were slowing everything down.

Matt's stride toward her took ages, her fumbling collection of her toiletries took much longer than it should.

But they kept going, moving, packing. Her laptop was the last thing she grabbed on the way out the door. It felt heavy and unbalanced in her grip.

"We need to get clear of the house. I need to think for myself," he said. She agreed with a nod and followed him out of their room.

Each step outside the room was like a slog through deep, sucking mud. Down the stairs, into the front hall, they pushed against whatever it was that wanted them to stay.

Faye appeared in the doorway to her office. "People never leave on Saturdays," she said. Her voice came slow and amused. Then she turned to empty space beside her and said, "Looks like you've frightened them away, Belle. Pity."

A husky feminine laugh swirled around their heads as Matt turned the doorknob and pulled for all he was worth. He had to get them out of here. He had to.

Whatever was driving him, she trusted his lead.

The door opened with a sudden bang, as if all resistance died.

Then they were running, full speed, down the drive. "It's half a mile to the road. Can you make it?" he asked, grabbing her shoulder. His duffel bag bounced against his back, while her laptop case wobbled heavily in her hand. She dropped her overnight bag and took his hand. Anything in there could be replaced at any department store.

"I'm a jogger; you bet your ass I can make a half mile."

"Good girl!" The dash to the gates was on.

An icy wind kicked up as they made it past the circular drive and hit the straightaway to the gate. The boughs from the trees that lined the drive touched each other over the hundred-year-old paving bricks.

Matt raised his forearm to break his way through. The optical illusion of the boughs opening for the cabs was gone. They had to fight for every foot. The wind played games, darting around them, blocking the path, causing headwinds that wailed in their ears.

"The spirits!" he said, while the words blew away on the wind. The cold gusts ran through her, from front to back, slamming into her chest. She froze from the inside out.

11

Carrie stumbled when her chest went numb, but Matt scooped her up into his arms and kept running. The cold bursts continue to pummel them both, dancing through her into him, then back again.

The wind blew hard and threatened to knock Matt to his knees. "Keep going," she said. "I can get down and run now."

He stopped long enough to let her slide to her feet and she took off at a dead run. The gates were in view, and a woman stood there. Tall, blond like Faye, but older. Dressed in an emerald green velvet dressing gown, she smiled serenely, apparently unperturbed by their zigzagging down the drive.

She waggled her fingers and the heavy iron gates creaked to swing open on their own.

"Don't look at her," Matt huffed beside her.

"She's beautiful."

"It's Belle, and she's the real mistress of Perdition."

The wind died as suddenly as it had come up. The cold disappeared and their need to run died with it.

Carrie stopped and put her hands on her knees to catch her

breath. The gates kept opening so she wasn't worried about being locked in. Not now.

"Sorry," the woman said, "sometimes my friends like to pester people. To them it's fun. But you two have provided more amusement than your share."

"We can leave?" Matt asked through lips that had turned blue with cold. He left the idea of amusing the spirits alone. She didn't want to mention it either, not with the gates open and freedom only a couple of yards away.

"Of course you can leave. This is Perdition House. Just because you check in doesn't mean you're trapped. You can always leave." She folded her hands. "And you're more than welcome to return."

"Like hell," they muttered at the same time.

Carrie unlocked the door to her apartment. Cozy but uninteresting, the place had no charm. She'd always planned to decorate, but after wrestling bamboo blinds onto the windows, she'd lapsed into complacency. "It's not much, but it's home," she said as she invited Matt inside.

He dropped his duffel bag to the floor and swept her into his arms. He walked her backward to her sofa, and she pulled him down to sit next to her. "Nice place," he said, before pulling her into a deep kiss.

At the hard feel of his lips, a familiar moistness built in her panties. She smiled at the knowledge of her body's response. "You've still got it!" she said when she could.

"I worried all the way here that we'd lost the spark." His eyes pulled at her heart, warming her through.

"Spark?" She climbed to straddle him, looping her arms around his neck. The rise of his cock cheered her. "What we have between us is more like a raging fire."

He tipped his forehead to hers. "I like it. Do you?"

"Very much."

292 / Bonnie Edwards

He looked relieved. "This is why I wanted us to get out today. I needed to know that what I feel is real and not put in my head by some spirit."

She thought of Belle waiting for them by the gates and shivered. "It is so creepy that after one night in that house we're both okay with the idea of talking to Belle Grantham, who's been dead for decades." Her words were so ridiculously outrageous she couldn't believe they were hers.

"I'm relieved we both saw her and responded to her. If she'd been a hallucination, we both wouldn't see her exactly the same way, right?"

They compared what they'd each seen at the gates, confirming the green velvet dressing gown and Belle's remarkable resemblance to Faye.

"I can't imagine being Faye and having to live with all those—" She shuddered, cutting off her thought.

"Speaking of Faye, did she convince you not to write your article?"

She thought fast. "My new angle is the house as a retreat for business women. No computers, cell phones or fax machines allowed." She raised an eyebrow in query. "Except the one I saw you using."

"Liam arranged for a brief window of opportunity for me to call my agent."

"There's what? A bubble of interference between the house and any satellites overhead?" It made sense, if you considered that most of the time the visitors were engaged in sexual matters. Leaving their work behind was essential to retreating from the world.

"Something like that. Number one, the house isn't wired for things like cable television or the Internet. Number two, Faye feels strongly about keeping the place quiet and restful. It's her home as much as it is a retreat."

Carrie nodded.

"Get back to your article. What did you find out?"

"The money from the auctions does go to charity. There's no double dealing or lying or fraud." So nobody ate as much as they thought they did. What woman would complain about that?

"The story of Perdition House will not be my stepping stone to a brilliant journalism career. I've accepted that." She stood and walked to the window. Gazing out, she saw not her own limited view of the city street below but the circular drive at the mansion. It must've been quite the sight in 1911. Delivery wagons and jalopies jostling for space while horses were tied up in front of a trough.

Matt came up behind her and tugged her to lean against his chest. She went because it might be the last time they shared a quiet moment. Just because she'd come to care deeply for him was no reason to hope he felt the same, no matter what he'd said in the heat of sex. He set his lips beside her ear.

"What will you tell the world about Perdition, Carrie?"

She hummed. "I can't tell the truth. I can't write that the real story spans generations and the veil between this life and the next. I can't tell readers that love is eternal, Matt. Whether the story is funny, sad or tragic, love has its own energy. Some of the women who worked there found love. On the spirit plane they need help to reunite with their lovers."

"So you won't expose the auctions?"

"I can't. It wouldn't be right. Anyone who's ever felt love would have to support what Faye's doing."

He tightened his hold on her and rocked her back and forth. His kiss on her earlobe set up a drumbeat of desire. She smiled and held her feelings for him to herself. If he was leaving there was no point telling him.

"I'm glad," he said, stirring the hair at her nape. "I'd hate to think we were responsible for the downfall of the house. Hell, it's been standing for close to a hundred years. Who are we to mess things up?"

She grinned and turned her face up to his. She gave him a quick kiss on his chin. "Right! Who are we to expose the place when we've been victims ourselves?"

"I'm no victim. I've been blessed."

"Really?"

"Hey, I'm a writer. Most of the time I'm holed up in my office alone or racing around the country researching. We never would've met if I hadn't gotten wind of these weekends." He frowned. "Come to think of it, I don't remember how I heard about them. I just knew I had to be accepted as one of the bachelors."

"It's possible the girls, as Faye calls them, put the idea of the article in my head just to get me there."

"Cool," he said, checking his watch. "Time's moving on."

"You're leaving?" She tried to keep the hurt out of her voice, but failed.

He slammed the palm of his hand onto his forehead. "Damn! I got so caught up in this idea that I didn't realize what you must be thinking."

The forehead slam looked hopeful, but she didn't want to get her hopes up. "What is it I'm thinking?"

"That I'm leaving you." He strode to her, palmed her shoulders and she felt a stab of fear as she looked into his serious gaze.

"Aren't you?"

"No! I'm leaving, yes, but you're coming with me."

"I am? Why?"

"Because I need your help."

"With?"

"Getting some research." His glance flickered away as if he were hiding something.

Suspicion rose. She was already learning how to read him. "What kind of research?"

"There's one type of sex club I couldn't infiltrate. As hard as I tried, I couldn't wangle an invitation. And I tried several in different parts of the country."

"And you think I'll be able to succeed where you failed?"

He grinned and alarm bells went off in her head. She was just discovering the man had a sneaky streak. "It's all in the name of research, Carrie, I swear."

More suspicion. "Why do I have the feeling I'm being conned?"

"Because you are," he admitted. "I'd pretty much given up on getting any information on lesbian clubs, but now—"

"Whoa!" she interrupted. "Hold on here . . ."

He laughed and grabbed her up into his arms. He swung her around while she considered his request. "No sex with women?"

"No."

"I just observe and report?"

"Yes."

"Then okay, I'll help you."

He stopped suddenly and squeezed her hard. His expression went joyful. Deep affection radiated through him and into her. She warmed and stilled, waiting for him to say whatever he had on his mind. "Marry me, Carrie. Spend your life with me."

"Is that your idea?"

"All mine, I swear."

"Oh, Matt." She kissed him, long and hard and deep.

Love is eternal.

Matt lifted his mouth and grinned down at her. "Love *is* eternal," he said. "Like mine for you."

"And like mine for you, Matt Crewe. I love you. And thank God we walked through the gates of Perdition."

* * *

Belle Grantham turned to her great-grandniece Faye and Faye's lover, Liam. "I believe we've averted a potential problem, dear. Thank you." She eyed Liam as warmly as a spirit could. "You handled Mr. Crewe beautifully."

"Always happy to serve," he said with a nod.

"Yes," Faye responded with a swirl of her fingertip on Liam's forearm. "I think Perdition's secrets are safe."

"At least for now," said Belle.

Here's a hot sneak peek at
HANDYMAN by Jodi Lynn Copeland,
coming soon from Aphrodisia!

1

Now, he was the kind of guy she needed to meet.

Parallel parked across the street from the Almost Family youth services building, Lissa Malone stopped examining her reflection in the vanity mirror of her Dodge Charger to watch the guy. He stood in front of the youth building, which was constructed of the same old-fashioned red brick as every other building in downtown Crichton, laughing with a lanky, long-haired blond kid in his early teens. The kid wouldn't be a relative, but a boy from the local community who was going through a rough patch and in need of an adult role model in the form of a foster friend.

Kind, caring and considerate enough to be that friend, by donating his free time to the betterment of the kid's life, the guy was the antithesis of every man she'd dated.

Make that every *straight* man. And, then again, he wasn't the complete opposite.

The way his faded blue Levi's hugged his tight ass and his biceps bulged from beneath the short sleeves of a slate gray T-shirt as he scruffed the kid's hair, the guy had as fine a body as her recent lovers. What he wasn't likely to have was their bad-ass hang-ups.

He was one of the good ones. A nice guy. The kind of guy Lissa had never gone for and never had any desire to.

There was something about those bad boys that called to her. Not just their bedside manner. Though she wasn't about to knock the red-hot thrill of being welcomed home from work by having her panties torn away and a stiff cock thrust inside her before she had a chance to say hello.

She shuddered with the memory of Haden, the brainless beefcake she ended up with following her latest dip in the bad boy pool, greeting her precisely that way three weeks ago. What Haden lacked in mentality, he more than made up for in ability. The guy could make her come with the sound of his voice alone.

Show me that sweet pussy, Liss.

Haden's deep baritone slid through her mind, spiking her pulse and settling dampness between her thighs. She caught her reflection in the vanity mirror as she shifted in the driver's seat. Her cheeks had pinkened—an unmanageable giveaway to her arousal—calling out her too many freckles.

Yeah, there was definitely something about those bad boys. Something she wouldn't be experiencing ever again.

Lissa wasn't the only woman Haden could bring to climax in seconds. As it turned out, she also wasn't the only woman he'd been bringing to climax the almost two months they dated. Really, it shouldn't have surprised her. With bad boys, something always ended up coming before her. Another woman. A massive ego. Or worst of all, the bad boy himself coming before her, then not bothering to stick around to see if she got off.

She was sick to hell of coming in second.

In the name of coming in first and being the center of a

man's attention if only for a little while, she was ready to give nice guys a try. Her housemate and ex-lover, Sam, claimed she wouldn't regret it, since what people were always saying about nice guys was true: they finished last and it was because they wanted their leading ladies to come in first.

A nice guy like the well-built Good Samaritan across the street, Lissa thought eagerly. Only, a glance back across the street revealed he wasn't standing there any longer. Neither was the kid.

"Well, shit." So much for opportunity knocking.

Not that she had time to do a meet and greet. She had an appointment with the owner of the Sugar Shack candy store for a potential interior redesign job. Besides, Mr. Nice Guy was likely one among a hundred like him who donated his time to Almost Family and similar non-profit services.

How many of those others had an ass and arms like his?

A dynamite ass and a killer set of arms, and probably a gorgeous wife or girlfriend to go with them.

Her eagerness flame fanned out, Lissa put her nice-guy hunt on hold. She returned her attention to the mirror for a quick teeth and facial inspection. Finding everything acceptable and her freckles returned to barely noticeable, she grabbed her black leather briefcase satchel from the passenger's seat and climbed out of the car.

The closest she'd been able to get a parking spot to the candy store was three blocks away. She was a stickler for arriving early, so reaching the place on time wouldn't require sprinting in her skirt and open-toe heels. Hooking the satchel's strap over her arm, she took off down the sidewalk.

One block in, footfalls pounded on the sidewalk behind her. Not an uncommon thing, given the number of people milling about the downtown area on a Friday afternoon. What was uncommon was how noisily they fell, like the person was purposefully trying to be loud.

Were they in step with hers?

Sam's thing was paranoia, not Lissa's. Only, it appeared her housemate was rubbing off on her. Her skin suddenly felt crawly. Her entire body went tense with the sensation of being watched. Followed. Stalked.

Oh, jeez! Could she be any more melodramatic?

This wasn't a dark-and-stormy-night scenario. The sun shone down from overhead and while June in Michigan didn't often equate to blistering temperatures, a warm, gentle breeze toyed with the yellow, green and white flowered silk overlay of her knee-length skirt. And then again, was the fact she was surrounded by a few dozen people.

To prove how ridiculous she was acting, Lissa stopped walking. The footfalls came again, once, and then fell silent.

Her breath dragged in.

What if she *was* being followed? The candy store was still a block and a half away. Sprinting the remainder of the distance might be the safest route. Yeah, right, it would. She was liable to snag a heel in a sidewalk crack and break her neck. *Then* she would have a reason to be concerned.

Ignoring the hasty beat of her heart, she faced her overactive imagination by spinning around . . . and there he was.

Mr. Nice Guy stood less than twenty feet away. Not following her or even eyeing her up, but standing in front of a coffee shop, peering into its storefront windows.

He moved toward the shop's door, pulling it open with a tinkling of overhead bells and placing his ass in her line of vision. Once more she appreciated the stellar view. This time it was more than appreciation though. This time, just before he turned and disappeared inside, he looked her way.

Lissa's heart skipped a beat with the glimpse of pure masculine perfection.

Stubble the same shade of wheat as his thick, wavy hair dusted an angular jaw line and coasted above a full, stubborn upper lip. Eyebrows a shade darker slashed in wicked arcs over vivid cobalt blue eyes. His cheeks sank in just enough to make him look lean, hungry and dangerous all at once. Then there was the way he filled out his jeans: his backside had nothing on his front half. Beneath the faded denim, muscles bulged and strained in all the right places. And she did mean *all* the right places.

If not for catching him joking around with the youth services kid, she would have mistaken him for a bad boy in a heartbeat. He wasn't. But, clearly, her body approved of him.

Heat raced into her face and her nipples stabbed to life, making her wish she hadn't relied on the built-in shelf bra of her yellow short-sleeve top to hold in her cleavage. Her breasts were way too big to be fully constrained by the flimsy little cotton bra sewn into shirts. For whatever reason, she allowed Sam to talk her in to giving one a try. Probably because when she slipped out of her bedroom wearing it, he'd taken one look at her chest and offered to give her a pre-appointment mouth job.

Coming from a gay guy that was a major compliment.

The bells over the coffee shop door sounded, emitting a gray-haired, sixty-something couple. Lissa glanced at her watch. Ten minutes till her appointment. A block and a half to go.

She could spend five minutes determining if Mr. Nice Guy was single and searching, and then huff it to the Sugar Shack. Or forgo the meet and greet, arrive at her appointment on time, and take Sam up on his mouth job offer when she arrived home.

As much as she loved Sam, there was no future for them beyond friendship. There probably wasn't one with the guy in the coffee shop either.

Lissa walked back to the shop anyway.

To the sound of tinkling bells, she pulled open the wood door with white and red stained glass coffee mugs designed into its window slats. Entering the shop, she looked up at the bells . . . and nearly slammed into Mr. Nice Guy.

He stood in front of a customer bulletin board, pinning business cards up with long-fingered hands that bore neither rings nor tan lines. After tacking the last card onto the board, he turned toward her, flashed a smile sexy enough to do a fluttering number on her sex, and moved right on past and out the door.

"Well, shit." *So much for opportunity knocking.* Even worse, she was starting to sound like a broken record.

She should forget about him and get to her appointment. But between his lack of a wedding ring and that sexy smile her eagerness flame was rekindled.

Lissa grabbed one of the newly posted business cards off the bulletin board. *Thad Davies, Handyman,* was written in black, and beneath it, in bold, blue lettering, *Loose Screws Construction.* Was the company name meant to be a double entendre, and exactly how handy of a man was Thad?

Handy enough to leave her his number.

Smiling, she tucked the business card into her satchel. Later, maybe she would give him a call. Or maybe she would pick up a box of Sam's favorite sweets while she was at the Sugar Shack and use them to bribe him in to making good on his mouth job offer.

"You're a bastard!"

Thad Davies sank back against the black metal rails of his headboard and sighed over the glaring brunette standing on the end of the bed's bare mattress.

Naked and flushed with the aftereffects of orgasm, she looked ready to beat the shit out of him. From what little he knew of her, she was nice enough. Her sweat-glistening tits were definitely nice, as they jostled around with her anger. That didn't mean he was ready to forget she was a client and sleep with her for free. "You play, you pay, sweetheart."

With a huff, she bounded off the end of the bed, flashing an ass that was just as nice and well rounded as her tits. "Don't call me that! And don't you *ever* come near me again."

She reached the tangle of sheets, covers and clothing, which had found their way to the floor in the midst of their wild screwing, and started kicking them apart.

Damn, he really didn't like upsetting women. It wasn't his fault they hired him for sex and ended up falling for him along the way. Not all of them did, but more than a couple had in the five months since the woman-pleasuring division of Loose Screws started up. "You called me," he reminded her.

The brunette stopped kicking to look at him, hurt evident in her eyes. "I *thought* we had something between us."

"We do. A business deal."

The hurt left her expression as cold fury took over. Soft pink lips, which less than ten minutes ago had been wrapped around his dick and delivering him to nirvana, pushed into a hard line. Giving the chaotic pile a final kick, she uncovered a slim red purse and yanked it up by the strap. "Consider the deal off," she bit out as she shoved her hand inside the purse and yanked out a handful of bills. "Don't expect any referrals to be coming your way."

Fifties and hundreds plastered him in the chest and rained down on the bed around him. Some people might feel cheap in a situation like this. For Thad, it was all in a day's work and if he happened to love his job most of the time . . . well, what man in his right mind wouldn't?

Pushing the bills off his chest, he moved to the edge of the bed and swung his legs over the side. He rolled the condom off his deflating shaft, tucked it into a tissue, and deposited it in the wastebasket between the bed and the short black oak dresser that doubled as a nightstand. "Don't you be forgetting that silence agreement you signed."

Midway through diving down to retrieve her bra and panties, the brunette's breath dragged in on a gasp. She glared at him. "Like I would tell anyone I had the poor taste to pay to fuck you."

"You got your money's worth. All six times." Today, she'd chosen to suck him off while he fulfilled her order of oral sex. The five times she employed his services before this, she'd been after her pleasure alone. The ecstatic cries centering each of those sessions said she'd enjoyed herself plenty.

With a final huff, she jerked the bra and panties off the floor and, not bothering to go back for her skintight white minidress, stormed out of the bedroom door. Less than twenty seconds later, the front door slammed. The short lapse of time told him she'd left his rental duplex buck naked.

The neighbors would have a coronary over that exit.

But to hell with what his neighbors thought. Thad had never been a saint a day in his life and he never intended to pretend otherwise, even if the ultraconservative city of Crichton and the surrounding county preferred him to do so.

He scrubbed a hand over his face, aware that line of thinking was a lie.

He didn't want to give a damn what his neighbors thought of him and whether they discovered he worked part time as a gigolo, but he didn't have any choice in the matter. Thanks to the economy being blown to shit and taking his job with the local automotive plant along with it, staying in the area meant making money by whatever means possible.

Loose Screws, the construction company he ran with two of his former plant coworkers, was taking off slowly. And business would continue to be slow until the economy bounced back. The cold, hard truth: most people didn't have the money to spend on building or remodeling.

Women did have money for sex. Or whatever else might tickle their fancy, or any other part of their mind and body.

Last week Benny pulled in a grand just for spending the afternoon alone with an eighty-year-old widow. Alone and naked, but still that was a helluva lot of dough for a few hours of small talk while being ogled by an old lady.

Speaking of his business partner, Thad should give Benny a call and see if he and Nash needed help at the current construction site. The job was a relatively small one. It was also nearly finished and the sooner it got done, the sooner they would get paid. Nash could avoid needing the cash, by sucking up his loathing for the wealthy and asking his affluent father for a handout the man was eager to give. Benny was doing whatever it took to keep his Alzheimer's-stricken foster mother in an upscale nursing home. Thad just liked to be able to afford to eat and make rent.

After going into the half bath adjoining his second-floor bedroom and getting washed up, Thad pulled on a pair of boxers and jeans, then headed downstairs to the kitchen. He lifted the cordless phone from the counter, planning to punch in Benny's cell number while he discovered what, if any, food waited in the refrigerator.

The phone rang before he could punch the first number. Pulling open the fridge door, he hit the phone's talk button. "Loose Screws. This is Thad."

"I need you," a low, husky feminine voice implored through the phone line.

One of the reasons he was able to charge as much as he did for his gigolo services was the shitload of testosterone the good Lord saw fit to gift him with. The carnal invitation that seemed to fill the woman's words had his blood pumping hot. His cock joined in, already hungry for more loving. Remembering this was the construction phone line didn't do a thing to calm his body. The woman-pleasuring division of Loose Screws originated because of someone calling the company, guessing it to be a hustler service by its name and hoping one of their employees might be interested in working as a stripper for a bachelorette party.

"Then you called the right place." Letting the refrigerator door shut, Thad focused on determining if she was after business or pleasure. "How might I be of service?"

"The way the ceiling's leaking, I think my roof's about ready to fall through. I need to get it fixed before the next rainstorm."

Serious words spoken in a sultry tone. Didn't tell him a damned thing. "Is this need business related?"

"It's personal."

If the sigh following her words was authentic, and not just a chirp in the phone line, it would suggest she was after pleasure. Loose Screws couldn't afford for him to be wrong. "So long as your place isn't too big, I might be able to squeeze you in. Lemme check the calendar."

Thad glanced at the hot rods and hotter babes calendar hanging on the refrigerator door. His next pleasure appointment wasn't until the following Thursday, with a woman old enough to be his mother. Tammy might be as old as his mother, but with her all-over tan, shoulder-length bleached blond hair and silicone-enhanced double Ds, she didn't look a thing like his mother. Unlike Benny's client widow, she wouldn't spend their time together staring at his naked body, but have her hands and mouth all over him.

What about the woman on the phone? Did her sexy voice go with her sexy mouth she had plans to put all over him? "Are you local?"

"According to Sam, I am."

"Come again?"

A throatily sensual laugh most women could only accomplish with a sore throat carried through the phone line. "I thought you said loco. Sam thinks I'm crazy, but he doesn't have much room to talk." Her voice returned to the low, husky tone, "I live about five miles out of town, in an older ranch-style."

"Sam live there, too?" More specifically, was Sam her man and crazy enough to take after Thad with a gun should he catch him doing his woman?

"Yeah. Though, he's stepping out pretty soon."

A female construction client wasn't bound to let on she would be alone when he arrived. That pretty much guaranteed it was pleasure services she sought. Until he had a better idea of her relationship with Sam, Thad wouldn't be providing those services—a quick drop by, however, would give him a chance to confirm she was after sex . . . while checking out the goods he would get to work with. "I'm busy later this afternoon, but I should have time to fit you in an inspection before then. What's the address?"

Her voice raised a little as she rattled off the address and told him the color of the house and surrounding landmarks. "By the way, my name's Lissa, or Liss. See you in a few."

Another sigh slipped through the phone line before it went dead. His cock gave a happy little jerk in response. Thad looked down at his groin. "Hate to break it to you, buddy, but she was talking to me. Unless you want Sam putting you out of commission permanently, you'd best not get any ideas about bringing Liss bliss."

Lissa did a little shimmy across her bedroom in potential outfit number four, a semi-sheer peach sundress that clung to her plentiful curves and required going braless with its open back and plunging scoop neck.

Sitting on the foot of her bed, Sam shook his head. "The ho-baby look's perfect for catching a bad boy, but you're chasing after a nice guy now."

Drawing a frustrated breath, she unzipped the dress, yanked

it over her head and tossed it on the bed next to him, where the previous rejects lay. It was damned good thing his personal taste ran to nice guys, since it was becoming increasingly clear she knew absolutely nothing about catching one herself.

Giving up on the closet, which contained a mix of moderately slutty bar clothes and casually refined work clothes and not one friggin' happy-medium outfit, Lissa tugged open her middle two dresser drawers and pulled out the first item in each: well worn, cut-off jean shorts and a v-neck, red tank top. Turning around, she jokingly lifted them for Sam's inspection.

Approval entered his brown eyes and he flashed his teeth in a smile. "Nice. Girl next door meets lady in red."

Fisting the clothes in her hands, she groaned. Of course, when she was trying to be funny, she would finally get it right.

He lifted her black bra from where she'd earlier flung it on the bed and tossed it to her. "You sure you don't want me to cancel my meeting and stick around for protection?"

She feigned a pout as she set the tank top on the dresser. After hooking the back clasps, she worked the bra around her body and her breasts into the cups. "If you followed through on your offer yesterday and went down on me, you wouldn't need to be worried about some stranger coming over while I'm home alone."

He gave her a sympathetic look. "Aw, honey, your kitty might have been happy for a few days, but in the end you would still be itching for more than I can give you."

As if that wasn't apparent by the fact she'd been parading around in nothing but skimpy panties for the last half hour and he hadn't even acted a little excited.

Because she enjoyed teasing him and knew he found it equally amusing, Lissa swiveled around to face the mirrored closet door. She bent down to slide her bare feet through the legs of the cut offs and made a show of wiggling her black panty-clad ass in his face. His smile emerged as she slowly straightened, trailing her fingertips along her inner thighs. The shorts settled into place over her ample hips and she dipped her first finger inside the right cuff and beneath the leg of her panties. Her breath caught with the flick of her fingertip between her pussy lips.

With a hearty laugh, Sam shook his head. "You're outrageous, Liss."

He might not be aroused by her behavior, but her body was turned on by the idea of him watching her finger herself. Part of her wanted to slide her shorts and panties down her legs and continue masturbating until she climaxed. A bigger part was aware of how soon Thad would be over. If she was really going to give this nice guy thing a try, she ought to practice at being a good girl in return.

Lissa pulled her finger free of her panties and shorts and grabbed the tank top from the dresser. She grinned at Sam's reflection. "I'm crazy and you love me for it." Sobering, she turned around and pulled on the tank top. "Thanks for offering to stay, but I'll be fine alone with him."

"Just promise me you will be careful. Even nice guys have their naughty days."

Really? Now, there was a tidbit of info she hadn't planned on, but was damned glad to hear. Maybe she wouldn't have to practice at being a good girl. Not if Thad was feeling naughty enough to put out on the first date.

As if they were even having a first date.

He was coming over to check out her ceiling and roof, while she spent the time confirming he was single and then casually convinced him they should see each other when business wasn't an issue. "He's coming over to look at the roof, not to get it on."

"So says you." Sam eyed the tank top's v-neck, and she looked down to discover her cleavage nearly bursting out—either the shirt had shrunk with the last washing, or she'd gained

weight. "So says me if after he see you in that top, he's still focused on the roof, you'd best be sending him my direct—" The
doorbell rang, cutting him off and, in the next instant, curving
his mouth in a sly smile. "I'll get it."

Lissa's heart sped up. Thad was five minutes early. Punctual-
ity was probably a trait common to nice guys, but it pleased her
all the same. Grabbing a brush off the dresser, she moved back
in front of the mirrored door and gave Sam's reflection a warning look. "Don't screw this up for me."

He placed a hand over his chest and sniffed. "I'm hurt."

"What you are is a drama queen. I mean it, Sammy. For all I
know, this guy could be the one." Or he might be married with
six kids. But, damn, she hoped not. "I don't want him running
away because you pinch his ass as soon as he clears the door."

He dropped the offended act to flash an intrigued grin. "I
only do that to the gorgeous ones, so I'll take that to mean
we're talking some serious eye candy."

She nodded at the open bedroom door. "Let him in and see
for yourself. Just don't get any nibbling ideas."

Typically Thad wasn't one for sizing another man up. But
then, typically he wasn't greeted at a potential pleasure client's
door by said client's husband. Or boyfriend. Or whatever the
hell the admittedly good-looking, clean-shaven, brown-haired
guy in the tailored black pants, matching tie and mint green
dress shirt was to Lissa. "You must be Sam."

With a nod, Sam slid his gaze the length of Thad, lingering a
little too long for comfort in the area of his groin. Sam returned
his attention to Thad's face to reveal an amused smile. "You
must be Mr. Nice Guy."

"Sam was just leaving," a low, throaty feminine voice said
from behind Sam.

Sam stepped back from the doorway and the owner of that

sexy voice came into view and had Thad hoping to hell she was Lissa and her interest in him was purely physical.

Pleasure clients rarely greeted him in casual clothes, preferring lingerie, tight dresses, or nothing at all. This woman's clothes were causal. The way she filled them out was anything but. From her generous breasts to her curvy hips and thighs, she was the type of woman the term hourglass figure was coined for.

She was remotely familiar.

A warm smile curved her lipstick-free lips. She swept a hank of loose copper, shoulder-length hair away from her face, tucking it behind her ear before extending her hand to him. "Lissa Malone."

Despite the fact he was no saint and the hellbent rebel years of his youth, Thad had always believed in God. Moments like this with natural beauties like her proved His existence that much more.

"Thad Davies." Her hand was warm in his, her skin soft. The scent of vanilla drifted to him. Not strong or perfumey, like so many of his clients wore, but the subtle scent of lotion or body wash. "So you're worried about getting wet?"

Sam gave a deep chuckle, reminding Thad of his presence. Moving next to Lissa, Sam pulled her into his arms and whispered something in her ear that had her laughing, as well. He released her to give Thad a look that could mean "hands off" as easily as "treat her right," then nodded a good-bye and took off down the covered porch to the sidewalk.

Lissa looked back at Thad. "*Should* I be worried?"

Between the sensual interest in her jade green eyes now and the sultry sound of her laughter moments ago, he suddenly remembered where he'd seen her before.

In his favorite wet dream. Had to be.

Sam left them alone, but his parting look didn't guarantee it

was with permission to fuck. Since Thad still wasn't 100 per-
cent sure that was the reason he was here, he played it safe.
"Possibly. I can only tell so much from what you said over the
phone."

Barefooted, she turned and started walking away. He closed
the door and followed, because what in the hell else was he
going to do?